Ernest Rhys

The Garden of Romance

romantic tales of all time

Ernest Rhys

The Garden of Romance
romantic tales of all time

ISBN/EAN: 9783337036065

Printed in Europe, USA, Canada, Australia, Japan

Cover: Foto ©Andreas Hilbeck / pixelio.de

More available books at **www.hansebooks.com**

The
Garden of Romance

Romantic Tales of
All Time

Chosen and Edited by Ernest Rhys

London
Kegan Paul, Trench, Trübner & Co. Ltd
Paternoster House, Charing Cross Road
1897

Preface

THE old taste for the TALE, pure and simple, which, stimulated by such writers as Mr. Kipling and M. de Maupassant, has grown anew of late years, is enough in itself to account for the present anthology. Within its limits will be found, as in a GARDEN, the fine flowers of the art, chosen with a preference for those of a romantic order, and transplanted from many lands and many times. From the East, where Romance may be said to have begun—whence we have taken an " Arabian Night "—to the extreme West, where Hawthorne and Edgar Poe gave the art a new effect ; from Sir Thomas Malory to Sir Walter Scott ; from Sterne to Hans Andersen ; we have ranged to get all the variety in excellence, and all the delight of stories wonderfully well told, to be had within so small a space. Most of the tales are so famous that they need give no account of themselves. To " Balin and Balan," let us remind the reader, however, Mr. Swinburne has lent lately a new interest, and a new excuse, if one be needed, for its being detached from the "Morte D'Arthur." Of the translated tales, we have taken an early seventeenth century version of "Cymon and Iphigenia," and Smollett's, of the "Story of Marcella;" while a new translation has been made for us by sympathetic hands of Hans Andersen's most touching "Pebersvendens Nathue" (Pepper-Vendor's or Old Bachelor's Nightcap).

E. R.

Contents

vii

The Garden of Romance

I

THE STORY OF THE LAME YOUNG MAN
Told by the Tailor

From The Arabian Nights

A MERCHANT, sire, of this city did me the honour two days since of inviting me to an entertainment which he gave yesterday morning to his friends ; I repaired to his house at an early hour, and found about twenty people assembled.

We were waiting for the master of the house, who was gone out on some sudden business, when we saw him arrive, accompanied by a young stranger, very neatly dressed, and of a good figure, but lame. We all rose, and to do honour to the master of the house, we begged the young man to sit with us on the sofa. He was just going to sit down, when, perceiving a barber, who was one of the company, he abruptly stepped back, and was going away. The master of the house, surprised at this, stopped him. "Where are you going?" said he; "I bring you here to do me the honour of being present at an entertainment I am going to give my friends, and you are scarcely entered before you want to go away!"   "In the name of God, sir," replied the stranger, "I entreat you not to detain me, but suffer me to depart. I cannot behold without horror that abominable barber who is sitting there; although he is born in a country where the complexion of the people is white, yet he bears the colour of an Ethiopian; and his mind is of a still deeper and more horrible dye than his visage."

We were all very much surprised at this speech, and began to conceive a very bad opinion of the barber, without knowing whether the young stranger had any just reason for speaking of him in such terms. We even went so far as to declare that we would not suffer at our table a man of whom we had heard so shocking a character. The master of the house begged the stranger to acquaint us with the occasion of his hatred to the barber. "Gentlemen," said the young man, "you must know that this barber was the cause of my being lame, and also of the most cruel affair that you can possibly conceive, which befell me; for this reason I have made a vow to quit instantly any place where he may be, and even not to reside in any town where he lives; for this reason I left Bagdad, where he was, and undertook so long a journey to come and settle myself in this city, where, being in the centre of Great Tartary, I flattered myself I should be secure of never beholding him again. However, contrary to my hopes and expectations, I find him here; this obliges me, gentlemen, to deprive myself of the honour of partaking of your feast. I will this day leave your city, and go to hide myself, if I can, in some place

where he can never again offend my sight." In saying
this, he was going to leave us, but the master of the
house still detained him, and entreated him to relate to
us the cause of the aversion he had against the barber,
who all this time kept his eyes fixed on the ground, and
was silent. We joined our entreaties to those of the
master of the house, and at last the young man, yielding
to our wishes, seated himself on the sofa, and began his
history in these words, having first turned his back towards
the barber, lest he should see him :

" My father, who lived in Bagdad, was of a rank to
aspire to the highest offices of state, but he preferred
leading a quiet and tranquil life to all the honours he
might deserve. I was his only child, and when he died
I had completed my education, and was of an age to
dispose of the large possessions he had bequeathed me.
I did not dissipate them in folly, but made such use of
them as procured me the esteem of every one.

" I had not yet felt any tender passion, and far from
being at all sensible to love, I will confess, perhaps to
my shame, that I carefully avoided the society of women.
One day, as I was walking in a street, I saw a great
number of ladies coming towards me ; in order to avoid
them, I turned into a little street that was before me,
and sat down on a bench that was placed near a door.
I was opposite to a window where there was a number
of very fine flowers, and my eyes were fixed on them,
when the window opened, and a lady appeared, whose
beauty dazzled me. She cast her eyes on me, and water-
ing the flowers with a hand whiter than alabaster, she
looked at me with a smile, which inspired me with as
much love for her as I had hitherto felt aversion towards

the rest of her sex. After having watered her flowers, and bestowed on me another look full of charms, which completed the conquest of my heart, she shut the window, and left me in a state of pain and uncertainty which I cannot describe.

"I should have remained thus a considerable time, had not the noise I heard in the street brought me to my senses again. I turned my head as I got up, and saw that it was one of the first cadis of the city, mounted on a mule, and accompanied by five or six of his people : he alighted at the door of the house where the young lady had opened the window, and went in, which made me suppose he was her father.

"I returned home in a state very different from that in which I had left it ; agitated by a passion so much the more violent from its being the first attack, I went to bed with a raging fever, which caused great affliction in my household. My relations, who loved me, alarmed by my sudden indisposition, came quickly to see me, and importuned me to acquaint them of the cause, but I was very careful to keep it secret. My silence increased their alarms, nor could the physicians dissipate their fears for my safety, because they knew nothing of my disease, which was only increased by the medicines they administered.

"My relations began to despair of my life, when an old lady of their acquaintance, being informed of my illness, arrived ; she considered me with a great deal of attention, and after she had thoroughly examined me, she discovered, I know not by what token, the cause of my disorder. She took them aside, and begged them to leave her alone with me, and to order my people to retire.

"The room being cleared, she seated herself near my pillow. 'My son,' said she, 'you have hitherto persisted in concealing the cause of your illness: nor do I require you to confess it: I have sufficient experience to penetrate into this secret, and I am sure you will not disown what I am going to declare. It is love which occasions your indisposition. I can probably assist your cure, provided you will tell me who is the happy lady that has been able to wound a heart so insensible as yours; for you have the reputation of not liking the ladies, and I have not been the last to perceive it; however, what I foresaw is at last come to pass, and I shall be delighted if I can be of any service in releasing you from your pain.'

"The old lady having finished this speech, waited to hear my answer; but although it had made a strong impression on me, I did not dare open my heart to her. I only turned towards her and uttered a deep sigh, without saying a word. 'Is it shame,' continued she, 'that prevents you from speaking, or is it want of confidence in my power to relieve you? Can you doubt the effects of my promise? I could mention to you an infinite number of young people of your acquaintance who have endured the same pain that you do, and for whom I have obtained consolation.'

"In short, the good lady said so many things to me, that at length I broke silence, and declared to her the cause of my pain. I acquainted her with the place where I had seen the object that had given birth to it, and related all the circumstances of the adventure. 'If you succeed,' continued I, 'and procure me the happiness of seeing this enchanting beauty, and of expressing to her the passion with which I burn, you may rely on my gratitude.' 'My son,' replied the old lady, 'I know the person you mention ; she is, as you justly suppose, the daughter of the principal cadi in this city. I am not surprised that you should love her ; she is the most beautiful, as well as most amiable, lady in Bagdad ; but what grieves me is, she is very haughty and difficult of access. You know that many of our officers of justice are very exact in making women observe the harsh laws which subject them to so irksome a restraint ; they are still more strict in their own families, and the cadi you saw is himself alone more rigid on this point than all the others put together. As they are continually preaching to their daughters the enormity of the crime of showing themselves to men, the poor things are in general so cautious of being guilty of it, that when necessity obliges them to walk in the streets, they make no use of their eyes but to guide them on their way ; I do not say that this is absolutely the case with the daughter of the principal cadi, yet I am much afraid of having as great obstacles to overcome on her side as on her father's. Would to Heaven you loved any other lady ! I should not have so many difficulties as I foresee to surmount. I will nevertheless employ all my address, but it will require time to succeed. At any rate, take courage, and place confidence in me.'

"The old lady left me, and as I reflected with anxiety on all the obstacles she had represented to me, the fear that she would not succeed possessed me, and increased my disease. She returned the following day, and I soon read in her countenance that she had no favourable intelligence to announce. She said, 'My son, I was not

mistaken; I have more to surmount than merely the
vigilance of a father; you love an insensible object, who
delights in letting those burn with unrequited passion
who suffer themselves to be charmed with her beauty;
she will not allow them the least relief; she listened to
me with pleasure whilst I talked to her only of the pain
she made you suffer, but no sooner did I open my mouth
to persuade her to allow you an interview, than she cast
an angry look at me, and said, 'You are very insolent
to attempt to make such a proposition; and I desire you
will never see me more, if it be only to hold such conversations as this.'

"'But let not that afflict you,' continued the old
lady; 'I am not easily discouraged, and provided you do
not lose your patience, I hope at last to accomplish my
design.' Not to protract my narration (said the young
man), I will only say that this good messenger made
several fruitless attempts in my favour with the haughty
enemy of my peace. The vexation I endured increased
my disorder to such a degree, that the physicians gave me
over. I was therefore considered as a man who was at
the point of death, when the old lady came to give me
new life.

"That no one might hear her, she whispered in my
ear, 'Think of the present you will make me for the
good news I bring you.' These words produced a wonderful effect; I raised myself in my bed, and replied
with transport, 'The present will not be deficient; what
have you to tell me?' 'My dear sir,' resumed she,
'you will not die this time, and I shall soon have the
pleasure of seeing you in perfect health, and well satisfied
with me; yesterday being Monday, I went to the lady

you are in love with, and found her in very good humour ;
I at first put on a mournful countenance, uttered an
abundance of sighs, and shed some tears. ' My good
mother,' said she, ' what is the matter ? Why are you in
such affliction ? ' ' Alas ! my dear and honourable lady,'
replied I, ' I am just come from the young gentleman I
spoke to you of the other day ; it is all over with him ;
he is at the point of death, and all for love of you ; it is
a great pity, I assure you, and you are very cruel.' ' I
do not know,' said she, ' why you should accuse me of
being the cause of his death ; how can I have contributed
to his illness ? ' ' How ? ' replied I ; ' did I not tell you
that he seated himself before your window just as you
opened it to water your flowers ? He beheld this prodigy
of beauty—these charms which your mirror reflects every
day ; from that moment he has languished for you, and
his disease is so augmented, that he is now reduced to
the pitiable state I have had the honour of describing to
you. You may remember, madam,' continued I, ' how
rigorously you treated me lately when I was going to tell
you of his illness, and propose to you a method of relieving him from his dangerous condition : I returned to
him after I left you, and he no sooner perceived from my
countenance that I did not bring a favourable account,
than his malady redoubled its violence. From that time,
madam, he has been in the most imminent danger of
death, and I do not know whether you could now save
his life even if you were inclined to take pity on him.'

    " ' This was what I said to her,' added the old lady.
' The fear of your death staggered her, and I saw her
face change colour. ' Is what you say to me quite true,'
said she ; ' and does his illness proceed only from his love

of me?' 'Ah, madam,' replied I, 'it is but too true; would to Heaven it were false!' 'And do you really think,' resumed she, 'that the hope of seeing and speaking to me could contribute to diminish the peril of his situation?' 'It very likely may,' said I; 'and if you desire me, I will try this remedy.' 'Well, then,' replied she, sighing, 'let him hope that he may see me, but he must not expect any other favours, unless he aspires to marry me, and my father gives his consent!' 'Madam,' said I, 'you are very good; I will go directly to this young gentleman, and announce to him that he will have the pleasure of seeing and conversing with you.' 'I do not know,' said she, 'that I can fix a more convenient time to do him this favour than on Friday next during the midday prayer. Let him observe when my father goes out to attend at the mosque; and then let him come immediately before this house, if he is well enough to go abroad. I shall see him arrive from my window, and will come down to let him in. We will converse together while prayers last, and he can retire before my father returns.'

"'This is Tuesday,' continued the old lady; 'between this and Friday you will be sufficiently recovered to encounter this interview.' Whilst the good lady was talking, I felt my disorder diminish, or rather by the time she concluded her discourse, I found myself quite recovered. 'Take this,' said I, giving her my purse, which was quite full, 'to you alone I owe my cure; I think this money better employed than all I have given to the physicians, who have done nothing but torment me during my illness.'

"The lady having left me, I found myself sufficiently strong to get up. My relations, delighted to see me so much better, congratulated me on my recovery, and took their leave.

"Friday morning being arrived, the old lady came whilst I was dressing, and making choice of the handsomest dress my wardrobe contained, 'I do not ask you,' said she, 'how you find yourself; the occupation you are engaged in sufficiently convinces me of what I am to think; but will not you bathe before you go to the principal cadi's?' 'That would take up too much time,' replied I; 'I shall content myself with sending for a barber to shave my head and beard.' I then ordered one of my slaves to seek one who was expert in his business, as well as expeditious.

"The slave brought me this unlucky barber, who is here present. After having saluted me, he said, 'Sir, by your countenance you seem to be unwell.' I replied that I was recovering from a very severe illness. 'I wish God may preserve you from all kinds of evils,' continued he, 'and may His grace accompany you everywhere.' 'I hope He will grant this wish,' said I, 'for which I am much obliged to you.' 'As you are now recovering from illness,' resumed he, 'I pray God that He will preserve you in health. Now tell me, what is your pleasure; I have brought my razors and my lancets; do you wish me to shave, or to bleed you?' 'Did I not tell you,' returned I, 'that I am recovering from illness? You may suppose then that I did not send for you to bleed me. Be quick and shave me, and do not lose time in talking, for I am in a hurry, and have an appointment precisely at noon.'

"The barber employed a great deal of time in undoing his apparatus, and preparing his razors; and then, instead of putting water into his basin, he drew out of his case an astrolabe, went out of my room, and walked into the middle of the court with a sedate step, to take the height of the sun. He returned with the same gravity, and on entering the chamber, ' You will, no doubt, be glad to learn, sir,' said he, ' that this Friday is the eighteenth day of the moon of Safar, in the year six hundred and fifty-three (the year of the Hegira, an epoch from which all the Mahometans reckon) since the retreat of our great prophet from Mecca to Medina, and in the year seven thousand three hundred and twenty of the epoch of the great Iskander with the two horns; and that the conjunction of Mars and Mercury signifies that you cannot choose a better time than the present day and present hour to be shaved. But on the other side, this conjunction forms a bad presage for you. It demonstrates to me, that you this day will encounter a great danger; not indeed of losing your life, but of an inconvenience which will remain with you all your days; you ought to be obliged to me for advertising you to be careful of this misfortune; I should be sorry that it befell you.'

" Judge, gentlemen, of my vexation, of having fallen in the way of this chattering and ridiculous barber; what a mortifying delay for a lover, who was preparing for a tender meeting with his mistress ! I was quite exasperated. ' I care very little,' said I angrily, ' either for your advice or your predictions; I did not send for you to consult you on astrology; you came here to shave me; therefore either perform your office, or take yourself away, that I may send for another barber.'

" ' Sir,' replied he, in a tone so phlegmatic, that I could scarcely contain myself, ' what reason have you to be angry? Do not you know that all barbers are not like me, and that you would not find another such, even if you had him made on purpose. You only asked for a barber, and in my person are united the best barber of Bagdad, an experienced physician, a profound chemist, a never-failing astrologer, a finished grammarian, a perfect rhetorician, a subtle logician; a mathematician, thoroughly accomplished in geometry, arithmetic, astronomy, and in all the refinements of algebra; an historian who is acquainted with the history of all the kingdoms in the universe. Besides these sciences, I am well instructed in all the points of philosophy; and have my memory well stored with all our laws and all our traditions. I am a poet, an architect; but what am I not? There is nothing in Nature concealed from me. Your late honoured father, to whom I pay a tribute of tears every time I think of him, was fully convinced of my merit. He loved me, caressed me, and never ceased quoting me in all companies, as the first man in the whole world. My gratitude and friendship for him attaches me to you; and urges me to take you under my protection, and insure you from all the misfortunes with which the planets may threaten you.'

"At this speech, notwithstanding my anger, I could not help laughing. 'When do you mean to have done, impertinent chatterer,' cried I, 'and when do you intend to begin shaving me?'

"'Sir,' replied the barber, 'you do me an injury by calling me a chatterer: every one, on the contrary, bestows on me the honourable appellation of silent. I had six brothers whom you might with some reason have termed chatterers, and that you may be acquainted with them, the eldest was named Bacbouc, the second Bakbarah, the third Bakbac, the fourth Alcouz, the fifth Alnaschar, and the sixth Schacabac. These were indeed most tiresome talkers, but I, who am the youngest of the family, am very grave and concise in my discourses.'

"Place yourselves in my situation, gentlemen; what could I do with so cruel a tormentor? 'Give him three pieces of gold,' said I to the slave who overlooked the expenses of my house, 'and send him away, that I may be at peace; I will not be shaved to-day.' 'Sir!' cried the barber at hearing this, 'what am I to understand, sir, by these words? It was not I who came to seek you; it was you who ordered me to come; and that being the case, I swear by the faith of a Mussulman, that I will not quit your house till I have shaved you. If you do not know my worth, it is no fault of mine; your late honoured father was more just to my merits. Every time when he sent for me to bleed him he used to make me sit down by his side, and then it was delightful to hear the clever things I entertained him with. I kept him in continual admiration; I enchanted him; and when I had done, 'Ah,' he would exclaim, 'you are an inexhaustible fund of science; no one can approach the profoundness of your knowledge.' 'My dear sir,' I used to reply, 'you do me more honour than I deserve. If I say a good thing, I am indebted to you for the favourable hearing you are so good as to grant me: it is your liberality that inspires me with those sublime ideas, which have the good fortune to meet your approbation.' One day, when he was quite charmed with an admirable discourse I had just concluded, 'Give him,' cried he, 'an hundred pieces of gold, and put on him one of my richest robes!' I received this present immediately; and at the same instant I drew out his horoscope, which I found to be one of the most fortunate in the world. I carried the proofs of my gratefulness still farther, for I cupped him instead of bleeding him with a lancet.'

"He did not stop here; he began another speech which lasted a full half-hour. Fatigued with hearing him, and vexed at finding the time pass without my getting forward, I knew not what more to say. 'No, indeed,' at length I exclaimed, 'it is not possible that there should exist in the whole world a man who takes a greater delight in enraging people.'

"I then thought I might succeed better by gentle means. 'In the name of God,' I said to him, 'leave off your fine speeches, and finish with me quickly: I have an affair of the greatest importance, which obliges me to go out, as I have already told you.' At these words he began to laugh. 'It would be very praiseworthy,' said he, 'if our minds were always wise and prudent; however, I am willing to believe, that when you put yourself in a passion with me, it was your late illness which occasioned this change in your temper; on this account, therefore, you are in need of some instructions, and you cannot do better than follow the example of your father and your grandfather: they used to come and consult me in all their affairs; and I may safely say without vanity, that they were always the better for my advice. Let me tell you, sir, that a man scarcely ever succeeds in any enterprise, if he has not recourse to the opinions of enlightened persons: no man becomes clever, says the proverb, unless he consults a clever man. I am entirely at your service, and you have only to command me.'

"'Cannot I then persuade you,' interrupted I, 'to desist from these long speeches, which tend to no purpose but to distract my head, and prevent me from keeping my appointment: shave me directly, or leave my house.' In saying this I arose, and angrily struck my foot against the ground.

"When he saw that I was really exasperated with him, 'Sir,' said he, 'do not be angry; we are going to begin directly.' In fact, he washed my head, and began to shave me; but he had not made four strokes with his razor when he stopped to say, 'Sir, you are hasty; you should abstain from these gusts of passion, which only come from the devil. Besides which, I deserve that you should have some respect for me on account of my age, my knowledge, and my striking virtues.'

"'Go on shaving me,' said I, interrupting him again, 'and speak no more.' 'That is to say,' replied he, 'that you have some pressing affair on your hands; I'll lay a wager that I am not mistaken.' 'Why, I told you so two hours ago,' returned I; 'you ought to have shaved me long since.' 'Moderate your ardour,' replied he; 'perhaps you have not considered well of what you are going to do; when one does anything precipitately, it is almost always a source of repentance. I wish you would tell me what this affair is that you are in such haste about, and I will give you my opinion on it; you have plenty of time, for you are not expected till noon, and it will not be noon these three hours.' 'That is nothing to me,' said I; 'people of honour, who keep their word, are always before the time appointed. But I perceive that in reasoning thus with you, I am imitating the faults of chattering barbers; finish shaving me quickly.'

"The more anxious I was for despatch, the less so was he to obey me. He left his razor to take up his astrolabe; and when he put down his astrolabe, he took up his razor.

"He got his astrolabe the second time, and left me half-shaved to go and see what o'clock it was precisely. He returned. 'Sir,' said he, 'I was certain I was not mistaken; it wants three hours to noon, I am well assured, or all the rules of astronomy are false.' 'Gracious heaven!' cried I, 'my patience is exhausted, I can hold out no longer. Cursed barber, ill-omened barber, I can hardly refrain from falling upon thee and strangling thee.' 'Softly, sir,' said he coolly, and without showing any emotion and anger, 'you seem to have no fear of bringing on your illness again; do not be so passionate, and you shall be shaved in a moment.' Saying this, he put the astrolabe in his case, took his razor, which he sharpened on the strop that was fastened to his girdle, and began to shave me; but whilst he was shaving me he could not help talking. 'If you would, sir,' said he, 'inform me what this affair is that will engage you at noon, I would give you some advice, which you might find serviceable.' To satisfy him I told him that some friends expected me at noon to regale me, and rejoice with me on my recovery.

"No sooner had the barber heard me mention a feast, than he exclaimed, 'God bless you on this day as well as on every other; you bring to my mind, that yesterday I invited four or five friends to come and regale with me to-day; I had forgotten it, and have not made any preparations for them.' 'Let not that embarrass you,' said I; 'although I am going out, my table is always well supplied, and I make you a present of all that is intended for it to-day; I will also give you as much wine as you want, for I have some most excellent in my cellar; but then you must be quick in finishing to shave me; and remember that instead of making you presents to hear you talk, as my father did, I give them to you to be silent.'

"He was not content to rely on my word. 'May God recompense you,' cried he, 'for the favour you do me; but show me directly these provisions, that I may judge if there will be enough to regale my friends handsomely; for I wish them to be satisfied with the good cheer I shall give them.' 'I have,' said I, 'a lamb, six capons, a dozen of fowls, and sufficient for four courses.' I gave orders to a slave to produce all that, together with four large jugs of wine. 'This is well,' replied the barber, 'but we shall want some fruit, and something for sauce to the meat.' I desired what he wanted to be given him. He left off shaving me to examine each thing separately, and as this examination took up nearly half-an-hour, I stamped and swore; but I might amuse myself as I pleased, the rascal did not hurry a bit the more. At length, however, he again took up the razor and shaved for a few minutes, then stopping suddenly, 'I should never have supposed, sir,' said he, 'that you had been of so liberal a turn; I begin to discover that your late father, of honoured memory, lives a second time in you; certainly I did not deserve the favours you heap on me, and I assure you that I shall retain an eternal sense of the obligation; for, sir, that you may know it in future, I will tell you that I have nothing but what I get from generous people like yourself, in which I resemble Zantout, who rubs people at the bath, and Sali, who sells little burnt peas about the streets, and Salouz, who sells beans, and Akerscha, who sells herbs, and Abou Mekares, who waters the streets to lay the dust, and Cassem, who belongs to the caliph's guard : all these people give no reception to melancholy ; they are neither sorrowful nor quarrelsome ; better satisfied with their fortune than the caliph himself in the midst of his court, they are always gay and ready to dance and sing, and they have each their peculiar dance and song, with which they entertain the whole city of Bagdad ; but what I esteem the most in them is, that they are none of them great talkers any more than your slave, who has the honour of speaking to you. Here, sir, I will give you the song and the dance of Zantout, who rubs the people at the bath ; look at me, and you will see an exact imitation.'

"The barber sung the song and danced the dance of Zantout ; and notwithstanding all I could say to make him cease his buffoonery, he would not stop till he had imitated in the same way all those he had mentioned. After that, 'Sir,' said he, 'I am going to invite all these good people to my house, and if you will take my advice, you will be of our party, and leave your friends, who are perhaps great talkers, and will only disturb you by their tiresome conversations, and will make you relapse into an illness still worse than that from which you are just recovered ; instead of which, at my house you will only enjoy pleasure.'

"Notwithstanding my anger, I could not avoid laughing at his folly. 'I wish,' said I, 'that I had no other engagement, and I would gladly accept your proposal ; I would with all my heart make one of your jolly set, but I must entreat you to excuse me, I am too much engaged to-day; I shall be more at liberty another day, and we will have this party: finish shaving me, and hasten to return, for perhaps your friends are already arrived.' 'Sir,' replied he, 'do not refuse me the favour I ask of you. Come and amuse yourself with the good company I shall have; if you had once been with such people, you would have been so pleased with them that you would give up your friends for them.' 'Say no more about it,' said I; 'I cannot be present at your feast.'

"I gained nothing by gentleness. 'Since you will not come with me,' replied the barber, 'you must allow me then to accompany you. I will go home with the provisions you have given me; my friends shall eat of them if they like, and I will return immediately. I cannot commit such an incivility as to suffer you to go alone—you deserve this piece of complaisance on my part.' 'Good Heaven,' exclaimed I, on hearing this, 'am I then condemned to bear this whole day so tormenting a creature! In the name of the great God,' said I to him, 'finish your tiresome speeches; go to your friends, eat and drink, and entertain yourselves, and leave me at liberty to go to mine. I will go alone, and do not want any one to accompany me; and indeed if you must know the truth, the place where I am going is not one in which you can be received—I only can be admitted.' 'You are joking, sir,' replied he; 'if your friends have invited you to an entertainment, what reason can prevent me from accompanying you? You will give them great pleasure, I am sure, by taking with you a man like me, who has the art of entertaining a company and making them merry. Say what you will, sir, I am resolved to go in spite of you.'

" These words, gentlemen, threw me into the greatest embarrassment. 'How can I possibly contrive to get rid of this infernal barber,' thought I to myself. 'If I continue obstinately to contradict him, our contest will never be finished.' I had already waited till they had called the people to noon prayers for the first time ; and as it was now almost the moment to set out, I determined therefore not to answer him a single word, and to appear as if I agreed to everything he said. He finished shaving me, and he had no sooner done than I said to him, ' Take some of my people with you to carry these provisions home ; then return here, I will wait, and not go without you.'

" He then went out, and I finished dressing myself as quickly as possible. I only waited till they called to prayers for the last time, when I hastened to commence my expedition ; but this malicious barber, who seemed aware of my intention, was satisfied with accompanying my people only within sight of his own house, and seeing them go in. He afterwards concealed himself at the corner of the street, to observe and follow me. In short, when I got to the door of the cadi, I turned round and perceived him at the end of the street. This sight put me into the greatest rage.

" The cadi's door was half open, and when I went in I saw the old lady who was waiting for me, and who, as soon as she had shut the door, conducted me to the apartment of the young lady with whom I was so much in love. But I had hardly begun to enter into any conversation with her before we heard a great noise in the street. The young lady ran to the window, and looking through the blinds, perceived that it was the cadi, her

father, who was already returning from prayers. I looked
out at the same time, and saw the barber seated exactly
opposite, and on the same bench from whence I had
beheld the lady the first time.

"I had now two subjects for alarm, the arrival of the
cadi, and the presence of the barber. The young lady
dissipated my fears on the first, by telling me that her
father very rarely came up into her apartment; but as
she had foreseen that such an interruption might take
place, she had prepared the means for my escape in case
of necessity; but the indiscretion of that unlucky barber
caused me great uneasiness, and you will soon perceive
that this disquietude was not without foundation.

"As soon as the cadi was returned home, he himself
inflicted the bastinado on a slave who had deserved it.
The slave uttered loud cries, which were distinguishable
even in the street. The barber thought I was the person
whom they were treating ill, and that these were my
cries. Fully persuaded of this, he began to call out as
loud as he could, to tear his clothes, throw dust upon his
head, and call for help to all the neighbours who ran out
to him. They inquired what was the matter, and what
assistance they could give him. 'Alas!' cried he, 'they
are assassinating my master, my dear lord;' and without
saying another word, he ran to my house, crying out in
the same way, and returned, followed by all my servants
armed with sticks. They knocked furiously at the door
of the cadi, who sent a slave to know what the noise was
about; but the slave, quite terrified, returned to his
master. 'My lord,' said he, 'above ten thousand men
will come into your house by force, and are already
beginning to break open the door.'

"The cadi ran himself to the door and inquired what they wanted. His venerable appearance did not inspire my people with any respect, and they insolently addressed him, 'Cursed cadi! thou dog! for what reason art thou going to murder our master? What has he done to thee?' 'My good people,' replied the cadi, 'why should I murder your master, whom I do not know, and who has never offended me? My door is open, you may come in and search my house.' 'You have given him the bastinado,' said the barber; 'I heard his cries not a minute ago.' 'But,' replied the cadi, 'as I said before, in what can your master have offended me, that I should ill-treat him thus? Is he in my house? and if he is, how could he get in, or who could have introduced him?' 'Thou wilt not make me believe thee with thy great beard, thou wicked cadi,' resumed the barber; 'I know what I say. Your daughter loves our master, and appointed a meeting in your house during the midday prayers; you no doubt received information of it, and returned quickly; you surprised him here, and ordered your slaves to give him the bastinado; but this wicked action shall not remain unpunished: the caliph shall be informed of it, and will execute a severe and speedy sentence on you. Give him his liberty, and let him come out directly, otherwise we will go in and take him from you to your shame.' 'There is no occasion to say so much about it,' said the cadi, 'nor to make such a bustle; if what you say is true, you have only to go in and search for him—I give you full permission.' The cadi had scarcely spoken these words when the barber and my people burst into the house, like a set of furious madmen, and began to seek for me in every corner.

" As I heard everything the barber said to the cadi, I endeavoured to find out some place to conceal myself in. I was unable to discover any other than a large empty chest, into which I immediately got, and shut the lid down upon me. After the barber had searched every other place, he did not fail coming into the apartment where I was. He went directly to the chest, and opened it; and as soon as he perceived that I was in it, he took it up and carried it away upon his head. He descended from the top of the staircase, which was very high, into a court, through which he quickly passed, and at last reached the street-door.

" As he was carrying me along the street, the lid of the chest unfortunately opened: I had not resolution enough to bear the shame and disgrace of being thus exposed to the populace who followed us; I jumped down, therefore, into the street in such a hurry that I hurt myself violently, and have been lame ever since. I did not at first perceive the full extent of my misfortune; I therefore made haste to get up, and run away from the people who were laughing at me. At the same time I scattered a handful or two of gold and silver, with which I had filled my purse, and while they were stopping to pick it up, I made my escape by passing through several private streets. But the cursed barber, taking advantage of the trick which I had made use of to get rid of the crowd, followed me so closely, that he never once lost sight of me; and all the time he continued calling aloud, ' Stop, sir, why do you run so fast? You know not how much I have felt for you on account of the ill-usage you have received from the cadi; and well I might, as you have been so generous to me and my friends, and we are under such obligations to you. Did I not truly inform you that you would endanger your life through your obstinacy, in not suffering me to accompany you? All this has happened to you through your own fault; and I know not what would have become of you if I had not obstinately determined to follow you, and observe which way you went. Where then, my lord, are you running? Pray wait for me.'

"It was in this manner that the unlucky barber kept calling out to me all through the street. He was not satisfied with having scandalised me so completely in the quarter of the town where the cadi resided, but seemed to wish that the whole city should become acquainted with my disgrace. This put me into such a rage that I could have stopped and strangled him, but that would only have increased my destruction. I therefore went another way to work. As I perceived that, by his calling out, the eyes of every one were attracted towards me, some looking out of their windows, and others stopping in the street to stare at me, I went into a khan, the master of which was known to me. I found him indeed at the door, where the noise and uproar had brought him. 'In the name of God,' I cried, 'do me the favour to prevent that mad fellow from following me in here.' He not only promised me to do so, but he kept his word, although it was not without great difficulty; for the obstinate barber attempted to force an entrance in spite of him. Nor did he retire before he uttered a thousand abusive words: and he continued to tell every one he met, till he reached his own house, the very great service he pretended to have done me.

"It was thus that I got rid of this tiresome man. The

master of the khan then entreated me to give him an account of my adventure. I did so; after which I asked him in my turn to let me have an apartment in his house till I was quite cured. 'You will be much better accommodated, sir,' he said, 'in your own house.' 'I do not wish to return there,' I answered, 'for that detestable barber will not fail to find me out; I shall then be pestered with him every day, and it would absolutely kill me with vexation to have him constantly before my eyes. Besides, after what has happened to me this day, I am determined not to remain any longer in this city. I will wander wherever my ill stars may direct me.' In short, as soon as I was cured, I took as much money as I thought would be sufficient for my journey, and gave the remainder of my fortune to my relations.

"I then set out from Bagdad, gentlemen, and arrived here. I had every reason, at least, to hope that I should not have met with this mischievous barber in a country so distant from my own; and I now discover him in your company. Be not therefore surprised at my anxiety and eagerness to retire. You may judge of the painful sensations the sight of this man causes me, through whose means I became lame and was reduced to the necessity of giving up my relations, my friends, and my country."

Having made his speech, the lame young man got up and went out. The master of the house conducted him to the door, assuring him that it gave him great pain to have been the cause, though innocently, of so great a mortification.

When the young man was gone (continued the tailor),

we still remained very much astonished at his history.
We cast our eyes towards the barber, and told him that
he had done wrong—if what we had just heard was true.
"Gentlemen," answered he, raising his head, which he
had till now kept towards the ground, "the silence which
I have imposed upon myself while this young man was
telling you his story ought to prove to you that he has
advanced nothing that was not the fact; notwithstanding,
however, all that he has told you, I still maintain that I
ought to have done what I did, and I leave you yourselves to judge of it. Was he not thrown into a situation of great danger, and, without my assistance, would he
so fortunately have escaped from it? He may, indeed,
think himself very happy to have got free from it with
only a lame leg. Was I not exposed to a much greater
danger, in order to get him from a house where I thought
he was so ill-treated? Has he, then, reason to complain
of me, and to attack me with so many injurious re-
proaches? You see what we get by serving ungrateful
people. He accuses me of being a chatterer; it is mere
calumny. Of seven brothers, of whom our family con-
sists, I am the very one who speaks least, and yet who
possesses the most wit. In order to convince you of
it, gentlemen, I have only to relate their story and my
own to you. I entreat you to favour me with your
attention."

"So soon as the barber had spoken," said the tailor,
"we plainly perceived the young man was not wrong
in accusing him of being a great chatterer. We nevertheless wished that he should remain with us, and
partake of the feast which the master of the house had

prepared for us. We then sat down at table, and continued to enjoy ourselves till the time of the last prayers before sunset. All the company then separated, and I returned to my shop, where I remained till it was time to shut it up and go to my house."

II

THE STORY OF CYMON AND IPHIGENIA

From The Decameron

Induction

Now began the sun to dart forth his golden beams, when
Fiammetta, incited by the sweet singing birds, which
since the break of day sate merrily chanting on the trees,
arose from her bed, as all the other ladies likewise did;
and the three young gentlemen descended down into the
fields, where they walked in a gentle pace on the green
grass, until the sun was risen a little higher. On many
pleasant matters they conferred together as they walked
in several companies, till at length the Queen, finding
the heat to enlarge itself strongly, returned back to the
castle, where, when they were all arrived, she commanded
that after this morning's walking their stomachs should
be refreshed with wholesome wines, and also divers sorts
of banqueting stuff. Afterward they all repaired into
the garden, not departing thence until the hour of dinner
was come : at which time the master of the household
having prepared everything in decent readiness, after a
solemn song was sung by order of the Queen, they were
seated at the table.

When they had dined to their own liking and contentment they began, in continuation of their former
order, to exercise divers dances, and afterward voices to
their instruments, and many pretty madrigals and roun-
delays. Upon the finishing of these delights the Queen
gave them leave to take their rest, when such as were so
minded went to sleep; others solaced themselves in the
garden. But after midday was past over, they met,
according to their wonted manner, and, as the Queen
had commanded, at the fair fountain, where she being
placed in her seat royal, and casting her eye upon
Pamfilo, she bade him begin the day's discourses of
happy success in love after disastrous and troublesome
accidents, who, yielding thereto with humble reverence,
thus began :

Many novels, gracious ladies, do offer themselves to
my memory wherewith to begin so pleasant a day as it is
her highness's desire that this should be, among which
plenty I esteem one above all the rest, because you may
comprehend thereby not only the fortunate conclusion
wherewith we intend to begin our day, but also how
mighty the forces of love are, deserving to be both
admired and reverenced. Albeit there are many, who
scarcely know what they say, do condemn them with
infinite gross imputations, which I purpose to disprove,
and, I hope, to your no little pleasing.

Cymon by falling in love became wise, and by force of arms winning his fair lady Iphigenia on the seas was afterwards imprisoned at Rhodes. Being delivered by one named Lysimachus, with him he recovered his Iphigenia again, and fair Cassandra, even in the midst of their marriage. They fled with them into Crete, where after they had married them, they were called home to their own dwelling.

ACCORDING to the ancient annals of the Cypriots, there sometime lived in Cyprus a noble gentleman, who was commonly called Aristippus, and exceeded all other of the country in the goods of fortune. Divers children he had, but (amongst the rest) a son, in whose birth he was more unfortunate than the rest, and continually grieved in regard that, having all complete perfections of beauty, good form, and many parts, surpassing all other youths of his age or stature, yet he wanted the real ornament of the soul—reason and judgment, being indeed a mere idiot or fool, and no better hope to be expected from him. His true name, according as he received it by baptism, was Galeso; but because whether by the laborious pains of his tutor's indulgence, with great care and fair endeavour of his parents, or by ingenuity of any other, he could not be brought to civility of life, understanding of letters, or common carriage of a reasonable creature; for his gross and deformed kind of speech, for his qualities also savouring rather of brutish feeling than any way derived from manly education; as an epithet of scorn and derision generally, they gave him the name of Cymon, which in their native country-language, and divers other beside, signifieth a very sot or fool, and so was he termed by every one.

This lost kind of life in him was no mean burthen of grief unto his noble father. All hope being already spent of any future happy recovery, he gave command, because he would not always have such a sorrow in his sight, that he should live at a farm of his own in a country village, among his peasants and plough-swains. This was not anyway distasteful to Cymon, but well agreed with his own natural disposition ; for their rural qualities and gross behaviour pleased him beyond the cities' civility. Cymon living thus at his father's country village, exercising nothing else but rural demeanour, such as then delighted him above all other, it chanced upon a day, about the hour of noon, as he was walking over the fields with a long staff on his neck, which commonly he used to carry, he entered into a small thicket, reputed the goodliest in all those quarters, and by reason it was then the month of May, the trees had their leaves fairly shot forth.

When he had walked through the thicket it came to pass that, even as good fortune guided him, he came into a fair meadow, on every side engirt with trees ; and in one corner thereof stood a goodly fountain, whose current was both cool and clear. Hard by it upon the green grass he espied a very beautiful damsel, seeming to be fast asleep, attired in such loose garments as hid very little of her white body ; only from the girdle downward she wore a kirtle made close unto her of interwoven delicate silk, and at her feet lay two other damsels sleeping, and a servant in the same manner. No sooner had Cymon fixed his eye upon her but he stood leaning on his staff, and viewed her advisedly, without speaking a word, and in no mean admiration, as if he had never seen the form of a woman before. He began then to feel in his rural understanding (whereunto never till now, either by painful instruction or any good means used to him, any honest civility had power of impression) a strange kind of humour to awake, which informed his gross and dull spirit that this damsel was the very fairest which any living man beheld.

Then he began to distinguish her parts, commending the tresses of her hair, which he imagined to be of gold, her forehead, nose, mouth, neck, arms, but, above all, her breasts, appearing as yet but only to show themselves like two little mountains. So that from being a rustic clownish lout he would needs now become a judge of beauty, coveting earnestly in his soul to see her eyes, which were veiled over with sound sleep that kept them fast enclosed together; and only to look on them he wished a thousand times that she would awake, for in his judgment she excelled all the women that ever he had seen, and doubted whether she were some goddess or no; so strangely was he metamorphosed from folly to a sensible apprehension, more than common. And so far did this sudden knowledge in him extend that he could conceive of divine and celestial things, and that they were more to be admired and reverenced than those of human or terrene consideration; wherefore the more gladly he contented himself to tarry till she awaked of her own accord. And although the time of stay seemed tedious to him, yet notwithstanding, he was overcome with such extraordinary contentment as he had no power to depart thence, but stood as if he had been glued to the ground.

After some indifferent respite of time, it chanced that

the young damsel, who was named Iphigenia, awaked
before any of the others with her, and lifting up her
head with her eyes wide open, she saw Cymon standing
before her leaning still on his staff. Whereat marvelling
not a little she said unto him, " Cymon, whither wan-
derest thou, or what dost thou seek for in this wood ? "
Cymon, who not only by his countenance but likewise
by his folly, nobility of birth, and wealthy possessions of
his father, was generally known throughout the country,
made no answer at all to the demand of Iphigenia ; but
so soon as he beheld her eyes open he began to observe
them with a constant regard, and was persuaded in his
soul that from them flowed such an unutterable singularity as he had never felt till then. Which the young
gentlewoman well noting, she began to wax fearful lest
these steadfast looks of his should incite his rusticity to
some attempt which might redound to her dishonour ;
wherefore awaking her women and servants, and they all
being risen, she said, " Farewell, Cymon, I leave thee to
thine own good fortune ; " whereto he presently replied,
saying, " I will go with you." Now although the gentlewoman refused his company as dreading some act of incivility from him, yet could she not devise any way to be
rid of him till he had brought her to her own dwelling,
where taking leave mannerly of her, he went directly
home to his father's house, saying nothing should compel
him to live any longer in the muddy country. And albeit
his father was much offended hereat, and all the rest of
his kindred and friends, yet not knowing how to help it,
they suffered him to continue there still, waiting to know
the cause of this his so sudden alteration from the course
of life which contented him so highly before.

c

Cymon being now wounded to the heart, where never any civil instruction could before get entrance, with love's piercing dart, by the bright beauty of Iphigenia, falling from one change to another, moved much admiration in his father, kindred, and all else that knew him. For first he requested of his father that he might be habited and respected like to his brethren, whereto right gladly he condescended. And frequenting the company of civil youths, observing also the carriage of gentlemen, especially such as were amorously inclined, he grew to a beginning in a short time, to the wonder of every one, not only to understand the first instruction of letters, but also became most skilful even amongst them that were best exercised in philosophy. And afterward, love to Iphigenia being the sole occasion of this happy alteration, not only did his harsh and clownish voice convert itself more mildly, but also he became a singular musician and could perfectly play on any instrument. Beside he took delight in the riding and managing of great horses, and finding himself of a strong and able body he used all kinds of military disciplines, as well by sea as on the land. And to be brief, because I would not seem tedious in the repetition of all his virtues, scarcely had he attained to the fourth year after he was thus fallen in love, but he became generally known to be the most civil, wise, and worthy gentleman, as well for all virtues enriching the mind as any whatsoever to beautify the body, that very hardly he could be equalled throughout the whole kingdom of Cyprus.

What shall we say then, virtuous ladies, concerning this Cymon? Surely nothing else but that those high and divine virtues infused into his gentle soul, were by

envious Fortune bound and shut up in some small angle
of his intellect, which being shaken and set at liberty by
Love, as having a far more potent power than Fortune
in quickening and reviving the dull and drowsy spirits,
so declared his mighty and sovereign authority in setting
free many fair and precious virtues unjustly detained,
and let the world's eye behold them truly, by manifest
testimony from whence he can deliver those spirits subjected to his power, and guide them, afterward, to the
highest degrees of honour. And although Cymon by
affecting Iphigenia failed in some particular things, yet
notwithstanding his father Aristippus, duly considering
that love had made him a man, whereas, before, he was
no better than a beast, not only endured all patiently,
but also advised him therein to take such courses as best
liked himself. Nevertheless Cymon, who refused to be
called Galesus, which was his natural name indeed, re-
membering that Iphigenia termed him Cymon, and coveting, under this title, to compass the issue of his honest
amorous desire, made many motions to Cipseus, the
father of Iphigenia, that he would be pleased to let him
have her in marriage. But Cipseus told him that he had
already passed his promise for her to a gentleman of
Rhodes, named Pasimunda, which promise he religiously
intended to perform.

The time being come which was concluded on for
Iphigenia's marriage, in regard that the affianced husband had sent for her, Cymon thus communed with his
own thoughts. "Now is the time," quoth he, "to let
my divine mistress see how truly and honourably I do
affect her, because, by her, I am become a man. But if
I could be possessed of her, I should grow more glorious

than the common condition of a mortal man, and have her I will, or lose my life in the adventure." Being thus resolved, he prevailed with divers young gentlemen, his friends, making them of his faction, and secretly prepared a ship furnished with all things for a naval fight, setting suddenly forth to sea, and hulling abroad in those parts by which the vessel should pass that must convey Iphigenia to Rhodes to her husband. After many honours done to them who were to transport her thence unto Rhodes, being embarked they set sail upon their voyage.

Cymon, who slept not in a business so earnestly importing him, set on them, the day following, with his ship, and standing aloft on the deck, cried out to them that had the charge of Iphigenia, saying, "Strike your sails, or else determine to be sunk in the sea." The enemies to Cymon, being nothing daunted with his words, prepared to stand upon their own defence; which made Cymon, after the former speeches delivered, and no answer returned, to command the grappling-irons to be cast forth, which took so fast hold on the Rhodians' ship that, whether they would or no, both the vessels joined close together. And he showing himself fierce like a lion, not tarrying to be seconded by any, stepped aboard the Rhodians' ship as if he made no respect at all of them, and having his sword ready drawn in his hand, incited by the virtue of unfeigned love, laid about him on all sides very manfully. Which when the men of Rhodes perceived, they cast down their weapons, and all of them, as it were, with one voice yielded themselves his prisoners, whereupon he said : " Honest friends, neither desire of booty, nor hatred to you, did occasion my departure from Cyprus, thus to assail you with drawn weapons, but that which hereto hath moved me is a matter highly importing to me, and very easy for you to grant and so enjoy your present peace. I desire to have fair Iphigenia from you, whom I love above all other ladies living, because I could not obtain her of her father to make her my lawful wife in marriage. Love is the ground of my instant conquest, and I must use you as my mortal enemies, if you stand upon any further terms with me, and do not deliver her as mine own, for your Pasimunda must not enjoy what is my right, first by virtue of my love, and now by conquest. Deliver her, therefore, and depart hence at your pleasure."

The men of Rhodes being rather constrained thereto than of any free disposition in themselves, with tears in their eyes delivered Iphigenia to Cymon, who beholding her in like manner to weep, thus spake unto her: "Noble lady, do not anyway discomfort yourself, for I am your Cymon, who have more right and true title to you, and much better do deserve you, by my long-continued affection to you, than Pasimunda can anyway plead, because you belong to him but only by promise." So bringing her aboard his own ship, where the gentlemen his companions gave her kind welcome, without touching anything else belonging to the Rhodians, he gave them free liberty to depart.

Cymon being more joyful by the obtaining of his heart's desire, than any other conquest else in the world could make him, after he had spent some time in comforting Iphigenia, who as yet sate sadly sighing, he consulted with his companions, who joined with him in opinion, that their safest course was by no means to return to Cyprus; and therefore all, with one accord, resolved to set sail for Crete, where every one made account, but especially Cymon, in regard of ancient and new combined kindred, as also very intimate friends, to find very worthy entertainment, and so to continue there safely with Iphigenia.   But fortune, who was so favourable to Cymon in granting him so pleasing a conquest, to show her inconstancy, so suddenly changed the inestimable joy of our jocund lover into as heavy sorrow and disaster.   For, four hours were not fully completed since his departure from the Rhodians, but dark night came upon them, and he sitting conversing with his fair mistress in the sweetest solace of his soul, the winds began to blow roughly, the seas swelled angrily, and a tempest rose impetuously, that no man could see what his duty was to do in such a great unexpected distress, nor how to warrant themselves from perishing.

If this accident were displeasing to poor Cymon, I think the question were in vain demanded ; for now it seemeth to him that the gods had granted his chief desire, to the end he should die with the greater anguish in losing both his love and life together.   His friends likewise felt the self-same afflictions, but especially Iphigenia, who wept and grieved beyond all measure, to see the ship beaten with such stormy billows as threatened her sinking every minute.   Impatiently she cursed the love of Cymon, greatly blamed his desperate boldness, and maintaining that so violent a tempest could never happen but only by the gods' displeasure, who would not permit him to have a wife against their will ; and therefore thus punished his proud presumption, not only in his unavoidable death, but also that her life must perish for company.

She continuing in these woeful lamentations, and the

mariners labouring all in vain because the violence of the tempest increased more and more, so that every moment they expected wrecking, they were carried contrary to their own knowledge, very near to the Isle of Rhodes, which they being no way able to avoid, and utterly ignorant of the coast, for safety of their lives they laboured to land there if possibly they might. Wherein fortune was somewhat furtherous to them, driving them into a small gulf of the sea, whereinto, but a little while before, the Rhodians, from whom Cymon had taken Iphigenia, were newly entered with their ship. Nor had they any knowledge each of other till the break of day, which made the heavens to look more clearly, and gave them discovery of being within a flight's shoot together. Cymon looking forth, and espying the same ship which he had left the day before, he grew exceeding sorrowful, as fearing that which after followed, and therefore he willed the mariners to get away from her by all their best endeavour, and let fortune afterwards dispose of them as she pleased, for into a worse place they could not come, nor fall into the like danger.

The mariners employed their utmost pains, and all proved but loss of time, for the wind was so stern, and the waves so turbulent, that still they drove them the contrary way; so that striving to get forth of the gulf, whether they would or no, they were driven on land, and instantly known to the Rhodians, whereof they were not a little joyful. The men of Rhodes being landed, ran presently to the near neighbouring villages, where dwelt divers worthy gentlemen, to whom they reported the arrival of Cymon, what fortune befell them at sea, and that Iphigenia might now be recovered again, with chastisement to Cymon for his bold insolence. They being very joyful of this good news, took so many men as they could of the same village, and ran immediately to the seaside, where Cymon being newly landed and his people, intending flight into a near adjoining forest for defence of himself and Iphigenia, they were all taken, led thence into the village, and afterward unto the chief city of Rhodes.

No sooner were they arrived, but Pasimunda, the intended husband for Iphigenia, who had already heard the tidings, went and complained to the senate, who appointed a gentleman of Rhodes, named Lysimachus, and being that year sovereign magistrate over the Rhodians, to go well provided for the apprehension of Cymon and his company, committing them to prison, which accordingly was done. In this manner the poor unfortunate lover Cymon lost his fair Iphigenia, having won her in so short a time before, and scarcely requited with so much as a kiss. But as for Iphigenia, she was royally welcomed by many lords and ladies of Rhodes, who so kindly comforted her that she soon forgot all her grief and trouble on the sea, remaining in company of those ladies and gentlemen until the day determined for her marriage.

At the earnest entreaty of divers Rhodian gentlemen who were in the ship with Iphigenia, and had their lives courteously saved by Cymon, both he and his friends had their lives likewise spared, although Pasimunda laboured importunately to have them all put to death ; only they were condemned to perpetual imprisonment, which, you must think, was most grievous to them, as being now hopeless of any deliverance. But in the meantime, while

Pasimunda was ordering his nuptial preparation, Fortune seeming to repent the wrongs she had done to Cymon, prepared a new accident whereby to comfort him in his deep distress, and in such manner as I will relate unto you.

Pasimunda had a brother, younger than he in years, but not a jot inferior to him in virtue, whose name was Ormisda, and long time the case had been in question for his taking to wife a fair young gentlewoman of Rhodes, called Cassandra, whom Lysimachus the governor loved very dearly, and hindered her marriage with Ormisda by divers strange accidents. Now Pasimunda perceiving that his own nuptials required much cost and solemnity, he thought it very convenient that one day might serve for both their weddings, which else would launch into more lavish expenses, and therefore concluded that his brother Ormisda should marry Cassandra at the same time as he wedded Iphigenia. Hereupon he consulted with the gentlewoman's parents, who liking the motion as well as he, the determination was set down, and one day to effect the duties of both.

When this came to the hearing of Lysimachus, it was greatly displeasing to him, because now he saw himself utterly deprived of all hope to attain the issue of his desire if Ormisda received Cassandra in marriage. Yet being a very wise and worthy man, he dissembled his distaste, and began to consider on some apt means whereby to disappoint the marriage once more, which he thought impossible to be done except it were by stealth; and that did not appear to him any difficult matter in regard of his office and authority, only it would seem dishonest in him by giving such an unfitting example.

Nevertheless, after long deliberation, honour gave way to love, and resolutely he concluded to steal her away, whatsoever became of it.

Nothing wanted now but a convenient company to assist him, and the order how to have it done. Then he remembered Cymon and his friends, whom he detained as his prisoners, and persuaded himself that he could not have a more faithful friend in such a business than Cymon was. Hereupon, the night following, he sent for him into his chamber, and being alone by themselves, thus he began : " Cymon," quoth he, " as the gods are very bountiful in bestowing their blessings on men, so do they therein most wisely make proof of their virtues, and such as they find firm and constant in all occurrences which may happen, them they make worthy, as valiant spirits, of the very best and highest merit. Now, they being willing to have more certain experience of thy virtues than those which heretofore thou hast shown within the bounds and limits of your father's possessions, which I know to be superabounding, perhaps do intend to present thee other occasions of more important weight and consequence.

" For first of all, as I have heard, by the piercing solicitudes of love, from a senseless creature they made thee to become a man endued with reason. Afterward, by adverse fortune, and now again by wearisome imprisonment, it seemeth that they are desirous to make trial whether thy manly courage be changed or no from that which heretofore it was, when thou hast won a matchless beauty and lost her again in so short a while. Wherefore if thy virtue be such as it hath been, the gods can never give thee any blessing more worthy any acceptance

than she whom they are now minded to bestow on thee;
in which respect, to the end that thou mayest reassume
thy wonted heroic spirit, and become more courageous
than ever heretofore, I will acquaint thee more at large.

"Understand then, noble Cymon, that Pasimunda, the
only glad man of thy misfortune, and diligent suitor
after thy death, maketh all haste he can possibly devise
to celebrate his marriage with thy fair mistress, because
he would plead possession of the prey, which Fortune,
when she smiled, did first bestow, and, afterward frown-
ing, took from thee again. Now, that it must needs
be very irksome to thee—at least if thy love be such
as I am persuaded it is—I partly can collect from myself,
being intended to be wronged by his brother Ormisda,
even in the self-same manner and on his marriage-
day, by taking from me fair Cassandra, the only jewel
of my love and life. For the prevention of two such
notorious injuries, I see that fortune hath left us no
other means but only the virtue of our courages, and
the help of our right hands, by preparing ourselves for
arms, opening a way to thee by a second seizure or
stealth, and to me the first, for absolute possession of
our divine mistresses. Wherefore, if thou art desirous
to recover thy loss, I will not only pronounce liberty to
thee—which I think thou dost little care for without
her—but dare also assure thee to have Iphigenia, so thou
wilt assist me in mine enterprise, and follow me in my
fortune, if the gods do let them fall into our power."

You may well imagine that Cymon's dismayed soul
was not a little cheered at these speeches, and therefore,
without craving any longer respite of time for answer,
thus he replied : "Lord Lysimachus, in such a business

as this is, you cannot have a faster friend than myself, at least if such good hap may betide me as you have more than half promised ; and therefore do no more but command what you would have to be effected by me, and make no doubt of my courage in the execution." Whereupon Lysimachus made this answer : " Know then, Cymon," quoth he, " that three days hence these marriages are to be celebrated in the houses of Pasimunda and Ormisda ; upon which day thou, thy friends, and myself, with some others, in whom I repose especial trust, by the friendly favour of night, will enter into their houses while they are in the midst of their jovial feasting, and seizing on the two brides, bear them thence to a ship which I will have lie in secret, waiting for our coming, and kill all such as shall presume to impeach us." This direction gave great contentment to Cymon, who remained still in prison without revealing a word to his own friends, until the appointed time was come.

Upon the wedding-day, performed with great and magnificent triumph, there was not a corner in the brethren's houses but it sung joy in the highest key. Lysimachus, after he had ordered all things as they ought to be, and the hour for despatch approached near, he made a division in three parts, of Cymon, of his followers, and his own friends, being all well armed under their outward habits. Having first used some encouraging speeches for more resolute prosecution of the enterprise, he sent one troop secretly to the port, that they might not be hindered of going aboard the ship when the urgent occasion should require it. Passing with the other two trains to Pasimunda, he left the one at the door, that such as were in the house might not shut them up fast, and so hinder their passage forth. Then with Cymon and the third band of confederates he ascended the stairs up into the hall, where he found the brides with store of ladies and gentlewomen all sitting in comely order at supper. Rushing in roughly among the attendants, down they threw the tables, and each of them laying hold of his mistress, delivered them into the hands of their followers, commanding that they should be carried aboard the ship for avoiding of further inconveniences.

This hurry and amazement being in the house—the brides weeping, the ladies lamenting, and all the servants confusedly wondering—Cymon and Lysimachus, with their friends, having their weapons drawn in their hands, made all opposers to give them way, and so gained the stairs for their own descending. There stood Pasimunda, with a huge long staff in his hand, to hinder their passage down the stairs, but Cymon saluted him so soundly on the head that, it being cleft in twain, he fell dead before his feet. His brother Ormisda came to his rescue, and sped likewise in the self-same manner as he had done ; so did divers others beside, whom the companions to Lysimachus and Cymon either slew outright or wounded.

So they left the house filled with blood, tears, and outcries, going on together without any hindrance, and so brought both the brides aboard the ship, which they rowed away instantly with their oars. For now the shore was full of armed people, who came in rescue of the stolen ladies, but all in vain, because they were launched into the main, and sailed on merrily towards Crete ; where being arrived they were worthily entertained by honourable friends and kinsmen, who pacified all unkindness between them and their mistresses ; and having accepted them in lawful marriage, there they lived in no mean joy and contentment, albeit there was a long and troublesome difference about these captures between Rhodes and Cyprus.

But yet in the end, by the means of noble friends and kindred on either side, labouring to have such discontentment appeased, endangering war between the kingdoms, after a limited time of banishment, Cymon returned joyfully with Iphigenia home to Cyprus, and Lysimachus with his beloved Cassandra unto Rhodes, each living in their several countries with much felicity.

III

THE STORY OF BALIN AND BALAN

By Sir Thomas Malory

AFTER the death of Uther Pendragon reigned Arthur his son, the which had great war in his days for to get all England into his hand.   For there were many kings within the realm of England, and in Wales, Scotland, and Cornwall.   So it befell on a time when King Arthur was at London, there came a knight and told the king tidings how that the King Ryons of North Wales had reared a great number of people, and were entered into the land, and burnt and slew the king's true liege people. "If this be true," said Arthur, "it were great shame unto mine estate but that he were mightily withstood."   "It is truth," said the knight, "for I saw the host myself." "Well," said the king, "let make a cry, that all the lords, knights, and gentlemen of arms, should draw unto a castle, called Camelot in those days, and there the king would let make a council general, and a great justs."

So when the king was come thither with all his baronage, and lodged as they seemed best, there was come a damsel the which was sent on message from the great lady. Lily of Avelion.   And when she came before King Arthur, she told from whom she came, and how she was sent on message unto him for these causes. Then she let her mantle fall that was richly furred; and then was she girt with a noble sword, whereof the king had marvel, and said, " Damsel, for what cause are ye girt with that sword? it beseemeth you not." "Now shall I tell you," said the damsel: "this sword that I am girt withal doth me great sorrow and cumbrance, for I may not be delivered of this sword but by a knight, but he must be a passing good man of his hands and of his deeds, and without villainy or treachery, and without treason. And if I may find such a knight that hath all these virtues, he may draw out this sword out of the sheath. For I have been at King Ryons'; it was told me there were passing good knights, and he and all his knights have assayed it, and none can speed." "This is a great marvel," said Arthur; "if this be sooth, I will myself assay to draw out the sword, not presuming upon myself that I am the best knight, but that I will begin to draw at your sword in giving example to all the barons, that they shall assay every one after other when I have assayed it." Then Arthur took the sword by the sheath and by the girdle, and pulled at it eagerly, but the sword would not out. "Sir," said the damsel, "ye need not to pull half so hard, for he that shall pull it out shall do it with little might." "Ye say well," said Arthur; "now assay ye, all my barons, but beware ye be not defiled with shame, treachery, nor guile." "Then it will not avail," said the damsel, " for he must be a clean knight without villainy, and of a gentle stock of father side and mother side." Most of all the barons of the Round Table that were there at that time assayed all by row, but there might none speed; wherefore the damsel made great sorrow out of measure, and said, "Alas! I wend in this court had been the best knights, without treachery or treason." "By my faith," saith Arthur, "here are good knights as I deem any been in the world, but their grace is not to help you, wherefore I am displeased."

Then fell it so that time there was a poor knight with King Arthur, that had been prisoner with him half a year and more, for slaying of a knight the which was cousin unto King Arthur. The name of this knight was called Balin, and by good means of the barons he was delivered out of prison, for he was a good man named of his body, and he was born in Northumberland. And so he went privily into the court, and saw this adventure, whereof it raised his heart, and he would assay it as other knights did, but for he was poor and poorly arrayed he put him not far in press; but in his heart he was fully assured to do as well, if his grace happed him, as any knight that there was. And as the damsel took her leave of Arthur and of all the barons, so departing, this knight, Balin, called unto her, and said, "Damsel, I pray you of your courtesy, to suffer me as well to assay as these lords; though I be poorly clothed, in mine heart meseemeth I am fully assured as some of these other lords, and meseemeth in my heart to speed right well." The damsel beheld the poor knight, and saw he was a likely man; but, because of his poor array, she thought he should be of no worship without villainy or treachery. And then she said to the knight Balin, "Sir, it is no need to put me to any more pain or labour, for it beseemeth not you to speed there, as others have failed." "Ah! fair damsel," said Balin, "worthiness and good graces, and good deeds, are not all only in raiment, but manhood and worship is hid within

D

man's person; and many a worshipful knight is not known
unto all people; and therefore worship and hardiness is
not in raiment and clothing." "By God!" said the
damsel, "ye say truth; therefore ye shall assay to do
what ye may." Then Balin took the sword by the girdle
and scabbard, and drew it out easily; and when he looked
upon the sword, it pleased him well. Then had the king
and all the barons great marvel, that Balin had done that
adventure; and many knights had great spite at Balin.
"Truly," said the damsel, "that is a passing good knight,
and the best man that ever I found, and most of worship,
without treason, treachery, or villainy, and many marvels
shall he achieve. Now, gentle and courteous knight," said
the damsel, "give me the sword again." "Nay," said
Balin, "for this sword will I keep, but it be taken from
me by force." "Well," said the damsel, "ye are not
wise to keep the sword from me; for ye shall slay with
the sword the best friend that ye have, and the man that
ye most love in this world; and the sword shall be your
destruction." "I shall take the adventure," said Balin,
"that God will ordain to me; but the sword ye shall not
have at this time, by the faith of my body." "Ye shall
repent it within a short time," said the damsel, "for I
would have the sword more for your avail than for mine,
for I am passing heavy for your sake; for ye will not
believe that the sword shall be your destruction, and that
is as great pity as ever I knew." With that the damsel
departed, making the greatest sorrow that might be.
Anon after Balin sent for his horse and his armour, and
so would depart from the court, and took his leave of
King Arthur. "Nay," said the king, "I suppose ye will
not depart so lightly from this fellowship. I believe ye

are displeased, that I have showed you unkindness; blame
me the less, for I was misinformed against you. But I
weened you had not been such a knight as ye are of worship and prowess; and if ye will abide in this court with
my good knights, I shall so advance you, that ye shall be
well pleased." "God thank your highness," said Balin,
"for your bounty and highness may no man praise half
to the value; but now at this time I must needs depart,
beseeching you alway of your good grace." "Truly,"
said King Arthur, "I am right wrath for your departing;
I beseech you, fair knight, that ye will not tarry long,
and ye shall be right welcome to me and all my barons,
and I shall amend all that is amiss, and that I have done
against you." "God thank your lordship," said Balin,
and therewith made him ready to depart. Then the
most part of the knights of the Round Table said, that
Balin did not this adventure all only by might, but by
witchcraft.

The meanwhile that this knight was making him ready
to depart, there came into the court a lady, which hight
the Lady of the Lake, and she came on horseback richly
beseen, and saluted King Arthur, and there she asked him
a gift that he had promised her when she gave him the
sword.

"That is sooth," said King Arthur, "a gift I promised
you; but I have forgotten the name of the sword which
ye gave me." "The name of it," said the lady, "is
Excalibur, that is as much to say as cut-steel." "Ye say
well," said King Arthur; "ask what ye will, and ye shall
have it, if it lie in my power to give it." "Well," said
the Lady of the Lake, "I ask the head of the knight that
hath won the sword, or else the damsel's head that brought

it; and though I have both their heads I care not, for he slew my brother, a full good knight and a true, and the gentlewoman was causer of my father's death." "Truly," said King Arthur, "I may not grant you neither of their heads with my worship; therefore ask what ye will else, and I shall fulfil your desire." "I will ask none other thing of you," said the lady. When Balin was ready to depart, he saw the Lady of the Lake there, by whose means was slain his own mother, and he had sought her three years. And when it was told him that she demanded his head of King Arthur, he went straight to her and said, "Evil be ye found, ye would have my head, and therefore ye shall lose yours;" and with his sword lightly he smote off her head in the presence of King Arthur. "Alas! for shame," said the king; "why have you done so? you have shamed me and all my court, for this was a lady that I was much beholden unto, and hither she came under my safe-conduct: I shall never forgive you that trespass." "My lord," said Balin, "me forethinketh much of your displeasure, for this lady was the untruest lady living; and by her enchantment and witchcraft she hath been the destroyer of many good knights, and she was the causer that my mother was burnt through her falsehood and treachery." "What cause soever ye had," said King Arthur, "ye should have forborne her in my presence; therefore think not the contrary, ye shall repent it, for such another despite had I never in my court afore; therefore withdraw you out of my court in all the haste ye may." Then Balin took up the head of the lady, and bare it with him to his hostel, and there he met with his squire, that was sorry he had displeased King Arthur; and so they rode forth out of the town. "Now," said

Balin, "we must here depart; take you this head and bear it to my friends, and tell them how I have sped, and tell my friends in Northumberland that my most foe is dead; also tell them now I am out of prison, and also what adventure did befall me at the getting of this sword." "Alas," said the squire, "ye are greatly to blame for to displease King Arthur." "As for that," said Balin, "I will hie me with all the haste I may to meet with Rience, and destroy him, or else to die therefor; and if it may happen me to win him, then will King Arthur be my good and gracious lord." "Where shall I meet with you?" said the squire. "In King Arthur's court," said Balin. So his squire and he departed at that time. Then King Arthur and all the court made great dole, and had great shame of the death of the Lady of the Lake. Then the king full richly buried her.

At that time there was in King Arthur's court a knight that was the king's son of Ireland, and his name was Lanceor; and he was a proud knight, and he counted himself one of the best knights of the court, and he had great spite at Balin for the achieving of the sword, that any should be accounted of more prowess than he was, and he asked King Arthur "if he would give him leave to ride after Balin, and to revenge the despite that he hath done." "Do your best," said King Arthur, "for I am right wrath with Balin; I would he were quit of the despite that he hath done to me and to my court." Then this Lanceor went to his hostel to make him ready; in the meanwhile came Merlin to King Arthur's court, and there it was told him of the adventure of the sword, and of the Lady of the Lake. "Now shall I say to you," said Merlin, "this damsel that here standeth, that brought the sword unto your court, I shall tell you the cause of her coming, she is the falsest damsel that liveth." "Say not so," said they; "she hath a brother, a passing good knight of prowess, and a full true man; and this damsel loved another that held her to paramour, and this good knight, her brother, met with the knight that held her to paramour, and slew him by force of his hands. When this false damsel understood this, she went to the lady Lily of Avelion, and besought her of help to be avenged on her brother. And so this lady Lily of Avelion took her this sword, which she brought with her, and told that there should no man draw it out of the scabbard, but if he were one of the best knights of this realm, and he should be hardy and full of prowess, and with that sword he should slay her brother. This was the cause that the damsel came into this court." "I know it as well as ye do," said Merlin; "would to God she had never come into this court, for she came never in fellowship or worship to do good, but alway great harm, and that knight which hath achieved the sword shall be destroyed by that sword; wherefore it shall be great damage, for there is not living a knight of more prowess than he is, and he shall do unto you my lord, King Arthur, great honour and kindness; and great pity it is, for he shall not endure but a while, and as for his strength and hardiness, I know not his match living." But the knight of Ireland armed him in all points, and dressed him his shield on his shoulder, and mounted upon horseback, and took his spear in his hand, and rode after as fast as his horse could run; and within a little on a mountain he had a sight of Balin, and with a loud voice he cried to him, and said, "Abide, knight, for ye shall abide,

whether ye will or will not; and the shield that is before
you shall not help you." When Balin heard that noise,
he turned his horse fiercely, and said, " Fair knight, what
will you with me; will ye joust with me?" " Yes," said
the Irish knight, " therefore am I come after you." " Peradventure," said Balin, " it had been better to have holden
you at home; for many a man weeneth to put his enemy
to rebuke, and often it falleth to himself. Of what court
be ye sent from?" " I am come from the court of King
Arthur," said the knight of Ireland, "that am come
hither for to revenge the despite that ye have done this
day to King Arthur and to his court."

" Well," said Balin, " I see well I must have ado with
you, which me forethinketh for to grieve King Arthur
or any of his knights, and your quarrel is full simple to
me," said Balin; " for the lady that is dead did great
damage, and else I would have been as loth as any knight
that liveth for to slay a lady." " Make you ready," said
the knight Lanceor, " and dress you to me; for one of
us shall abide in the field." Then they took their spears
in all the haste they might, and came together as fast as
their horses might drive, and the king's son of Ireland
smote Balin upon his shield, that his spear went all to
shivers. And Balin smote him with such a might, that
it went through his shield and perished the hawberk, and
so pierced through his body and the horse croup; and
Balin anon turned his horse fiercely, and drew out his
sword, and wist not that he had slain him, and then he
saw him lie as a dead corpse.

Then he looked by him, and was ware of a damsel
that came riding as fast as her horse might gallop upon
a fair palfrey. And when she espied that Sir Lanceor

was slain, then she made sorrow out of measure, and said, " O Balin ! two bodies hast thou slain and one heart, and two hearts in one body, and two souls thou hast lost." And therewith she took the sword from her love that lay dead, and as she took it she fell to the ground in a swoon : and when she arose, she made great dole out of measure, which sorrow grieved Balin passing sore, and went to her for to have taken the sword out of her hands, but she held it so fast, that in nowise he might take the sword out of her hands, but if he should have hurt her ; and suddenly she set the pommel of the sword to the ground, and ran herself through the body. And when Balin saw her dead, he was passing heavy in his heart, and ashamed that so fair a damsel had destroyed herself for the great love she had unto Sir Lanceor. " Alas ! " said Balin, " me repenteth sore the death of this knight, for the love of this damsel ; for there was much true love between them both," and for sorrow he might no longer behold them, but turned his horse and looked toward a forest, and there he espied the arms of his brother Balan ; and when they were met, they put off their helms and kissed together, and wept for joy and pity. " Then," said Balan, " I weened little to have met with you at this sudden adventure ; I am right glad of your deliverance out of your dolorous prisoning, for a man told me in the Castle of Fourstones that ye were delivered, and that man had seen you in King Arthur's court ; and there-fore I came hither into this country, for here I supposed to find you." And anon Balin told unto his brother of all his adventures of the sword, and of the death of the Lady of the Lake, and how King Arthur was displeased with him ; " wherefore he sent this knight after me that lieth here dead, and the death of this damsel grieveth me full sore." "So doth it me," said Balan; "but ye must take the adventure that God will ordain unto you." "Truly," said Balin, "I am right heavy of mind that my lord, King Arthur, is displeased with me, for he is the most worshipfullest knight that reigneth now on the earth, and his love I will get, or else I will put my life in adventure; for King Rience, of North Wales, lieth at a siege at the Castle Terabil, and thither will we draw in all haste, to prove our worship and prowess upon him." "I will well," said Balan, "that we do so, and we will help each other as brethren ought to do."

"Brother," said Balin, "let us go hence, and well be we met." The meanwhile as they talked there came a dwarf from the city of Camelot on horseback, as fast as he might, and found the dead bodies; wherefore he made great dole, and drew his hair for sorrow, and said, "Which of you knights hath done this deed?" "Whereby asketh thou it?" said Balin. "For I would wit," said the dwarf. "It was I," said Balin, "that slew this knight in my defence; for hither came he to chase me, and either I must slay him or me; and this damsel slew herself for his love, which me sore repenteth, and for her sake I shall owe all women the better love and favour." "Alas!" said the dwarf, "thou hast done great damage unto thyself; for this knight, that is here dead, was one of the most valiantest men that lived, and trust thou well, Balin, that the kin of this knight will chase thee through the world till they have slain thee." "As for that," said Balin, "I fear it not greatly; but I am right heavy, because I have displeased my sovereign lord, King Arthur, for the death of this knight." So,

as they talked together, there came a man of Cornwall
riding by them, which was named King Marke; and when
he saw these two bodies dead, and understood how they
were dead by one of the two knights abovesaid, then
made King Marke great sorrow for the true love that
was between them, and said, "I will not depart from
hence till I have on this earth made a tomb." And
there he pitched his pavilions, and sought through all
the country to find a tomb. And in a church they
found one was rich and fair, and then the king let put
them both in the earth, and put the tomb on them, and
wrote both their names on the tomb, "Here lieth Lanceor the king's son of Ireland; that at his own request
was slain by the hands of Balin, and how his lady Colombe,
and paramour, slew herself with her love's sword, for dole
and sorrow."

The meanwhile as this was doing, came Merlin unto
King Marke, and seeing all his doing, said, "Here in
this place shall be the greatest battle between two knights
that ever was or ever will be, and the truest lovers, and
yet none of them shall slay other;" and there Merlin
wrote their names upon the tomb with letters of gold,
that should fight in that place, whose names were Launcelot du Lake, and Tristram de Liones. "Thou art a
marvellous man," said King Marke unto Merlin, "that
speakest of such marvels; thou art a boisterous fellow,
and an unlikely, to tell of such deeds. What is thy
name?" said King Marke. "At this time," said Merlin,
"I will not tell; but at that time, when Sir Tristram
shall be taken with his sovereign lady, then ye shall know
and hear my name, and at that time ye shall hear tidings
that shall not please you. Then," said Merlin to Balin,

"thou hast done thyself great hurt, because thou did not save this lady that slew herself, that might have saved her if thou had would." "By the faith of my body," said Balin, "I could not, nor might not save her: for she slew herself suddenly." "Me repenteth," said Merlin; "because of the death of that lady, thou shalt strike a stroke the most dolorous that ever man stroke, except the stroke of our Lord: for thou shalt hurt the truest knight, and the man of the most worship that now liveth, and through that stroke three kingdoms shall be in great poverty, misery, and wretchedness twelve years, and the knight shall not be whole of that wound in many years." And then Merlin took his leave of Balin. "Then," said Balin, "if I wist it were sooth that ye say, I should do such a perilous deed as that, I would slay myself to make thee a liar." And therewith anon Merlin suddenly vanished away: then Balin and his brother took their leave of King Marke.

"First," said the king, "tell me your name." "Sir," said Balin, "ye may see he beareth two swords, thereby ye may call him the knight of the two swords." And so departed King Marke, and rode to Camelot to King Arthur; and Balin and his brother took the way to King Rience, and as they rode together they met with Merlin disguised, but they knew him not. "Whither ride ye?" said Merlin. "We have little to do," said the two knights, "for to tell thee." "But what is thy name?" said Balin. "As at this time," said Merlin, "I will not tell thee." "It is full evil seen," said the two knights, "that thou art a true man, when thou wilt not tell thy name." "As for that," said Merlin, "be it as it may; but I can tell you wherefore ye ride this way, for to

meet King Rience : but it will not avail you, without you
have my counsel." "Ah!" said Balin, "ye are Merlin :
we will be ruled by your counsel." "Come on," said
Merlin ; "ye shall have great worship, and look that
ye do knightly ; for ye shall have great need." "As for
that," said Balin, "dread ye not : we will do what we may."

Then Merlin lodged them in a wood amongst leaves,
beside the highway, and took off the bridles of their
horses, and put them to grass, and laid them down to
rest them till it was nigh midnight. Then Merlin bade
them arise and make them ready ; for the king was nigh
them that was stolen away from his host, with threescore
of his best knights : and twenty of them rode before,
to warn the Lady de Vance that the king was coming ;
for that night King Rience should have been with her.
"Which is the king?" said Balin. "Abide," said
Merlin ; "here in a straight way ye shall meet with him."
And therewith he showed Balin and his brother where he
rode. Anon Balin and his brother met with the king,
and smote him down, and wounded him fiercely, and laid
him to the ground ; and there they slew on the right
hand and on the left, and slew more than forty of his
men, and the remnant fled. Then went they again to
King Rience, and would have slain him, if he had not
yielded him to their grace. Then said the king again,
"Knights, full of prowess, slay me not ; for by my life
ye may win, and by my death shall ye win nothing."
Then said these two knights, "Ye say sooth and troth ; "
and so laid him on a horse-litter. With that Merlin
was vanished, and came to King Arthur aforehand, and
told him how his most enemy was taken and discomfited.
"By whom?" said King Arthur. "By two knights,"

said Merlin, "that would please your lordship, and to-morrow ye shall know what they be." Anon after came the knight with the two swords, and Balan, his brother, and brought with them King Rience, and there delivered him to the porters, and charged them with him, and so they two returned again in the springing of the day. King Arthur came to King Rience and said, " Sir king, you are welcome ; by what adventure came ye hither ? " " Sir," said King Rience, " I came hither by a hard adventure." " Who won you ? " said King Arthur. " Sir," said Rience, " the knight with the two swords and his brother, which are two marvellous knights of prowess." " I know them not," said King Arthur ; " but much I am beholden unto them." " Ah ! " said Merlin, " I shall tell you it is Balin that achieved the sword, and his brother Balan, a good knight ; there liveth not a better in prowess and worthiness, and it shall be the greatest dole of him that ever was of knight, for he shall not long endure." " Alas ! " said King Arthur, " that is a great pity ; for I am greatly beholden unto him, and I have full evil deserved it unto him for his kindness." " Nay," said Merlin, " he shall do much more for you, and that shall ye know ere it be long. But, sir, are ye purveyed ? " said Merlin ; " for to-morrow the host of Nero, King Rience's brother, will set upon you afore dinner with a mighty host ; therefore, make you ready, for I will depart from you."

Then King Arthur made ready his host in ten battles ; and Nero was ready in the field, afore the Castle Terabil, with a mighty host ; for he had ten battles, with much more people than King Arthur had. So Nero himself had the vanguard with the most party of his people : and Merlin came to King Lot of the Isle of the Orkney,

and held him with a tale of prophecy, till Nero and his
people were destroyed. And there Sir Kaye, the seneschal,
did passing well, that all the days of his life he had thereof
worship ; and Sir Herves de Revel did marvellous deeds
with King Arthur : and King Arthur slew that day twenty
knights, and maimed forty. At that time came in the
knight with the two swords, and his brother, Balan ; but
they two did so marvellously, that the king and all the
knights had great marvel thereof : and all that beheld
them said, that they were sent from heaven as angels, or
as devils from hell ; and King Arthur said himself, that
they were the best knights that ever he saw ; for they gave
such strokes that all men had wonder of them. In the
meantime came one to King Lot and told him that, while
he tarried there, Nero was destroyed and slain with all his
people. "Alas! I am ashamed," said King Lot, "for,
through my default, is slain many a worshipful man : for,
if we had been together, there had been no host under
heaven that had been able to match us. This flatterer,
with his prophesy, hath mocked me." All that did Merlin ; for he knew well that, if King Lot had been there
with his body at the first battle, King Arthur and all his
people should have been destroyed and slain ; and Merlin
knew well that one of the kings should be dead that day,
and loth was Merlin that any of them both should be
slain ; but of the twain he had liever King Lot had been
slain than King Arthur.

"Now what is best to do?" said King Lot ; "whether
is it better for to treat with King Arthur, or to fight? for
the most part of our people are slain and destroyed."
"Sir," said a knight, "set upon King Arthur ; for he
and his men are weary of fighting, and we be fresh."

"As for me," said King Lot, "I would that every knight would do his part as I will do mine." And then they advanced their banners, and smote together, and all to-shivered their spears; and King Arthur's knights, with the help of the knight of the two swords, and his brother, Balan, put King Lot and his host to the worst. But always King Lot held him in the foremost, and did great deeds of arms; for all his host was borne up by his hands, for he abode and withstood all knights. Alas! he might not ever endure, the which was great pity that so worthy a knight as he was should be overmatched, and that of late time afore had been a knight of King Arthur's, and had wedded King Arthur's sister; and, because King Arthur cast his love upon her and therewith begat Mordred, therefore King Lot held against King Arthur. So there was a knight, that was called the knight with the strange beast, and at that time his right name was Pellinore, which was a good man of prowess; and he smote a mighty stroke at King Lot as he fought with his enemies: and he failed of his stroke, and smote the horse's neck, that he fell to the ground with King Lot. And therewith Sir Pellinore smote him a great stroke through the helm, and hewed him to the brows: then all the host of Orkney fled for the death of King Lot, and there was slain many a mother's son. But King Pellinore bare the blame of the death of King Lot: wherefore, Sir Gawaine revenged the death of his father the tenth year after he was made knight, and slew King Pellinore with his own hands. Also there was slain at the battle twelve kings on King Lot's side with Nero, and all were buried in the church of St. Stevens, in Camelot; and the remnant of knights and of others were buried in a great rock.

So, at the interment, came King Lot's wife, Morgause, with her four sons, Gawaine, Agravaine, Gaheris, and Gareth. Also there came thither King Urience, Sir Ewaine's father, and Morgan le Fay, his wife, that was King Arthur's sister: all these came to the interment. But of all these twelve knights King Arthur let make the tomb of King Lot passing richly, and his tomb stood by itself apart. And then King Arthur let make twelve images of latten and of copper, and made them to be overgilt with fine gold, in sign and token of the twelve kings; and every image held a taper of wax, which burnt night and day. And King Arthur was made in sign of a figure standing above them all, with a sword drawn in his hand; and all the twelve figures had countenances like unto men that were overcome. All this made Merlin by his subtle craft, and there he said to King Arthur, "When I am dead the twelve tapers shall burn no longer; and, soon after this, the adventures of the Holy Sancgreal shall come among you, and shall also be achieved." Also he told unto King Arthur, how Balin, the worshipful knight, should give the dolorous stroke, whereof shall fall great vengeance. "And where is Balin, and Balan, and Pellinore?" said King Arthur.

"As for Sir Pellinore," said Merlin, "he will meet with you anon; and as for Balin, he will not be long from you; but the other brother, Balan, will depart, and ye shall see him no more." "Now, by my faith," said King Arthur, "they are two marvellous knights, and namely, Balin passeth of prowess far of any knight that ever I found; for I am much beholden unto him. Would to God that he would abide still with me." "Sir," aid Merlin, "look that ye keep well the scabbard of

Excalibur; for, as I told you, ye shall lose no blood as long as ye have the scabbard upon you, though ye have as many wounds upon your body as ye may have." So afterwards, for great trust, King Arthur betook the scabbard to Morgan le Fay, his sister; and she loved another knight better than her husband, King Urience, or King Arthur. And she would have had King Arthur slain: and, therefore, she let make another scabbard like it by enchantment, and gave the scabbard of Excalibur to her love, a knight named Sir Accolon, which after had nigh slain King Arthur. After this, Merlin told unto King Arthur of the prophecy that there should be a great battle beside Salisbury, and that Mordred, his own son, should be against him: also he told him, that Basdemegus was his cousin, and german unto King Urience.

Within a day or two King Arthur was somewhat sick, and he let pitch his pavilion in a meadow, and there he laid him down on a pallet to sleep, but he might have no rest. Right so he heard a great noise of a horse; and therewith the king looked out at the porch of the pavilion's door, and saw a knight coming by him making great sorrow. "Abide, fair sir," said King Arthur, "and tell me wherefore thou makest this sorrow." "Ye may little amend it," said the knight, and so passed forth unto the castle of Meliot. Anon after there came Balin; and, when he saw King Arthur, anon he alighted off his horse, and came to the king on foot, and saluted him. "By my head," said King Arthur, "ye be welcome, sir. Right now came riding this way a knight making great sorrow, and I cannot tell for what cause; wherefore, I would desire you, of your courtesy and gentleness, that ye will fetch that knight again, either by force, or else by his

E

good will." "I will do more for your lordship than that," said Balin, and so rode more than a pace, and found the knight with a damsel in a forest, and said, "Sir knight, ye must come with me unto my lord, King Arthur, for to tell him the cause of your sorrow." "That will I not," said the knight; "for it would scath me greatly, and do you none avail." "Sir," said Balin, "I pray you make you ready; for ye must needs go with me, or else I will fight with you, and bring you by force, and that were I loth to do." "Will ye be my warrant," said the knight to Balin, "if I go with you?" "Yea," said Balin, "or else I will die therefor." And so he made him ready to go with the good knight, Balin, and left there the damsel: and, as they were afore King Arthur's pavilion, there came one invisible, and smote the knight that went with Balin throughout the body with a spear.

"Alas!" said the knight, "I am slain under your conduct and guard, with a traitorous knight, called Garlon; therefore, take my horse, the which is better than yours, and ride to the damsel, and follow the quest that I was in, whereas she will lead you, and revenge my death when ye may best." "That shall I do," said Balin, "and thereof I make a vow to you by my knighthood." And so he departed from this knight, making great sorrow. So King Arthur let bury this knight richly, and made a mention upon the tomb how there was slain Herleus le Berbeus, and also how the treachery was done by the knight, Garlon. But ever the damsel bore the truncheon of the spear with her that Sir Herleus was slain with.

So Balin and the damsel rode into the forest, and

there met with a knight that had been on hunting; and
that knight asked Balin for what cause he made so great
sorrow. "Me list not to tell you," said Balin. "Now,"
said the knight, "and I were armed as ye be I would
fight with you." "That should little need," said Balin;
"for I am not afraid to tell it you:" and he told him all
the cause how it was. "Ah!" said the knight, "is this
all? here I ensure you, by the faith of my body, never
to depart from you as long as my life lasteth." And so
they went to the hostel and armed him, and so rode
forth with Balin; and as they came by a hermitage, fast
by a churchyard, there came the knight Garlon invisible,
and smote this good knight, Perin de Mountbelyard, with
a spear through the body. "Alas!" said the knight, "I
am slain by this traitor knight that rideth invisible."
"Alas!" said Balin, "it is not the first despite that he
hath done to me." And there the hermit and Balin
buried the knight under a rich stone and a tomb royal;
and, on the morrow, they found letters of gold written,
how Sir Gawaine shall revenge King Lot's death, his
father, upon King Pellinore. And anon, after this,
Balin and the damsel rode till they came to a castle;
and there Balin alighted, and he and the damsel weened
to have gone into the castle. And anon, as Balin came
within the gate, the portcullis fell down at his back.
and there came many men about the damsel, and would
have slain her. And, when Balin saw that, he was so
grieved, because he might not help the damsel: and then
he went upon the walls, and leaped over into the ditch,
and hurt him not. And anon he pulled out his sword,
and would have foughten with them. And they all said
"that they would not fight with him; for they did

nothing but the old custom of the castle." And told
him how their lady was sick, and had lain many years,
and she might not be whole, but if she had a silver dish
full of blood, of a clean maid, and a king's daughter;
and, therefore, the custom of the castle is, that there
shall none pass this way but she shall bleed of her blood
a silver dish full.   "Well," said Balin, "she shall bleed
as much as she may bleed; but I will not that she lose
her life, while my life lasteth."   And so Balin made her
to bleed by her good will; but her blood helped not the
lady.   And so he and she rested there all that night, and
had their right good cheer; and, on the morrow, they
passed on their way.   And as it telleth afterwards, in the
Sancgreal, that Sir Percivale's sister helped that lady with
her blood, whereof she died.

Then they rode three or four days, and never met
with adventure; and by hap they were lodged with a
gentleman that was a rich man, and well at ease.   And,
as they sat at their supper, Balin heard one complain
grievously by him in a chair.   "What noise is this?"
said Balin.   "Forsooth," said his host, "I will tell you:
I was but late at a jousting, and there I jousted with a
knight, that is brother unto King Pellam, and twice I
smote him down; and then he promised to quit me on
my best friend, and so he wounded my son that cannot
be whole till I have of that knight's blood : and he rideth
always invisible, but I know not his name."   "Ah!"
said Balin, "I know that knight, his name is Garlon;
he hath slain two knights of mine in the same manner,
therefore I had rather meet with that knight than all
the gold in this realm, for the despite that he hath done
me."   "Well," said his host, "I shall tell you: King

Pellam, of Listeneise, hath made a cry, in all this country, of a great feast that shall be within twenty days, and no knight may come there but if he bring his wife with him, or his paramour ; and that knight, your enemy and mine, ye shall see that day." "Then I behove you," said Balin, " part of his blood to heal your son withal." "We will be forward to-morrow," said his host. So, on the morrow, they rode all three towards Pellam, and had fifteen days' journey or they came thither ; and that same day began the great feast, and they alighted and stabled their horses, and went into the castle : but Balin's host might not be let in, because he had no lady. Then was Balin well received, and brought to a chamber, and unarmed him ; and there were brought him robes to his pleasure, and would have had him leave his sword behind him. "Nay," said Balin, "that will I not do ; for it is the custom of my country for a knight always to keep his weapon with him, and that custom will I keep, or else I will depart as I came." Then they gave him leave to wear his sword. And so he went to the castle, and was set among knights of worship, and his lady afore him. Soon Balin asked a knight, " Is there not a knight in this court whose name is Garlon ? " " Yonder he goeth," said the knight, " he with that black face : he is the marvailest knight that is now living, for he destroyeth many good knights, for he goeth invisible." " Ah ! well," said Balin, " is that he ? " Then Balin advised him long, " If I slay him here I shall not escape, and if I leave him now, peradventure I shall never meet with him again at such a good time, and much harm he will do, and he live." Therewith this Garlon espied that this Balin beheld him, and then he came and smote Balin on the face with the back of his hand, and said, " Knight, why beholdest thou me so? for shame; therefore eat thy meat, and do that thou came for." " Thou sayest sooth," said Balin; " this is not the first despite that thou hast done me; and, therefore, I will do that I came for;" and rose up so fiercely, and cleaved his head to the shoulders. "Give me the truncheon," said Balin to his lady, " wherewith he slew your knight." Anon she gave it him, for always she bare that truncheon with her. And therewith Balin smote him through the body, and said openly, " With that truncheon thou hast slain a good knight, and now it sticketh in thy body." And then Balin called to him his host, saying, " Now may ye fetch blood enough for to heal your son withal."

Anon all the knights rose up from the table for to set on Balin; and King Pellam himself arose up fiercely, and said, " Knight, why hast thou slain my brother? thou shalt die, therefore, ere thou depart." "Well," said Balin, " then do it yourself." "Yes," said King Pellam, " there shall no man have to do with thee but myself, for the love of my brother." Then King Pellam caught in his hand a grim weapon, and smote eagerly at Balin; but Balin put the sword between his head and the stroke, and therewith his sword burst in sunder. And when Balin was weaponless, he came into a chamber for to seek some weapon, and so from chamber to chamber, and no weapon could he find; and always King Pellam followed him, and at the last he entered into a chamber that was mar- vellously well dight and richly, and a bed arrayed with cloth of gold, the richest that might be thought, and one lying therein, and thereby stood a table of clean gold, with four pillars of silver that bare up the table, and upon the table stood a marvellous spear, strangely wrought. And when Balin saw the spear, he gat it in his hand, and turned him to King Pellam, and smote him passingly sore with that spear, that King Pellam fell down in a swoon; and therewith the castle rove and the walls brake, and fell to the earth, and Balin fell down, so that he might not stir hand nor foot: and so the most part of the castle that was fallen down, through that dolorous stroke, lay upon King Pellam and Balin three days.

Then Merlin came thither and took up Balin, and gat him a good horse, for his horse was dead, and bade him ride out of that country. "I would have my damsel," said Balin. "Lo," said Merlin, "where she lieth dead." And King Pellam lay so many years sore wounded, and might never be whole till Galahad, the haute prince, healed him in the quest of the Sancgreal; for in that place was part of the blood of our Lord Jesus Christ, that Joseph of Arimathea brought into this land, and there himself lay in that rich bed. And that was the same spear that Longius smote our Lord to the heart; and King Pellam was nigh of Joseph's kin, and that was the most worshipful man that lived in those days: and great pity it was of his hurt, for the stroke turned him to great dole, vexation, and grief. Then departed Balin from Merlin, and said, "In this world we shall never meet more." So he rode forth through the fair countries and cities, and found the people dead on every side. And all that were alive, cried, "O Balin! thou hast caused great damage in these countries, for the dolorous stroke that thou gavest unto King Pellam, three countries are destroyed; and doubt not but the vengeance will fall on thee at the last." When Balin was past the countries he was passing faint; so he rode eight days ere he met with adventures, and at the last he came into a fair forest, in a valley, and was aware of a tower, and there beside he saw a great horse of war tied to a tree, and there beside sat a fair knight on the ground, and made great mourning: and he was a likely man, and well made. Balin said, "God save you, why be ye so heavy? tell me, and I will amend it, and I may to my power." "Sir knight," said he, " again thou doest me great grief; for I was in merry thoughts, and now thou puttest me to more pain." Balin went a little from him, and looked on his horse. Then Balin heard him say thus: "Ah! fair lady, why have ye broken my promise; for ye promised me to meet me here by noon, and I may curse you that ever ye gave me this sword; for with this sword I will slay myself." And he pulled it out, and therewith Balin started to him, and took him by the hand. "Let go my hand," said the knight, " or else I shall slay thee." "That shall not need," said Balin, "for I shall promise you my help to get you your lady, if you will tell me where she is?" "What is your name?" said the knight. "My name is Balin le Savage." "Ah! sir, I know you well enough; you are the knight with the two swords, and the man of most prowess of your hands living." "What is your name?" said Balin. "My name is Garnish of the Mount, a poor man's son; but, by my prowess and hardiness, a duke hath made me a knight, and gave me lands: his name is Duke Hermel, and his daughter is she that I love, and she me, as I deemed." "How far is she hence?" said Balin. "But six mile," said the knight. "Now ride we hence," said these two knights. So they rode more than a pace till they came to a fair castle, well walled and ditched. "I will into the castle," said Balin, "and look if she be there." So he went in, and searched from chamber to chamber, and found her bed, but she was not there; then Balin looked into a fair little garden, and under a laurel tree he saw her lie upon a quilt of green samite, and a knight with her, and under their heads grass and herbs. When Balin saw her with the foulest knight that ever he saw, and she a fair lady, then Balin went through all the chambers again, and told the knight how he found her, as she had slept fast, and so brought him in the place where she lay fast sleeping.

And when Garnish beheld her so lying, for pure sorrow his mouth and nose burst out on bleeding, and with his sword he smote off both their heads, and then he made sorrow out of measure and said, "O Balin, much sorrow hast thou brought unto me, for hadst thou not shown me that sight I should have passed my sorrow." "Forsooth," said Balin, "I did it to this intent that it should better thy courage, and that ye might see and know her falsehood, and to cause you to leave love of such a lady: truly I did none other but as I would ye did to me." "Alas!" said Garnish, "now is my sorrow double that I may not endure: now have I slain that I most loved in all my life." And therewith suddenly he rove himself on his own sword unto the hilts. When Balin saw that, he dressed him thenceward, lest folks would say he had slain them, and so he rode forth, and within three days he came by a cross, and thereon were letters of gold written that said, "It is not for any knight alone to ride toward this castle." Then saw he an old hoar gentleman coming toward him that said, "Balin le Savage, thou passest thy bounds to come this way, therefore turn again and it will

avail thee." And he vanished away anon ; and so he heard
an horn blow as it had been the death of a beast. "That
blast," said Balin, "is blown for me, for I am the prize,
yet am I not dead." Anon withal he saw an hundred
ladies and many knights, that welcomed him with fair
semblance, and made him passing good cheer unto his
sight, and led him into the castle, and there was dancing
and minstrelsy, and all manner of joy. Then the chief
lady of the castle said, "Knight with the two swords, ye
must have ado with a knight hereby that keepeth an
island, for there may no man pass this way but he must
joust or he pass." "That is an unhappy custom," said
Balin, "that a knight may not pass this way but if he
joust." "Ye shall not have ado but with one knight," said
the lady. "Well," said Balin, "since I shall, thereto am
I ready, but travelling men are oft weary, and their horses
also ; but though my horse be weary my heart is not
weary. I would be fain there my death should be."
"Sir," said a knight to Balin, "methinketh your shield
is not good, I will lend you a bigger : therefore I pray
you ;" and so he took the shield that was unknown, and
left his own, and so rode unto the island, and put him
and his horse in a great boat, and when he came on the
other side he met with a damsel, and she said, "O knight
Balin, why have ye left your own shield? alas ! ye have
put yourself in great danger, for by your shield ye should
have been known : it is great pity of you as ever was of
knight, for of thy prowess and hardiness thou hast no
fellow living." "Me repenteth," said Balin, "that ever
I came within this country, but I may not turn now again
for shame, and what adventure shall fall to me, be it life
or death, I will take the adventure that shall come to

me." And then he looked on his armour, and understood he was well armed, and therewith blessed him, and mounted upon his horse.

Then afore him he saw come riding out of a castle a knight, and his horse trapped all red, and himself in the same colour. When this knight in the red beheld Balin, him thought it should be his brother Balin, because of his two swords, but because he knew not his shield, he deemed it was not he. And so they aventred their spears, and came marvellously fast together, and they smote each other in the shields, but their spears and their course were so big that it bare down horse and man, that they lay both in a swoon. But Balin was bruised sore with the fall of his horse, for he was weary of travel. And Balan was the first that rose on foot and drew his sword, and went toward Balin, and he arose and went against him, but Balan smote Balin first, and he put up his shield, and smote him through the shield and cleft his helm. Then Balin smote him again with that unhappy sword, and well nigh had felled his brother Balan, and so they fought there together till their breaths failed. Then Balin looked up to the castle, and saw the towers stand full of ladies. So they went to battle again, and wounded each other dolefully, and then they breathed oft-times, and so went unto battle, that all the place there as they fought was blood red. And at that time there was none of them both but they had smitten either other seven great wounds; so that the least of them might have been the death of the mightiest giant in the world. Then they went to battle again so marvellously, that doubt it was to hear of that battle; for the great bloodshedding, and their hawberks unnailed, that naked they were on every side: at the last Balan, the

younger brother, withdrew him a little, and laid him
down. Then said Balin le Savage, "What knight art
thou? for ere now I found never no knight that matched
me." "My name is," said he, "Balan, brother to the
good knight Balin." "Alas!" said Balin, "that ever
I should see this day." And therewith he fell backward
in a swoon. Then Balan went on all four, feet and
hands, and put off the helm of his brother, and might
not know him by the visage, it was so full hewn and
bebled; but when he awoke, he said, "O Balan, my
brother, thou hast slain me, and I thee, wherefore all
the wide world shall speak of us both." "Alas!" said
Balan, "that ever I saw this day, that through mishap I
might not know you; for I espied well your two swords,
but because ye had another shield, I deemed you had
been another knight." "Alas!" said Balin, "all that
made an unhappy knight in the castle, for he caused me
to leave mine own shield to the destruction of us both;
and if I might live I would destroy that castle for the ill
customs." "That were well done," said Balan, "for I
had never grace to depart from them, since that I came
hither, for here it happened me to slay a knight that
kept this island, and since might I never depart, and no
more should ye, brother, and ye might have slain me, as
ye have, and escaped yourself with your life." Right so
came the lady of the tower with four knights and six
ladies, and six yeomen unto them, and there she heard
how they made their mourn either to other, and said,
"We came both out of one womb, and so shall we lie
both in one pit." So Balan prayed the lady of her gentleness, for his true service, that she would bury them both
in that place where the battle was done. And she granted

them, with weeping cheer, and said, "It should be done richly, and in the best manner." "Now will ye send for a priest, that we may receive the sacrament and blessed body of our Lord Jesus Christ." "Yea," said the lady, "it shall be done." And so she sent for a priest, and gave them their rites. "Now," said Balin, "when we are buried in one tomb, and the inscription made over us how two brethren slew each other, there will never good knight, nor good man, see our tomb, but they will pray for our souls." And so all the ladies and gentlewomen wept for pity. And anon Balan died, but Balin died not till the midnight after, and so were buried both; and the lady let make an inscription of Balan, how he was there slain by the hands of his own brother: but she knew not Balin's name.

On the morrow came Merlin, and let write Balin's name upon the tomb, with letters of gold: "Here lieth Balin le Savage, that was the Knight with the Two Swords, and he that smote the Dolorous Stroke." Merlin let make there also a bed, that there should never man lie in but he went out of his wit; yet Launcelot du Lake fordid that bed through his nobleness. And anon, after as Balin was dead, Merlin took his sword, and took off the pommel, and set on another pommel. Then Merlin had a knight that stood afore him to handle that sword, and he assayed, but he could not handle it. Then Merlin laughed. "Why laugh ye?" said the knight. "This is the cause," said Merlin: "there shall never no man handle this sword but the best knight of the world, and that shall be Launcelot, or else Galahad, his son; and Launcelot, with his sword, shall slay the man that in this world he loved best, that shall be Sir Gawaine." All this he let write in the pommel of the sword. Then Merlin let make a bridge of iron and of steel into that island, and it was but half a foot broad : and there shall never man pass that bridge, nor have hardiness to go over, but if he were a passing good man, and a good knight, without treachery or villainy. Also, the scabbard of Balin's sword, Merlin left it on this side the island, that Galahad should find it. Also, Merlin let make, by his subtlety and craft, that Balin's sword was put in marble stone, standing upright, as great as a millstone, and the stone hoved always above the water, and did many years : and so, by adventure, it swam down the stream to the city of Camelot. And that same day Galahad, the haughty prince, came with King Arthur; and so Galahad brought with him the scabbard, and achieved the sword that was there in the marble stone, hoving upon the water; and, on Whitsunday, he achieved the sword as it is rehearsed in the book of the Sancgreal. Soon after this was done Merlin came to King Arthur, and told him of the dolorous stroke that Balin gave to King Pellam, and how Balin and Balan fought together the marvailest battle that ever was heard of, and how they were buried both in one tomb. "Alas," said King Arthur, "this is the greatest pity that ever I heard tell of two knights; for in the world I know not such two knights as they were." Thus endeth the tale of Balin and Balan, two brethren, born in Northumberland, good knights.

THE STORY OF MARCELLA

FROM DON QUIXOTE

"Do you know what has happened in our town, comrades?" said one of the lads who brought them victuals
from the village, entering the hut. When one of them
answered, "How should we?" "Know then," continued
he, "that the famous student Chrysostom died this
morning; and it is murmured about, that his death was
occasioned by his love for that devilish girl Marcella,
daughter of William the rich; she that roves about these
plains in the habit of a shepherdess." "For Marcella,
said you?" cried one. "The same," answered the goatherd, "and it is certain that, in his last will, he ordered
himself to be buried in the field, like a Moor (God
bless us!), at the foot of the rock hard by the cork-tree
spring; for, the report goes, and they say he said so
himself, as how the first time he saw her was in that
place; and he has also ordained many other such things,
as the clergy say, must not be accomplished, nor is it right
they should be accomplished; for truly, they seem quite
heathenish. To all which objections his dear friend, Ambrosio the student, who also dressed himself like a shepherd, to keep him company, replies that he will perform

everything without fail that Chrysostom has ordered ; and the whole village is in an uproar about it. But it is believed, that everything, at last, will be done according to the desire of Ambrosio, and all the rest of the shepherds, his friends ; and that to-morrow he will be interred with great pomp in the very spot I have mentioned. I am resolved, therefore, as it will be a thing well worth seeing, to go thither without fail, even though I thought I should not be able to return to the village that night." "We will do so too," replied the goatherds, "and cast lots to see which of us must stay and take care of our flocks." "You are in the right, Pedro," said one, "but, there will be no occasion to use that shift ; for I myself will stay and take care of the whole, and you must not impute my tarrying to virtue, or the want of curiosity, but to the plaguy thorn that ran into my foot the other day, and hinders me from walking." "We are obliged to thee, however," answered Pedro, whom Don Quixote desired to tell him who that same dead shepherd and living shepherdess were.

To this question the goatherd replied, "All that he knew of the matter was, that the deceased was the son of a rich farmer, who lived in the neighbourhood of a village in these mountains ; that he had studied in Salamanca many years, at the end of which he had returned to his family with the character of a great scholar ; in particular, they said, he was very knowing in the science of the stars, and what passed betwixt the sun and moon, and the heavens ; for, he had punctually foretold the clipse of them both !" "The obscuration of those two great luminaries," said the knight, "is called the eclipse, and not the clipse, friend." But Pedro, without

troubling his head with these trifles, proceeded saying,
" he likewise foresaw when the year would be plentiful
or staril." "You mean sterile," said Don Quixote.
"Sterile, or staril," replied Pedro, "comes all to the
same purpose ; and I say, that his father and his friends,
taking his advice, became very rich ; for, they gave credit
to his words, and followed his counsel in all things.
When he would say, this year you must sow barley, and
no wheat ; here you must sow carabances, but no barley ;
next year there will be a good harvest of oil ; but for
three years to come there will not be a drop." "That
science," replied Don Quixote, "is called astrology."
"I know not how it is called," replied Pedro, "but
this I know, that he knew all this, and much more. In
short, not many months after he came from Salamanca,
he appeared all of a sudden in shepherd-weeds, with his
woolly jacket, and a flock of sheep, having laid aside the
long dress of a student. And he was accompanied by a
friend of his in the same habit, whose name was Ambrosio, and who had been his fellow-student at college.
I forgot to tell you, that Chrysostom the defunct was
such a great man at composing couplets, that he made
carols for Christmas-eve, and plays for the Lord's-day,
which were represented by the young men in our village :
and everybody said, that they were tip-top. When the
people of the village saw the two scholars, so suddenly
clothed like shepherds, they were surprised, and could
not guess their reason for such an odd chance. About
that time, the father of this Chrysostom dying, he inherited great riches, that were in moveables and in lands,
with no small number of sheep more or less, and a great
deal of money : all of which, this young man remained

F

desolate lord and master; and truly he deserved it all; for he was an excellent companion, very charitable, a great friend to good folks, and had a most blessed countenance. Afterwards it came to be known, that his reason for changing his garb, was no other than with a view of strolling through the woods and deserts after that same shepherdess Marcella, whose name my friend mentioned just now, and with whom the poor defunct Chrysostom was woundily in love: and I will now tell you, for it is necessary that you should know who this wench is; for, mayhap, nay even without a mayhap, you never heard of such a thing in all the days of your life, though you be older than St. Paul." [1]   "Say Paul's," replied Don Quixote, offended at the goatherd's perverting of words.   "St. Paul was no chicken," replied Pedro, "and if your worship be resolved to correct my words every moment, we shall not have done in a twelvemonth." "I ask your pardon, friend," said the knight; "I only mention this, because there is a wide difference between the person of St. Paul, and a church that goes by his name: but, however, you made a very sensible reply; for, to be sure, the saint lived long before the church was built: therefore go on with your story, and I promise not to interrupt you again."

"Well then, my good master," said the goatherd, "there lived in our village a farmer, still richer than Chrysostom's father; his name was William, and God gave him, over and above great wealth, a daughter, who at

---

[1] In the original Spanish, the goatherd, instead of saying as old as Sarah, says as old as Sarna, which in that language signifies the itch; but as it is impossible to preserve these mistakes in the translation, I have substituted another in its room, which I apprehend is equally expressive.—[S.]

her birth was the death of her mother, the most worthy
dame in all the country.   Methinks I see her now with
that face of hers, which seemed to have the sun on one
side, and the moon on the other; she was an excellent
housewife, and a great friend to the poor, for which
reason I believe her soul is enjoying the presence of God
in paradise.   Her husband died of grief for the loss of
so good a wife, leaving his daughter Marcella, young
and rich, to the care of an uncle, who has got a living
in our village.   The girl grew up with so much beauty,
that she put us in mind of her mother, who had a great
share, and yet it was thought it would be surpassed by
the daughter's.   It happened accordingly, for when she
came to the age of fourteen or fifteen, nobody could
behold her without blessing God for having made so
beautiful a creature; and everybody almost grew desperately in love with her.   Her uncle kept her up with
great care; but, for all that, the fame of her exceeding
beauty spread in such a manner, that both for her person
and her fortune, not only the richest people in our town,
but likewise in many leagues about, came to ask her in
marriage of her uncle, with much importunity and solicitation.   But he who, to give him his due, was a good
Christian, although he wanted to dispose of her as soon
as she came to an age fit for matrimony, would not give
her away without her own consent; neither had he a
view in deferring her marriage, to the gain and advantage
which he might enjoy in managing the girl's fortune.
And truly I have heard this spoken in more companies
than one, very much to the praise of the honest priest.
For I would have you know, sir traveller, that in these
small towns, people intermeddle and grumble about

everything.   And this you may take for certain, as I
know it to be so, that a clergyman must be excessively
good indeed, if he can oblige his flock to speak well of
him, especially in country villages."   "You are certainly
in the right," said Don Quixote, "and pray go on, for
your story is very entertaining, and you, honest Pedro,
relate it with a good grace."   "May I never want God's
grace," said the shepherd, "for, that is the main chance;
and you must know, moreover, that though the uncle
proposed to his niece, and described the good qualities
of each in particular who asked her in marriage, desiring
her to give her hand to some one, or other, and choose
for herself; she never would give him any other answer,
but that she did not choose to marry, for she was too
young to bear the burden of matrimony.   On account
of these excuses, which seemed to have some reason in
them, her uncle forbore to importune her, and waited
till she should have more years and discernment to make
choice of her own company; for, he said, and to be sure,
it was well said, that parents should never dispose of their
children against their own inclinations.   But, behold, when
we least thought of it, the timorous Marcella, one day,
appeared in the habit of a shepherdess; and without im-
parting her design to her uncle, or anybody in the village,
for fear they might have dissuaded her from it, she took
to the field with her own flock, in company with the
other damsels of the village.   As she now appeared in
public, and her beauty was exposed to the eyes of everybody, you cannot conceive what a number of rich youths,
gentlemen, and farmers, immediately took the garb of
Chrysostom, and went wooing her through the fields.
One of these suitors, as you have heard, was the deceased,

who, they say, left off loving to adore her; and you must not think, that because Marcella took this free and unconfined way of living, she brought the least disparagement upon her chastity and good name; on the contrary, such is the vigilance with which she guards her honour, that of all those who serve and solicit her, not one has boasted, nor indeed can boast with any truth, that she has given him the smallest hope of accomplishing his desire; for, though she neither flies, or avoids the company and conversation of the shepherds, but treats them in a courteous and friendly manner, whenever any of them comes to disclose his intention, let it be ever so just and holy, even marriage itself, she throws him from her, like a stone from a sling, and being of this disposition, does more damage in this country than if a pestilence had seized it; for, her affability and beauty allures all the hearts of those that converse with her to serve and love her, but her coyness and plain-dealing drives them even to the borders of despair; therefore, they know not what to say, but upbraid her with cruelty and ingratitude, and give her a great many such titles, as plainly show the nature of her disposition: and if your worship was but to stay here one day, you would hear these hills and dales resound with the lamentations of her rejected followers. Not far from this place there is a tuft of about a dozen of tall beeches, upon every one of which you may read engraved the name of Marcella, and over some a crown cut out in bark, as if her lover would have declared that Marcella wears, and deserves to wear, the crown of all earthly beauty. Here one shepherd sighs, there another complains; in one place you may hear amorous ditties, in another the dirges of despair; one lover sits musing through all the hours of the night, at the foot of some tall ash, or rugged rock, and there, without having closed his weeping eyes, shrunk up as it were, and entranced in his own reflections, he is found by the rising sun ; a second, without giving respite or truce to his sighs, exposed to the heat of the most sultry summer's sun, lies stretched upon the burning sand, breathing his complaints to pitying heaven ; and over this and that, and these and those, the free, the unconcerned, the fair Marcella triumphs. We who are acquainted with her disposition, wait with impatience to see the end of all this disdain, and long to know what happy man will tame such an unsociable humour, and enjoy such exceeding beauty. As everything that I have accounted is true to a tittle, I have no reason to doubt the truth of what our comrades said concerning the cause of Chrysostom's death ; and therefore, I advise you, sir, not to fail being to-morrow at his burial, which will be worth seeing ; for Chrysostom had a great many friends, and the spot in which he ordered himself to be buried is not more than half a league from hence."

"I will take care to be present," said the knight, "and thank you heartily for the pleasure you have given me in relating such an interesting story." "Oh! as for that," cried the goatherd, "I do not know one half of what has happened to the lovers of Marcella ; but, to-morrow perhaps, we may light upon some shepherd on the road who is better acquainted with them. In the meantime you will do well to go to sleep under some cover, though the remedy I have applied is such, that you have nothing else to fear."

Sancho Panza, who wished the goatherd's loquacity

at the devil, earnestly entreated his master to go to sleep
in Pedro's hut. This request the knight complied with,
and spent the greatest part of the night in thinking of
his lady Dulcinea, in imitation of Marcella's lovers;
while Sancho Panza, taking up his lodging betwixt
Rozinante and his ass, slept soundly, not like a discarded
lover, but like one who had been battered and bruised
the day before.

Scarce had Aurora disclosed herself through the bal-
conies of the east, when five of the six goatherds arising,
went to waken Don Quixote, and told him, that if he
continued in his resolution of going to see the famous
funeral of Chrysostom, they would keep him company.
The knight, who desired nothing better, arose, and commanded Sancho to saddle his horse and pannel his ass
immediately. This order was executed with great dis-
patch, and they set out without loss of time. They had
not travelled more than a quarter of a league, when, upon
crossing a path, they saw coming towards them six shepherds, clothed in jackets of black sheep-skin, and crowned
with garlands of cypress, and bitter-bay, each having a
club of holly in his hand. Along with them came also
two gentlemen on horseback, very well equipped for
travel, accompanied by three young men on foot.

When they advanced they saluted one another, and
understanding, upon inquiry, that they were all bound
to the place of interment, they joined company, and
travelled together. One of the horsemen said to his
companion, "Signor Vivaldo, we shall not have reason
to grudge our tarrying to see this famous funeral, which
must certainly be very extraordinary, by the strange
account we have received from these people of the dead

shepherd and the murderous shepherdess." "I am of
the same opinion," answered Vivaldo, "and would not
only tarry one day, but even four or five, on purpose to
see it." Don Quixote asking what they had heard of
Marcella and Chrysostom, the traveller replied, that early
in the morning they had met with these shepherds, of
whom inquiring the cause of their being clothed in such
melancholy weeds, they had been informed of the coyness
and beauty of a certain shepherdess called Marcella, and
the hapless love of many who courted her, together with
the death of that same Chrysostom to whose funeral they
were going. In short, he recounted every circumstance
of what Pedro had told Don Quixote before.

This conversation being ended, another began by
Vivaldo's asking Don Quixote why he travelled thus in
armour in a peaceable country? To this question the
knight replied, "The exercise of my profession will not
permit, or allow me to go in any other manner. Revels,
feasting, and repose were invented by effeminate courtiers;
but toil, anxiety, and arms are peculiar to those whom
the world calls knights-errant, of which order I, though
unworthy, and the least, am one." He had no sooner
pronounced these words than all present took him for
a madman : but, in order to confirm their opinion, and
discover what species of madness it was, Vivaldo desired
to know what he meant by "knights-errant." "What!"
said Don Quixote, "have you never read the annals and
history of England, which treat of the famous exploits
of Arthur, who at present, in our Castilian language, is
called King Artus, and of whom there is an ancient tradi-
tion, generally believed all over Great Britain, that he did
not die, but was, by the art of enchantment, metamor-

phosed into a raven : and, that the time will come when
he shall return, and recover his sceptre and throne. For
which reason, it cannot be proved, that from that period
to this, any Englishman has killed a raven. In the reign
of that excellent king was instituted that famous order
of chivalry, called the Knights of the Round Table ; and
those amours punctually happened, which are recounted
of Don Lancelot of the Lake, with Queen Ginevra, by
the help and mediation of that sage and venerable duenna
Quitaniona ; from whence that delightful ballad, so much
sung in Spain, took its rise :

> ' For never sure was any knight,
>   So serv'd by damsel or by dame,
>   As Lancelot, that man of might,
>   When he at first from Britain came : '

with the rest of that most relishing and delicious account
of his amours, and valiant exploits. From that time the
order of knight-errantry was extended, as it were, from
hand to hand, and spread through divers and sundry parts
of the world, producing, among many other worthies
celebrated for their achievements, the valiant Amadis
de Gaul, with all his sons and nephews even to the fifth
generation ; the courageous Fleximarte of Hircania, the
never-enough-to-be-commended Tirante the White, and
he whom, in this our age, we have as it were seen, heard,
and conversed with, the invincible and valorous knight
Don Belianis of Greece. This, gentlemen, is what I
meant by knight-errant ; and such as I have described is
the order of chivalry, which, as I have already told you,
I, though a sinner, have professed, and the very same
which those knights I mentioned professed, I profess

also. On which account, I am found in these deserts and solitudes, in quest of adventures, fully determined to lift my arm, and expose my person to the greatest danger, that my destiny shall decree, in behalf of the needy and oppressed."

By this declaration, the travellers were convinced that the knight had lost his wits, and easily perceived the species of folly which had taken possession of his brain, and which struck them with the same surprise that always seizes those who became acquainted with our knight. Vivaldo, who was a person of discretion, and a great deal of archness, in order to travel agreeably the rest of the road which they had to go, till they should come to the place of interment, wanted to give him an opportunity of proceeding in his extravagance, and in that view said to him, " Sir knight-errant, methinks your worship professes one of the strictest orders upon earth, nay, I will affirm, more strict than that of the Carthusian friars."

" The order of the Carthusians," answered Don Quixote, " may be as strict, but that it is as beneficial to mankind, I am within a hair's-breadth of doubting ; for, to be plain with you, the soldier who executes his captain's command, is no less valuable than the captain who gave the order : I mean, that the monks pray to God for their fellow-creatures in peace and safety : but, we soldiers and knights put in execution that for which they pray, by the valour of our arms, and the edge of our swords ; living under no other cover than the cope of heaven, set up in a manner as marks for the intolerable heat of the sun in summer, and the chilling breath of frosty winter : we are therefore God's ministers, and the arms by which he executes his justice upon earth ; and as the circumstances of war, and what has the least affinity and concern with it, cannot be accomplished without sweat, anxiety, and fatigue ; it follows, that those who possess it are doubtless more subject to toil than those who, in rest and security, implore the favour of God for persons who can do nothing for themselves : not that I would be thought to say, or imagine, the condition of a knight-errant is equal to that of a recluse monk ; I would only infer from what we suffer, that it is without doubt more troublesome, more battered, more famished, more miserable, ragged, and lousy ; for, the knights-errant of past times certainly underwent numberless misfortunes in the course of their lives : and if some of them came to be emperors by the valour of their arms, considering the blood and sweat it cost them, in faith, it was a dear purchase ; and if those who attained such a supreme station, had been without their sage enchanters to assist them, they might have been defrauded of their desires, and grievously baulked of their expectations."

"I am very much of your opinion," answered the traveller, "but there is one thing among you knights-errant that I cannot approve of, and that is, when any great and dangerous adventure occurs, in which you run a manifest risk of losing your lives, in the instant of engagement, you never think of recommending your souls to God, as every Christian ought to do on such occasions ; but, on the contrary, put up your petitions to your mistresses, with as much fervour and devotion as if they were your deities ; a circumstance which, in my opinion, smells strong of paganism." "Sir," replied Don Quixote, "that practice must in no degree be

altered ; and woe be to that knight-errant who should
do otherwise ; for, according to the practice and custom
of chivalry, every knight, when he is upon the point of
achieving some great feat, must call up the idea of his
mistress, and turning his eyes upon her with all the gentleness of love, implore, as it were, by his looks, her favour
and protection in the doubtful dilemma in which he
is about to involve himself : nay, even though nobody
should hear him, he is obliged to mutter between his
teeth an ejaculation, by which he heartily and confi-
dently recommends himself to her good wishes : and of
this practice we have innumerable examples in history ;
but I would not have you think, that we are to forbear
recommending ourselves to God also ; there will be time
and opportunity enough for that duty, in the course of
action."

   " But, nevertheless," said the traveller, " I have still
one scruple remaining, which is, that I have often read
of a dispute between two knights, which proceeding to
rage from one word to another, they have turned about
their steeds, to gain ground for a good career, and then
without any more ceremony, returned to the encounter
at full gallop, recommending themselves to their mistresses by the way ; and the common issue of such an
engagement is, that one of them is thrown down over
his horse's crupper, stuck through and through with his
adversary's lance, while the other with difficulty avoids
a fall by laying hold of his horse's mane : now, I cannot
comprehend how the dead man could have time to recommend himself to God in the course of so sudden an
attack ; surely it would have been better for his soul if,
instead of the words he uttered in his career, he had put

up a petition to heaven, according to the duty and obligation of every Christian; especially, as I take it for
granted, that every knight-errant has not a mistress, for
all of them cannot be in love." "That's impossible,"
answered Don Quixote : "I affirm that there never could
be a knight-errant without a mistress; for to be in love
is as natural and peculiar to them as the stars are to the
heavens. I am very certain, that you never read an history that gives an account of a knight-errant without an
amour ; for he that has never been in love would not be
held as a legitimate member, but some adulterate brood,
who had got into the fortress of chivalry, not through
the gate, but over the walls, like a thief in the night."

"Yet, notwithstanding," said the traveller, "I have
read that Don Galaor, brother of the valiant Amadis de
Gaul, never had any known mistress to whom he could
recommend himself: and he was not disregarded, but
looked upon as a very valiant and famous knight."
"Signor," answered our hero Don Quixote, "one swallow
makes not a spring : besides, to my certain knowledge,
that knight was privately very much in love: indeed he
made love to every handsome woman who came in his
way; for that was his natural disposition, which he by
no means could resist : in short, it is very well attested
that he had one mistress, whom he enthroned as sovereign
of his heart, and to whom he recommended himself with
great caution and privacy, because he piqued himself upon
being a secret knight."

"Since then it is essential to every knight to be in
love, we may conclude that your worship being of that
profession, is no stranger to the passion ; and if you do
not value yourself upon being as secret a knight as Don

Galaor, I earnestly entreat you, in behalf of myself and the rest of the company, to tell us the name, country, station, and qualities of your mistress, who must think herself extremely happy in reflecting that all the world knows how much she is beloved and adored by so valiant a knight as your worship appears to be."

Here Don Quixote uttered a grievous sigh, saying : " I am not positively certain, whether or not that beauteous enemy of mine, takes pleasure in the world's knowing I am her slave ; this only I can say, in answer to the question you asked with so much civility, that her name is Dulcinea ; her native country, a certain part of Valencia called Toboso ; her station must at least be that of a princess, since she is queen and lady of my soul ; her beauty, supernatural, in that it justifies all those impossible and chimerical attributes of excellence, which the poets bestow upon their nymphs ; her hair is of gold, her forehead the Elysian fields, her eyebrows heavenly arches, her eyes themselves suns, her cheeks roses, her lips of coral, her teeth of pearl, her neck alabaster, her breast marble, her hands ivory, her skin whiter than snow, and those parts which decency conceals from human view are such, according to my belief and apprehension, as discretion ought to enhance above all comparison."

"I wish we knew her lineage, race, and family," replied Vivaldo. To this hint the knight answered, "She is not descended of the ancient Caii, Curtii, and Scipios of Rome, nor of the modern Colonas and Ursini, nor of the Moncadas and Requesnes of Catalonia, much less of the Rebellas and Villanovas of Valencia : or the Palafaxes, Nucas, Rocabertis, Corellas ; Lunas, Alagones, Urreas, Fozes and Gurreas of Arragon, or the Cerdas, Manriquez,

Mendozas and Gusmans of Castile, or the Alencastros, Pallas and Menesis of Portugal: but she sprung from the family of Toboso de la Mancha, a lineage which, though modern, may give a noble rise to the most illustrious families of future ages; and let no man contradict what I say, except upon the conditions expressed in that inscription placed by Cerbino under the trophy of Orlando's arms—

> 'That knight alone these arms shall move,
> Who dares Orlando's prowess prove.'"[1]

"Although I myself am descended from the Cachopines[2] of Laredo," said the traveller, "I won't presume

[1] When a knight challenged the whole world, he wore an emprize, consisting of a gold chain, or some other badge of love and chivalry; and sometimes this emprize was fixed in a public place to attract the attention of strangers: when any person accepted the challenge for a trial of chivalry, called the combat of courtesy, he touched this emprize; but, if he tore it away, it was considered as a resolution to fight the owner to extremity or outrance. The combat of courtesy is still practised by our prize-fighters and boxers, who shake hands before the engagement, in token of love.

But no defiance of this kind could be either published or accepted without the permission of the prince, at whose court the combatants chanced to be. Accordingly we are told by Oliver de la Marche, that the lord of Ternant having published a defiance at the court of Burgundy, in the year 1445, Galiat asked the duke's permission to touch the challenger's emprize, which, being granted, he advanced and touched it, saying to the bearer, while he bowed very low, "Noble knight, I touch your emprize, and, with God's permission, will do my utmost to fulfil your desire either on horseback or on foot." The lord of Ternant humbly thanked him for his condescension, said he was extremely welcome, and promised to send him that same day a cartel, mentioning the arms they should use.

[2] Cachopines is the name given to Europeans by the Indians of Mexico.

to compare with that of Toboso de la Mancha ; though, to be plain with you, I never before heard of any such generation." "How, not heard ?" replied Don Quixote. The rest of the company jogged on, listening with great attention to this discourse, and all of them, even the very goatherds, by this time, were convinced, that our knight's judgment was grievously impaired. Sancho alone believed that everything his master said was true ; because he knew his family, and had been acquainted with himself from his cradle. The only doubt that he entertained was of this same beautiful Dulcinea del Toboso ; for never had such a name, or such a princess, come within the sphere of his observation, although he lived in the neighbourhood of that place.

While they travelled along, conversing in this manner, they perceived about twenty shepherds descending through a cleft made by two high mountains. They were all clad in jackets of sheep-skin, covered with black wool, and each of them crowned with a garland, which was composed, as it afterwards appeared, partly of cypress, and partly of yew : six of the foremost carried a bier, upon which they had strewed a variety of branches and flowers. And this was no sooner perceived by one of the goatherds, than he said, "These are the people who carry the corpse of Chrysostom, and the foot of that mountain is the place where he ordered himself to be interred."

Upon this information they made haste, and came up just at the time that the bearers, having laid down the body, began to dig the grave with pick-axes on one side of a flinty rock. They received our travellers with great courtesy, and Don Quixote, with his company, went towards the bier, to look at the dead body, which was covered with flowers, clad in shepherd's weeds, and seemingly thirty years old. Notwithstanding he was dead, they could plainly perceive that he had been a man of an engaging aspect, and genteel stature; and could not help wondering at the sight of a great many papers, both sealed and loose, that lay round him in the coffin.

While the new comers were observing this phenomenon, and the shepherds busied in digging a grave, a wonderful and universal silence prevailed, till such time as one of the bearers said to another: "Consider, Ambrosio, if this be the very spot which Chrysostom mentioned, that his last will may be punctually fulfilled." "This," answered Ambrosio, "is the very place in which my unhappy friend has often recounted to me the story of his misfortunes. Here it was he first beheld that mortal enemy of the human race; here also did he first declare his amorous and honourable intention; and here, at last, did Marcella signify her disgust and disdain, which put an end to the tragedy of his wretched life: and in this place, as a monument of his mishap, did he desire to be deposited in the bowels of eternal oblivion."

Then addressing himself to Don Quixote and the travellers, he thus proceeded: "This corse, gentlemen, which you behold with compassionate eyes, was the habitation of a soul, which possessed an infinite share of the riches of heaven: this is the body of Chrysostom, who was a man of unparalleled genius, the pink of courtesy and kindness; in friendship a very phœnix, liberal without bounds, grave without arrogance, gay without meanness; and, in short, second to none in everything that was good, and without second in all that was unfortunate. He loved, and was abhorred; he adored, and was disdained;

G

he implored a savage; he importuned a statue; he hunted the wind; cried aloud to the desert; he was a slave to the most ungrateful of women; and the fruit of his servitude was death, which overtook him in the middle of his career; in short, he perished by the cruelty of a shepherdess, whom he has eternalised in the memory of all the people in this country; as these papers which you gaze at would show, if he had not ordered me to commit them to the flames as soon as his body shall be deposited in the earth."

"You will use them then with more cruelty and rigour," said Vivaldo, "than that of the author himself; seeing it is neither just nor convenient to fulfil the will of any man, provided it be unreasonable. Augustus Cæsar would have been in the wrong had he consented to the execution of what the divine Mantuan ordered on his death-bed. Wherefore, Signor Ambrosio, while you commit the body of your friend to the earth, you ought not likewise to consign his writings to oblivion; nor perform indiscreetly, what he in his affliction ordained: on the contrary, by publishing these papers, you ought to immortalise the cruelty of Marcella, that it may serve as an example in time to come, and warn young men to shun and avoid such dangerous precipices; for I, and the rest of this company, already know the history of that enamoured and unhappy friend, the nature of your friendship, the occasion of his death, together with the orders that he left upon his death-bed; from which lamentable story, it is easy to conclude how excessive must have been the cruelty of Marcella, the love of Chrysostom, the faith of your friendship, and the check which those receive, who precipitately run through the path exhibited to them by idle and mischievous love. Last night, we understood the death of Chrysostom, who, we are informed, was to be buried in this place; and therefore, out of curiosity and concern, have turned out of our way, resolving to come, and see with our eyes, what had affected us so much in the hearing: and in return for that concern, and the desire we felt in remedying it, if it had been in our power, we entreat thee, O discreet Ambrosio! at least, for my own part, I beg of thee not to burn these papers, but allow me to preserve some of them."

Accordingly, without staying for an answer, he reached out his hand, and took some of those that were nearest him: which Ambrosio perceiving, said, "Out of civility, Signor, I will consent to your keeping what you have taken up; but to think that I will fail to burn the rest, is a vain supposition." Vivaldo being desirous of seeing the contents, immediately opened one entitled " A Song of Despair," which Ambrosio hearing, said, " That is the last poem my unhappy friend composed; and that you may see, Signor, to what a pass his misfortunes had reduced him, read it aloud, and you'll have time enough to finish it before the grave be made!" " That I will do with all my heart," said Vivaldo, and everybody present being seized with the same desire, they stood around him in a circle, and he read what follows, with an audible voice :—

A SONG OF DESPAIR.

I.

" Since then thy pleasure, cruel maid!
Is, that thy rigour and disdain
Should be from clime to clime convey'd;
All hell shall aid me to complain!

The torments of my heart to tell,
  And thy achievements to record,
My voice shall raise a dreadful yell,
  My bowels burst at every word:
Then listen to the baleful sound
  That issues from my throbbing breast,
Thy pride, perhaps, it may confound,
  And yield my madd'ning soul some rest.

II.

Let the snake's hiss and wolf's dire howl,
  The bull's harsh note, the lion's roar,
The boding crow and screeching owl,
  The tempest rattling on the shore,
The monster's scream, the turtle's moan,
  The shrieks of the infernal crew,
Be mingled with my dying groan,
  A concert terrible and new!
The hearer's senses to appal,
  And reason from her throne depose;
Such melody will suit the gall
  That from my burning liver flows!

III.

Old Tagus with his yellow hair,
  And Betis with her olive wreath,
Shall never echo such despair,
  Or listen to such notes of death,
As here I'll utter and repeat,
  From hill to dale, from rock to cave,
In wilds untrod by human feet,
  In dungeons dreary as the grave.
The beasts of prey that scour the plain,
  Shall thy more savage nature know,
The spacious earth resound my strain;
  Such is the privilege of woe!

IV.

Disdain is death, and doubt o'erturns
    The patience of the firmest mind ;
But, jealousy still fiercer burns,
    Like all the flames of hell combin'd.
The horrors of that cursed fiend,
    In absence to distraction rage,
And all the succour hope can lend,
    The direful pangs will not assuage.
Such agonies will surely kill ;
    Yet, 'spite of absence, doubts, and scorn,
I live a miracle, and still
    Those deadly flames within me burn !

V.

Hope's shadow ne'er refresh'd my view,
    Despair attends with wakeful strife ;
The first let happier swains pursue,
    The last my comfort is for life.
Can hope and fear at once prevail,
    When fear on certainty is fed ?
To shut mine eyes will not avail,
    When thunder bursts around my head.
When cold disdain in native dye,
    Appears, and falsehood's cunning lore
Perverts the tale of truth, shall I
    Against despondence shut the door ?

VI.

O jealousy ! love's tyrant lord,
    And thou soul-chilling, dire disdain !
Lend me the dagger and the cord,
    To stab remembrance, strangle pain.
I die bereft of hope in death,
    Yet still those are the freest souls,
(I'll vouch it with my latest breath)
    Whom love's old tyranny controls.

My fatal enemy is fair,
In body and in mind, I'll say,
And I have earn'd the woes I bear :
By rigour love maintains the sway.

VII.

With this opinion let me fall
A prey to unrelenting scorn :
No fun'ral pomp shall grace my pall,
No laurel my pale corse adorn.
O thou ! whose cruelty and hate
The tortures of my breast proclaim,
Behold how willingly to fate
I offer this devoted frame.
If thou, when I am past all pain,
Should'st think my fall deserves a tear,
Let not one single drop distain
Those eyes so killing and so clear.

VIII.

No ! rather let thy mirth display
The joys that in thy bosom flow ;
Ah ! need I bid that heart be gay
Which always triumph'd in my woe.
Come then, for ever barr'd of bliss,
Ye, who with ceaseless torment dwell,
And agonising, howl and hiss
In the profoundest shades of hell ;
Come, Tantalus, with raging thirst,
Bring, Sisyphus, thy rolling stone,
Come, Tityus, with thy vulture curst,
Nor leave Ixion rack'd, alone :

IX.

The toiling sisters, too, shall join,
And my sad, solemn dirge repeat,
When to the grave my friends consign
These limbs denied a winding sheet;

Fierce Cerberus shall clank his chain,
  In chorus with chimæras dire:
What other pomp, what other strain
  Should he who dies of love, require?
Be hush'd, my song, complain no more
  Of her whose pleasure gave thee birth;
But let the sorrows I deplore
  Sleep with me in the silent earth."

This ditty of Chrysostom was approved by all the hearers: but he who read it observed, that it did not seem to agree with the report he had heard of Marcella's virtue and circumspection; inasmuch as the author complained of jealousy, absence, and suspicion, which tended to the prejudice of her morals and reputation. To this objection Ambrosio, as one that was acquainted with the most secret sentiments of his friend, answered, "Signor, for your satisfaction in this point, it is necessary you should know, that the forlorn shepherd composed this song in the absence of Marcella, from whose presence he had gone into voluntary exile, in order to try if he could reap the usual fruits of absence, and forget the cause of his despair; and as one in that situation is apt to be fretted by every circumstance, and invaded by every apprehension, poor Chrysostom was harassed by groundless jealousy and imaginary fears, which tormented him as much as if they had been real; for which reason, this circumstance ought not to invalidate the fame of Marcella's virtue, against which, exclusive of her cruelty, arrogance, and disdain, envy itself hath not been able to lay the least imputation."

"That may be very true," replied Vivaldo, who, being about to read another of the papers he had saved from the flames, was diverted from this purpose by a wonderful vision, for such it seemed, that all of a sudden presented itself to their eyes. This was no other than the shepherdess Marcella, who appeared upon the top of the rock, just above the grave they were digging, so beautiful that she surpassed all report. Those who had never seen her before, gazed with silent admiration ; nor were the rest who had been accustomed to see her, less astonished at her appearance. But no sooner did Ambrosio perceive her than, with indignation in his looks, he cried :

"Comest thou hither, fierce basilisk of these mountains ! to see if the wounds of this unhappy youth, whom thy cruelty hath slain, will bleed at thy approach ? or art thou come to rejoice in the exploits of thy barbarity, and from the top of that mountain behold, like another Nero, the flames which thy impiety hath kindled ? or inhumanly to trample upon this unfortunate corse, as the unnatural daughter insulted the dead body of her father Tarquin ? Tell us, at once, the cause of thy approach, and deign to signify thy pleasure, that I, who know how devoutly Chrysostom obeyed thee, when alive, may, now that he is dead, dispose his friends to yield the same obedience."

"I come not," answered Marcella, "for any of the purposes you have mentioned, Ambrosio ; but rather personally to demonstrate how unreasonably I am blamed for the death and sufferings of Chrysostom. I beg, therefore, that all present will give me the hearing, as it will be unnecessary to spend much time, or waste many words, to convince those that are unprejudiced, of the truth. Heaven, you say, hath given me beauty, nay, such a share of it as compels you to love me, in spite of your resolutions to the contrary ; from whence you draw this infer-

ence, and insist upon it, that it is my duty to return your
passion. By the help of that small capacity which nature
has bestowed upon me, I know that which is beautiful is
lovely; but I can by no means conceive why the object,
which is beloved for being beautiful, is bound to be
enamoured of its admirer; more especially, as it may
happen that this same admirer is an object of disgust
and abhorrence; in which case, would it be reasonable
in him to say, 'I love thee because thou art beautiful, and
thou must favour my passion, although I am deformed'?
But, granting the beauty equal on both sides, it does not
follow that the desires ought to be mutual; for all sorts
of beauty do not equally affect the spectator; some, for
example, delighting the eye only, without captivating the
heart. And well it is for mankind that things are thus
disposed, otherwise there would be a strange perplexity
and confusion of desires, without power of distinguishing
and choosing particular objects; for beauty, being infinitely diversified, the inclination would be infinitely
divided, and I have heard that true love must be un-
divided and unconstrained; if this be the case, as I believe it is, why should I constrain my inclination, when
I am under no other obligation so to do, but your saying
that you are in love with me? Otherwise tell me, if
heaven that made me handsome had created me a monster
of deformity, should I have had cause to complain of you
for not loving me? Besides, you are to consider that I
did not choose the beauty I possess; such as it is, God
was pleased of His own free will and favour to bestow it
upon me, without any solicitation on my part. Therefore, as the viper deserves no blame for its sting, although
it be mortal, because it is the gift of nature; neither

ought I to be reviled for being beautiful; for beauty in a virtuous woman is like a distant flame and a sharp sword afar off, which prove fatal to none but those who approach too near them. Honour and virtue are the ornaments of the soul; without which the body, though ever so handsome, ought to seem ugly; if chastity, then, be one of the virtues which chiefly adorns and beautifies both body and soul, why should she that is beloved, lose that jewel for which she is chiefly beloved, merely to satisfy the appetite of one who, for his own selfish enjoyment, employs his whole care and industry to destroy it? I was born free, and to enjoy that freedom have I chosen the solitude of these fields. The trees on these mountains are my companions; and I have no other mirror than the limpid streams of these crystal brooks. With the trees and the streams I share my contemplation and my beauty: I am a distant flame and a sword afar off: those whom my eyes have captivated, my tongue has undeceived: and if hope be the food of desire, as I gave none to Chrysostom or to any other person, so neither can his death, nor that of any other of my admirers, be justly imputed to my cruelty, but rather to their own obstinate despair. To those who observe that his intentions were honourable, and that, therefore, I was bound to comply with them, I answer, when he declared the honesty of his designs in that very spot where now his grave is digging, I told him my purpose was to live in perpetual solitude, and let the earth alone enjoy the fruits of my retirement, and the spoils of my beauty. Wherefore, if he, notwithstanding this my explanation, persevered without hope, and sailed against the wind, it is no wonder that he was overwhelmed in the gulf of his

rashness. Had I cajoled him, I should have been per-
fidious; had I gratified his inclination, I should have
acted contrary to my own reason and resolution. But,
because he persisted after I had explained myself, and
despaired before he had cause to think I abhorred him,
I leave you to judge whether or not it be reasonable to
lay his misfortune at my door. Let him whom I have
deceived complain, and let him despair to whom I have
broke my promise : if I call upon any man, he may
depend upon me : if I admit of his addresses, he may
rejoice in his success; but why should I be styled a bar-
barous homicide by him whom I never soothed, deceived,
called, or admitted? Hitherto Heaven has not thought
fit that I should love by destiny, and the world must
excuse me from loving by election. Let this general
declaration serve as an answer to all those who solicit
me in particular, and henceforward give them to understand, that whosoever dies for me perishes not by jealousy
or disdain, for she who never gave her love, can never
give just cause of jealousy ; neither ought her plain-dealing to be interpreted into disdain. Let him who terms
me a fierce basilisk, shun me as an evil being ; if any man
thinks me ungrateful, let him refuse his services when I
ask them. If I have disowned any one, let him renounce
me in his turn; and let him who has found me cruel,
abandon me in distress : this fierce basilisk, this ungrateful, cruel, supercilious wretch, will neither seek, serve,
own, nor follow you in any shape whatever. If Chrysostom perished by the impatience of his own extrava-
gant desire, why should my innocent reserve be inveighed
against? If I have preserved my virginity in these deserts,
why should he that loves me, wish me to lose it among

mankind? I have riches of my own, as you all know, and covet no man's wealth. I am free, and will not be subjected : I neither love nor hate any man ; I do not cajole this one, nor teaze that ; nor do I joke with one or discourse with another, but amuse myself with the care of my goats, and the innocent conversation of the shepherdesses belonging to the neighbouring villages. My desires are bounded by these mountains; or if my meditation surpasses these bounds, it is only to contemplate the beauty of the heavens, those steps by which the soul ascends to its original mansion." So saying, without waiting for any reply, she turned her back and vanished into a thicket on a neighbouring mountain, leaving all that were present equally surprised with her beauty and discretion.

Some of the bystanders being wounded by the powerful shafts that were darted from her fair eyes, manifested an inclination to follow her, without availing themselves of the ingenious declaration they had heard, which, being perceived by Don Quixote, who thought this a proper occasion for exercising his chivalry in defence of distressed damsels, he laid his hand upon the hilt of his sword, and in a lofty and audible voice pronounced, " Let no person, of whatsoever rank or degree, presume to follow the beautiful Marcella, on pain of incurring my most furious indignation. She has demonstrated, by clear and undeniable arguments, how little, if at all, she is to be blamed for the death of Chrysostom, and how averse she is to comply with the desires of any of her admirers ; for which reason, instead of being pursued and persecuted, she ought to be honoured and esteemed by all virtuous men, as the only person in the universe

who lives in such a chaste and laudable intention."
Whether it was owing to these menaces of the knight,
or to the advice of Ambrosio, who desired them to perform the last office to their deceased friend, not one of
the shepherds attempted to stir from the spot, until the
grave being finished, and the papers burnt, the body of
poor Chrysostom was interred, not without abundance of
tears shed by his surviving companions. The grave was
secured by a large fragment of the rock which they rolled
upon it, till such time as a tombstone could be made,
under the direction of Ambrosio, who was resolved to
have the following epitaph engraved upon it—

> "The body of a wretched swain,
>   Kill'd by a cruel maid's disdain,
> In this cold bed neglected lies.
>   He liv'd, fond hapless youth ! to prove
> The inhuman tyranny of love,
>   Exerted in Marcella's Eyes."

Having strewed the place with a profusion of flowers
and branches, everybody present condoled, and took leave
of the afflicted executor ; and Don Quixote bade farewell
to his kind landlords, as well as to the travellers.

THE STORY OF LE FEVRE

It was some time in the summer of that year in which
Dendermond was taken by the Allies, which was about
seven years before my father came into the country, and
about as many after the time that my uncle Toby and
Trim had privately decamped from my father's house in
town, in order to lay some of the finest sieges to some of
the finest fortified cities in Europe, when my uncle Toby
was one evening getting his supper, with Trim sitting
behind him at a small sideboard. I say sitting, for, in
consideration of the Corporal's lame knee (which sometimes gave him exquisite pain), when my uncle Toby
dined or supped alone, he would never suffer the Corporal to stand ; and the poor fellow's veneration for his
master was such that, with a proper artillery, my uncle
Toby could have taken Dendermond itself with less
trouble than he was able to gain this point over him ;
for many a time, when my uncle Toby supposed the
Corporal's leg was at rest, he would look back, and
detect him standing behind him with the most dutiful
respect. This bred more little squabbles betwixt them
than all other causes for five-and-twenty years together ;

but this is neither here nor there. Why did I mention it ? Ask my pen : it governs me ;—I govern not it.

He was one evening sitting thus at his supper, when the landlord of a little inn in the village came into the parlour, with an empty phial in his hand, to beg a glass or two of sack. " 'Tis for a poor gentleman, I think of the army," said the landlord, " who has been taken ill at my house four days ago, and has never held up his head since, or had a desire to taste anything, till just now, that he has a fancy for a glass of sack and a thin toast. *'I think,'* says he, taking his hand from his forehead, *' it would comfort me.'*

"If I could neither beg, borrow, nor buy such a thing," added the landlord, "I would almost steal it for the poor gentleman, he is so ill. I hope in God he will still mend," continued he; "we are all of us concerned for him."

" Thou art a good-natured soul, I will answer for thee," cried my uncle Toby; "and thou shalt drink the poor gentleman's health in a glass of sack thyself, and take a couple of bottles with my service, and tell him he is heartily welcome to them, and to a dozen more, if they will do him good.

"Though I am persuaded," said my uncle Toby, as the landlord shut the door, " he is a very compassionate fellow, Trim, yet I cannot help entertaining a high opinion of his guest too. There must be something more than common in him, that, in so short a time, should win so much upon the affections of his host." "And of his whole family," added the Corporal, " for they are all concerned for him." "Step after him," said my uncle Toby; "do, Trim ; and ask if he knows his name."

"I have quite forgot it truly," said the landlord, coming back into the parlour with the Corporal; "but I can ask his son again." "Has he a son with him, then?" said my uncle Toby. "A boy," replied the landlord, "of about eleven or twelve years of age; but the poor creature has tasted almost as little as his father; he does nothing but mourn and lament for him night and day. He has not stirred from the bed-side these two days."

My uncle Toby laid down his knife and fork, and thrust his plate from before him, as the landlord gave him the account; and Trim, without being ordered, took away, without saying one word, and, in a few minutes after, brought him his pipe and tobacco.

"Stay in the room a little," said my uncle Toby.

"Trim," said my uncle Toby, after he lighted his pipe and smoked about a dozen whiffs. Trim came in front of his master, and made his bow; my uncle Toby smoked on, and said no more. "Corporal!" said my uncle Toby. The Corporal made his bow. My uncle Toby proceeded no farther, but finished his pipe.

"Trim!" said my uncle Toby, "I have a project in my head, as it is a bad night, of wrapping myself up warm in my *roquelaure*, and paying a visit to this poor gentleman." "Your Honour's *roquelaure*," replied the Corporal, "has not once been had on since the night before your Honour received your wound, when we mounted guard in the trenches before the gate of St. Nicholas; and, besides, it is so cold and rainy a night that, what with the *roquelaure*, and what with the weather, 'twill be enough to give your Honour your death, and bring on your Honour's torment in your groin." "I fear so," replied my uncle Toby, "but I am not at rest in my mind, Trim, since the account the landlord has given me. I wish I had not known so much of this affair," added my uncle Toby, "or that I had known more of it. How shall we manage it?" "Leave it, an' please your Honour, to me," quoth the Corporal. "I'll take my hat and stick, and go to the house and reconnoitre, and act accordingly; and I will bring your Honour a full account in an hour." "Thou shalt go, Trim," said my uncle Toby, "and here's a shilling for thee to drink with his servant." "I shall get it all out of him," said the Corporal, shutting the door.

My uncle Toby filled his second pipe; and had it not been that he now and then wandered from the point, with considering whether it was not full as well to have the curtain of the *ténaille* a straight line as a crooked one,—he might be said to have thought of nothing else but poor Le Fevre and his boy the whole time he smoked it.

It was not till my uncle Toby had knocked the ashes out of his third pipe that Corporal Trim returned from the inn, and gave him the following account :—

"I despaired at first," said the Corporal, "of being able to bring back your Honour any kind of intelligence concerning the poor sick Lieutenant." "Is he in the army, then?" said my uncle Toby. "He is," said the Corporal. "And in what regiment?" said my uncle Toby. "I'll tell your Honour," replied the Corporal, "everything straight forwards, as I learnt it." "Then, Trim, I'll fill another pipe," said my uncle Toby, "and not interrupt thee till thou hast done; so sit down at thy

H

ease, Trim, in the window-seat, and begin thy story again." The Corporal made his old bow, which generally spoke as plain as a bow could speak it, *Your Honour is good:*—and having done that, he sat down, as he was ordered, and began the story to my uncle Toby over again in pretty near the same words.

"I despaired at first," said the Corporal, "of being able to bring back any intelligence to your Honour about the Lieutenant and his son;—for, when I asked where his servant was, from whom I made myself sure of knowing everything which was proper to be asked—" ["That's a right distinction, Trim," said my uncle Toby.] "I was answered, an' please your Honour, that he had no servant with him; that he had come to the inn with hired horses, which, upon finding himself unable to proceed (to join, I suppose, the regiment) he had dismissed the morning after he came. 'If I get better, my dear,' said he, as he gave his purse to his son to pay the man, 'we can hire horses thence.' 'But, alas! the poor gentleman will never go hence,' said the landlady to me, 'for I heard the death-watch all night long; and, when he dies, the youth, his son, will certainly die with him, for he is broken-hearted already.'

"I was hearing this account," continued the Corporal, "when the youth came into the kitchen, to order the thin toast the landlord spoke of. 'But I will do it for my father myself,' said the youth. 'Pray let me save you the trouble, young gentleman,' said I, taking up a fork for the purpose, and offering him my chair to sit down upon by the fire, whilst I did it. 'I believe, sir,' said he, very modestly, 'I can please him best myself.' 'I am sure,' said I, 'his Honour will not like the toast the

worse for being toasted by an old soldier.' The youth
took hold of my hand, and instantly burst into tears."
" Poor youth ! " said my uncle Toby, "he has been bred
up from an infant in the army; and the name of a
soldier, Trim, sounded in his ears like the name of a
friend ! I wish I had him here."

" I never, in the longest march," said the Corporal,
" had so great a mind for my dinner, as I had to cry with
him for company. What could be the matter with me,
an' please your Honour?" "Nothing in the world,
Trim," said my uncle Toby, blowing his nose, " but that
thou art a good-natured fellow."

" When I gave him the toast," continued the Corporal, " I thought it was proper to tell him I was Captain Shandy's servant, and that your Honour (though a
stranger) was extremely concerned for his father ; and
that if there was anything in your house or cellar " [" And
thou might'st have added my purse, too," said my uncle
Toby] " he was heartily welcome to it. He made a very
low bow (which was meant to your Honour) but no
answer, for his heart was full; so he went upstairs with
the toast. ' I warrant you, my dear,' said I, as I opened
the kitchen door, ' your father will be well again.' Mr.
Yorick's curate was smoking a pipe by the kitchen fire,
but said not a word, good or bad, to comfort the youth.
I thought it wrong," added the Corporal. "I think so
too," said my uncle Toby.

" When the Lieutenant had taken his glass of sack
and toast, he felt himself a little revived, and sent down
into the kitchen to let me know that, in about ten
minutes, he should be glad if I would step upstairs. ' I
believe,' said the landlord, ' he is going to say his prayers;

for there was a book laid upon the chair by his bedside, and, as I shut the door, I saw his son take up a
cushion.'

"'I thought,' said the Curate, 'that you gentlemen of
the army, Mr. Trim, never said your prayers at all.' 'I
heard the poor gentleman say his prayers last night,' said
the landlady, 'very devoutly, and with my own ears, or I
could not have believed it.' 'Are you sure of it?' replied
the Curate. 'A soldier, an' please your reverence,' said
I, 'prays as often (of his own accord) as a parson; and
when he is fighting for his king, and for his own life, and
for his honour too, he has the most reason to pray to
God of any one in the whole world.'" "'Twas well said
of thee, Trim," said my uncle Toby. "'But when a
soldier,' said I, 'an' please your reverence, has been
standing for twelve hours together in the trenches, up to
his knees in cold water, or engaged,' said I, 'for months
together in long and dangerous marches; harassed, perhaps, in his rear to-day; harassing others to-morrow;
detached here, countermanded there; resting this night
out upon his arms, beat up in his shirt the next; benumbed in his joints; perhaps without straw in his tent
to kneel on; must say his prayers *how* and *when* he
can — I believe,' said I, for I was piqued, quoth the
Corporal, for the reputation of the army—'I believe,
an' please your reverence,' said I, 'that when a soldier
gets time to pray, he prays as heartily as a parson, though
not with all his fuss and hypocrisy.'" "Thou should'st
not have said that, Trim," said my uncle Toby, "for
God only knows who is a hypocrite, and who is not. At
the great and general review of us all, Corporal, at the
day of judgment (and not till then), it will be seen who

have done their duties in this world, and who have not; and we shall be advanced, Trim, accordingly." "I hope we shall," said Trim. "It is in the Scripture," said my uncle Toby; "and I will show it thee to-morrow. In the meantime we may depend upon it, Trim, for our comfort," said my uncle Toby, "that God Almighty is so good and just a Governor of the world that, if we have but done our duties in it, it will never be inquired into whether we have done them in a red coat or a black one." "I hope not," said the Corporal. "But go on, Trim," said my uncle Toby, "with thy story."

"When I went up," continued the Corporal, "into the Lieutenant's room, which I did not do till the expiration of the ten minutes, he was lying in his bed, with his head raised upon his hand, with his elbow upon the pillow, and a clean white cambric handkerchief beside it. The youth was just stooping down to take up the cushion, upon which I supposed he had been kneeling; the book was laid upon the bed, and, as he arose, in taking up the cushion with one hand, he reached out his other to take it away at the same time. 'Let it remain there, my dear,' said the Lieutenant.

"He did not offer to speak to me till I had walked up close to his bedside. 'If you are Captain Shandy's servant,' said he, 'you must present my thanks to your master, with my little boy's thanks along with them, for his courtesy to me. If he was of Leven's,' said the Lieutenant. I told him your Honour was. 'Then,' said he, 'I served three campaigns with him in Flanders, and remember him; but 'tis most likely, as I had not the honour of any acquaintance with him, that he knows nothing of me. You will tell him, however, that the

person his good-nature has laid under obligations to him
is one Le Fevre, a lieutenant in Angus's;—but he knows
me not,' said he, a second time, musing; 'possibly he
may my story,' added he. 'Pray tell the Captain that I
was the ensign at Breda whose wife was most unfortunately killed with a musket-shot, as she lay in my arms
in my tent.' 'I remember the story, an' please your
Honour,' said I, 'very well.' 'Do you so?' said he,
wiping his eyes with his handkerchief, 'then well may I.'
In saying this, he drew a little ring out of his bosom,
which seemed tied with a black riband about his neck,
and kissed it twice. 'Here, Billy,' said he. The boy
flew across the room to the bedside, and falling down
upon his knee, took the ring in his hand, and kissed it
too, then kissed his father, and sat down upon the bed
and wept."

"I wish," said my uncle Toby, with a deep sigh, "I
wish, Trim, I was asleep."

"Your Honour," replied the Corporal, "is too much
concerned. Shall I pour your Honour out a glass of sack
to your pipe?" "Do, Trim," said my uncle Toby.

"I remember," said my uncle Toby, sighing again,
"the story of the ensign and his wife, with a circumstance
his modesty omitted; and particularly well that he, as well
as she, upon some account or other (I forget what) was universally pitied by the whole regiment; but finish the story
thou art upon." "'Tis finished already," said the Corporal, "for I could stay no longer; so wished his Honour
good night. Young Le Fevre rose from off the bed, and
saw me to the bottom of the stairs; and, as we went down
together, told me that they had come from Ireland, and
were on their route to join the regiment in Flanders.

But, alas !" said the Corporal, "the Lieutenant's last day's march is over!" "Then what is to become of his poor boy?" cried my uncle Toby.

It was to my uncle Toby's eternal honour—though I tell it only for the sake of those who, when cooped in betwixt a natural and a positive law, know not, for their souls, which way in the world to turn themselves—that, notwithstanding my uncle Toby was warmly engaged at that time in carrying on the siege of Dendermond, parallel with the Allies, who pressed theirs on so vigorously that they scarce allowed him time to get his dinner, that nevertheless he gave up Dendermond, though he had already made a lodgment upon the counterscarp, and bent his whole thoughts towards the private distresses at the inn ; and, except that he ordered the garden gate to be bolted up, by which he might be said to have turned the siege of Dendermond into a blockade, he left Dendermond to itself, to be relieved or not by the French king, as the French king thought good, and only considered how he himself should relieve the poor Lieutenant and his son.

That kind Being, who is a friend to the friendless, shall recompense thee for this.

"Thou hast left this matter short," said my uncle Toby to the Corporal, as he was putting him to bed,— "and I will tell thee in what, Trim. In the first place, when thou madest an offer of my services to Le Fevre,— as sickness and travelling are both expensive, and thou knewest he was but a poor Lieutenant, with a son to subsist as well as himself out of his pay, that thou didst not make an offer to him of my purse; because had he stood in need, thou knowest, Trim, he had been as welcome to it as myself." "Your Honour knows," said the Corporal, "I had no orders." "True," quoth my uncle Toby,—"thou didst very right, Trim, as a soldier—but certainly very wrong as a man.

"In the second place, for which, indeed, thou hast the same excuse," continued my uncle Toby, "when thou offeredst him whatever was in my house, thou shouldst have offered him my house too. A sick brother officer should have the best quarters, Trim; and if we had him with us, we could tend and look to him. Thou art an excellent nurse thyself, Trim; and what with thy care of him, and the old woman's, and his boy's, and mine together, we might recruit him again at once, and set him upon his legs.

"In a fortnight or three weeks," added my uncle Toby, smiling, "he might march." "He will never march, an' please your Honour, in this world," said the Corporal. "He *will* march," said my uncle Toby, rising up from the side of the bed with one shoe off. "An' please your Honour," said the Corporal, "he will never march but to his grave." "He *shall* march," cried my uncle Toby, marching the foot which had a shoe on, though without advancing an inch, "he *shall* march to his regiment." "He cannot stand it," said the Corporal. "He shall be supported," said my uncle Toby. "He'll drop at last," said the Corporal, "and what will become of his boy?" "He *shall not* drop," said my uncle Toby firmly. "A-well-a-day!—do what we can for him," said Trim, maintaining his point, "the poor soul will die." "*He shall not die, by G—*," cried my uncle Toby.

The *accusing spirit*, which flew up to heaven's

chancery with the oath, blushed as he gave it in;—and the *recording angel*, as he wrote it down, dropped a tear upon the word, and blotted it out for ever.

My uncle Toby went to his bureau, put his purse into his breeches pocket, and, having ordered the Corporal to go early in the morning for a physician, he went to bed and fell asleep.

The sun looked bright, the morning after, to every eye in the village but Le Fevre's and his afflicted son's; the hand of death pressed heavy upon his eyelids; and hardly could the wheel at the cistern turn round its circle, when my uncle Toby, who had risen up an hour before his wonted time, entered the Lieutenant's room, and without preface or apology, sat himself down upon the chair by the bedside, and, independently of all modes and customs, opened the curtain in the manner an old friend and brother officer would have done it, and asked him how he did, how he had rested in the night, what was his complaint, where was his pain, and what he could do to help him; and, without giving him time to answer any one of these inquiries, went on, and told him of the little plan which he had been concerting with the Corporal the night before for him.

"You shall go home directly, Le Fevre," said my uncle Toby, "to my house, and we'll send for a doctor to see what's the matter; and we'll have an apothecary; and the Corporal shall be your nurse; and I'll be your servant, Le Fevre."

There was a frankness in my uncle Toby, not the *effect* of familiarity, but the *cause* of it, which let you at once into his soul, and showed you the goodness of his nature. To this there was something in his looks, and

voice, and manner superadded which eternally beckoned
to the unfortunate to come and take shelter under him;
so that, before my uncle Toby had half finished the kind
offers he was making to the father, had the son insensibly
pressed up close to his knees, and had taken hold of the
breast of his coat, and was pulling it towards him. The
blood and spirits of Le Fevre, which were waxing cold
and slow within him, and were retreating to their last
citadel, the heart, rallied back, the film forsook his
eyes for a moment; he looked up wistfully in my uncle
Toby's face, then cast a look upon his boy; and that
ligament, fine as it was, was never broken!

Nature instantly ebbed again;—the film returned to
its place;—the pulse fluttered;—stopped;—went on,—
throbbed,—stopped again,—moved, stopped. Shall I go
on? No!

I am so impatient to return to my own story, that
what remains of young Le Fevre's, that is, from this turn
of his fortune to the time my uncle Toby recommended
him for my preceptor, shall be told in a very few words
in another page. All that is necessary to be added to
this is as follows :—

That my uncle Toby, with young Le Fevre in his
hand, attended the poor Lieutenant, as chief mourners,
to his grave.

That the governor of Dendermond paid his obsequies
all military honours, and that Yorick, not to be behind-
hand, paid him all ecclesiastic, for he buried him in his
chancel. And it appears, likewise, he preached a funeral
sermon over him. I say it appears, for it was Yorick's
custom, which I suppose a general one with those of his
profession, on the first leaf of every sermon which he

composed, to chronicle down the time, the place, and the occasion of its being preached : to this he was ever wont to add some short comment or stricture upon the sermon itself,—seldom, indeed, much to its credit. For instance, "This sermon upon the Jewish dispensation—I don't like it at all; though I own there is a world of water-landish knowledge in it; but 'tis all tritical, and most tritically put together. This is but a flimsy kind of composition. What was in my head when I made it ?

"*N.B.* The excellency of this text is that it will suit any sermon; and of this sermon, that it will suit any text.

"For this sermon I shall be hanged, for I have stolen the greatest part of it. Doctor Paidagunes found me out. ☞ Set a thief to catch a thief."

On the back of half-a-dozen I find written, *So, so,* and no more; and upon a couple *moderato;* by which, as far as one may gather, from Altieri's Italian Dictionary, but mostly from the authority of a piece of green whipcord, which seemed to have been the unravelling of Yorick's whip-lash, with which he has left us the two sermons marked *moderato* and the half-dozen of *So, so,* tied fast together in one bundle by themselves, one may safely suppose he meant pretty nearly the same thing.

There is but one difficulty in the way of this conjecture, which is this, that the *moderatos* are five times better than the *so, so's;* show ten times more knowledge of the human heart; have seventy times more wit and spirit in them (and, to rise properly in my climax), discover a thousand times more genius; and, to crown all, are infinitely more entertaining than those tied up with them; for which reason, whenever Yorick's *dramatic*

sermons are offered to the world, though I shall admit
but one out of the whole number of the *so, so's*, I shall,
nevertheless, adventure to print the two *moderatos* without
any sort of scruple.

What Yorick could mean by the words *lentamente*,
tenutò, *grave*, and sometimes *adagio*, as applied to
theological compositions, and with which he has characterised some of these sermons, I dare not venture to guess.
I am more puzzled still upon finding *a l'octavo alta!*
upon one; *Con strepito* upon the back of another; *Sci-
cilliana* upon a third; *Alla capella* upon a fourth; *Con
l'arco* upon this; *Senza l'arco* upon that. All I know
is that they are musical terms, and have a meaning; and,
as he was a musical man, I will make no doubt but that,
by some quaint application of such metaphors to the
compositions in hand, they impressed very distinct ideas
of their several characters upon his fancy, whatever they
may do upon that of others.

Amongst these there is that particular sermon which
has unaccountably led me into this digression, the funeral
sermon upon poor Le Fevre, wrote out very fairly, as if
from a hasty copy. I take notice of it the more because
it seems to have been his favourite composition. It is
upon mortality, and is tied lengthways and crossways
with a yarn thrum, and then rolled up and twisted
round with a half-sheet of dirty blue paper, which seems
to have been once the cast cover of a general review,
which to this day smells horribly of horse-drugs. Whether
these marks of humiliation were designed, I something
doubt, because at the end of the sermon (and not at the
beginning of it), very different from his way of treating
the rest, he had wrote—*Bravo!*

Though not very offensively, for it was at two inches, at least, and a half's distance from and below the concluding line of the sermon, at the very extremity of the page, and in that right hand corner of it which, you know, is generally covered with your thumb; and, to do it justice, it is wrote besides with a crow's quill, so faintly, in a small Italian hand, as scarcely to solicit the eye towards the place, whether your thumb is there or not, so that, from the *manner of it*, it stands half excused, and being wrote moreover with very pale ink, diluted almost to nothing—'tis more like a *ritratto* of the shadow of Vanity than of Vanity herself—of the two; resembling rather a faint thought of transient applause, secretly stirring up in the heart of the composer, than a gross mark of it coarsely obtruded upon the world.

With all these extenuations, I am aware that, in publishing this, I do no service to Yorick's character as a modest man; but all men have their failings! and what lessens this still farther, and almost wipes it away, is this, that the word was struck through some time afterwards (as appears from a different tint of the ink) with a line quite across it, in this manner, ~~Bravo!~~ as if he had retracted, or was ashamed of the opinion he had once entertained of it.

These short characters of his sermons were always written, excepting in this one instance, upon the first leaf of his sermon, which served as a cover to it, and usually upon the inside of it, which was turned towards the text; but at the end of his discourse, where, perhaps, he had five or six pages, and sometimes, perhaps, a whole score to turn himself in, he took a larger circuit, and indeed a much more mettlesome one, as if he had snatched the

occasion of unlacing himself with a few more frolicksome
strokes at vice than the straitness of the pulpit allowed.
These, though, hussar-like, they skirmish lightly, and
out of all order, are still auxiliaries on the side of
Virtue. Tell me then, Mynheer Vander Blonederdon-
dergewdenstronke, why they should not be printed together?

When my uncle Toby had turned everything into
money, and settled all accounts betwixt the agent of the
regiment and Le Fevre, and betwixt Le Fevre and all
mankind, there remained nothing more in my uncle
Toby's hands than an old regimental coat and sword; so
that my uncle Toby found little or no opposition from
the world in taking administration. The coat, my uncle
Toby gave the Corporal. "Wear it, Trim," said my
uncle Toby, "as long as it will hold together, for the
sake of the poor Lieutenant. And this," said my
uncle Toby, taking up the sword in his hand, and drawing it out of the scabbard as he spoke, "and this, Le
Fevre, I'll save for thee; 'tis all the fortune," continued
my uncle Toby, hanging it up upon a crook, and pointing
to it, "'tis all the fortune, my dear Le Fevre, which God
has left thee; but if He has given thee a heart to fight
thy way with it in the world, and thou dost it like a man
of honour, 'tis enough for us."

As soon as my uncle Toby had laid a foundation,
and taught him to inscribe a regular polygon in a circle,
he sent him to a public school, where, excepting Whit-
suntide and Christmas, at which times the Corporal was
punctually despatched for him, he remained to the spring
of the year Seventeen; when the stories of the Emperor's
sending his army into Hungary against the Turks, kind-

ling a spark of fire in his bosom, he left his Greek and Latin, without leave, and, throwing himself upon his knees before my uncle Toby, begged his father's sword, and my uncle Toby's leave along with it, to go and try his fortune under Eugene. Twice did my uncle Toby forget his wound and cry out, " Le Fevre, I will go with thee, and thou shalt fight beside me!" and twice he laid his hand upon his groin, and hung down his head in sorrow and disconsolation.

My uncle Toby took down the sword from the crook, where it had hung untouched ever since the Lieutenant's death, and delivered it to the Corporal to brighten up; and, having detained Le Fevre a single fortnight to equip him, and contract for his passage to Leghorn, he put the sword into his hand. "If thou art brave, Le Fevre," said my uncle Toby, "this will not fail thee; but Fortune," said he, musing a little, "Fortune may; and if she does," added my uncle Toby, embracing him, "come back again to me, Le Fevre, and we will shape thee another course."

The greatest injury could not have oppressed the heart of Le Fevre more than my uncle Toby's paternal kindness; he parted from my uncle Toby as the best of sons from the best of fathers: both dropped tears; and, as my uncle Toby gave him his last kiss, he slipped sixty guineas, tied up in an old purse of his father's, in which was his mother's ring, into his hand, and bid God bless him.

VI

THE TAPESTRIED CHAMBER

By Sir Walter Scott [1]

ABOUT the end of the American war, when the officers
of Lord Cornwallis's army, which surrendered at York-
town, and others, who had been made prisoners during
the impolitic and ill-fated controversy, were returning to
their own country, to relate their adventures and repose
themselves after their fatigues, there was amongst them a
general officer, to whom Miss S. gave the name of Browne,
but merely, as I understood, to save the inconvenience of
introducing a nameless agent in the narrative. He was
an officer of merit, as well as a gentleman of high consideration for family and attainments.

Some business had carried General Browne upon a
tour through the western counties, when, in the conclusion

[1] The present writer heard the following events related, more than
twenty years since, by the celebrated Miss Seward of Litchfield, who to
her numerous accomplishments added, in a remarkable degree, the power
of narrative in private conversation. In its present form the tale must
necessarily lose all the interest which was attached to it by the flexible
voice and intelligent features of the gifted narrator. Yet still, read aloud
to an undoubting audience by the doubtful light of the closing evening, or
in silence by a decaying taper, and amidst the solitude of a half-lighted
apartment, it may redeem its character as a good ghost story.

of a morning stage, he found himself in the vicinity of a small country town, which presented a scene of uncommon beauty, and of a character peculiarly English.

The little town, with its stately old church, whose tower bore testimony to the devotion of ages long past, lay amidst pasture and corn-fields of small extent, but bounded and divided with hedgerow timber of great age and size. There were few marks of modern improvement. The environs of the place intimated neither the solitude of decay nor the bustle of novelty; the houses were old, but in good repair; and the beautiful little river murmured freely on its way to the left of the town, neither restrained by a dam nor bordered by a towing-path.

Upon a gentle eminence nearly a mile to the southward of the town were seen, amongst many venerable oaks and tangled thickets, the turrets of a castle as old as the wars of York and Lancaster, but which seemed to have received important alterations during the age of Elizabeth and her successors. It had not been a place of great size; but whatever accommodation it formerly afforded was, it must be supposed, still to be obtained within its walls; at least such was the inference which General Browne drew from observing the smoke arise merrily from several of the ancient wreathed and carved chimney-stalks. The wall of the park ran alongside of the highway for two or three hundred yards; and, through the different points by which the eye found glimpses into the woodland scenery, it seemed to be well stocked. Other points of view opened in succession, now a full one of the front of the old castle, and now a side glimpse at its particular towers; the former rich in

I

all the *bizarrerie* of the Elizabethan school, while the simple and solid strength of other parts of the building seemed to show that they had been raised more for defence than ostentation.

Delighted with the partial glimpses which he obtained of the castle through the woods and glades by which this ancient feudal fortress was surrounded, our military traveller was determined to inquire whether it might not deserve a nearer view, and whether it contained family pictures or other subjects of curiosity worthy of a stranger's visit; when, leaving the vicinity of the park, he rolled through a clean and well-paved street, and stopped at the door of a well-frequented inn.

Before ordering horses to proceed on his journey, General Browne made inquiries concerning the proprietor of the château which had so attracted his admiration, and was equally surprised and pleased at hearing in reply a nobleman named whom we shall call Lord Woodville. How fortunate! Much of Browne's early recollections, both at school and at college, had been connected with young Woodville, whom, by a few questions, he now ascertained to be the same with the owner of this fair domain. He had been raised to the peerage by the decease of his father a few months before, and, as the General learned from the landlord, the term of mourning being ended, was now taking possession of his paternal estate in the jovial season of merry autumn, accompanied by a select party of friends to enjoy the sports of a country famous for game.

This was delightful news to our traveller. Frank Woodville had been Richard Browne's fag at Eton, and his chosen intimate at Christ Church; their pleasures and their tasks had been the same; and the honest soldier's heart warmed to find his early friend in possession of so delightful a residence, and of an estate, as the landlord assured him with a nod and a wink, fully adequate to maintain and add to his dignity. Nothing was more natural than that the traveller should suspend a journey which there was nothing to render hurried, to pay a visit to an old friend under such agreeable circumstances.

The fresh horses, therefore, had only the brief task of conveying the General's travelling carriage to Woodville Castle. A porter admitted them at a modern Gothic lodge, built in that style to correspond with the castle itself, and at the same time rang a bell to give warning of the approach of visitors. Apparently the sound of the bell had suspended the separation of the company bent on the various amusements of the morning; for, on entering the court of the château, several young men were lounging about in their sporting dresses, looking at and criticising the dogs which the keepers held in readiness to attend their pastime. As General Browne alighted, the young lord came to the gate of the hall, and for an instant gazed, as at a stranger, upon the countenance of his friend, on which war, with its fatigues and its wounds, had made a great alteration. But the uncertainty lasted no longer than till the visitor had spoken, and the hearty greeting which followed was such as can only be exchanged betwixt those who have passed together the merry days of careless boyhood or early youth.

"If I could have formed a wish, my dear Browne," said Lord Woodville, "it would have been to have you here, of all men, upon this occasion, which my friends are good enough to hold as a sort of holiday. Do not think you have been unwatched during the years you have been absent from us. I have traced you through your dangers, your triumphs, your misfortunes, and was delighted to see that, whether in victory or defeat, the name of my old friend was always distinguished with applause."

The General made a suitable reply, and congratulated his friend on his new dignities, and the possession of a place and domain so beautiful.

"Nay, you have seen nothing of it as yet," said Lord Woodville, "and I trust you do not mean to leave us till you are better acquainted with it. It is true, I confess, that my present party is pretty large, and the old house, like other places of the kind, does not possess so much accommodation as the extent of the outward walls appears to promise. But we can give you a comfortable old-fashioned room; and I venture to suppose that your campaigns have taught you to be glad of worse quarters."

The General shrugged his shoulders and laughed. "I presume," he said, "the worst apartment in your château is considerably superior to the old tobacco-cask in which I was fain to take up my night's lodging when I was in the Bush, as the Virginians call it, with the light corps. There I lay, like Diogenes himself, so delighted with my covering from the elements that I made a vain attempt to have it rolled on to my next quarters; but my commander for the time would give way to no such luxurious provision, and I took farewell of my beloved cask with tears in my eyes."

"Well, then, since you do not fear your quarters," said Lord Woodville, "you will stay with me a week at least. Of guns, dogs, fishing-rods, flies, and means of sport by sea and land we have enough and to spare; you cannot pitch on an amusement but we will pitch on the means of pursuing it. But if you prefer the gun and pointers, I will go with you myself, and see whether you have mended your shooting since you have been amongst the Indians of the back settlements."

The General gladly accepted his friendly host's proposal in all its points. After a morning of manly exercise, the company met at dinner, where it was the delight of Lord Woodville to conduce to the display of the high properties of his recovered friend, so as to recommend him to his guests, most of whom were persons of distinction. He led General Browne to speak of the scenes he had witnessed; and as every word marked alike the brave officer and the sensible man, who retained possession of his cool judgment under the most imminent dangers, the company looked upon the soldier with general respect, as on one who had proved himself possessed of an uncommon portion of personal courage, that attribute, of all others, of which everybody desires to be thought possessed.

The day at Woodville Castle ended as usual in such mansions. The hospitality stopped within the limits of good order; music, in which the young lord was a proficient, succeeded to the circulation of the bottle; cards and billiards, for those who preferred such amusements, were in readiness; but the exercise of the morning required early hours, and not long after eleven o'clock the guests began to retire to their several apartments.

The young lord himself conducted his friend, General Browne, to the chamber destined for him, which answered the description he had given of it, being comfortable, but old-fashioned. The bed was of the massive form used in the end of the seventeenth century, and the curtains of faded silk, heavily trimmed with tarnished gold. But then the sheets, pillows, and blankets looked delightful to the campaigner, when he thought of his mansion, the cask. There was an air of gloom in the tapestry hangings, which, with their worn-out graces, curtained the walls of the little chamber, and gently undulated as the autumnal breeze found its way through the ancient lattice-window, which pattered and whistled as the air gained entrance. The toilet, too, with its mirror, turbaned after the manner of the beginning of the century with a coiffure of murrey-coloured silk, and its hundred strange-shaped boxes, providing for arrangements which had been obsolete for more than fifty years, had an antique, and in so far a melancholy, aspect. But nothing could blaze more brightly and cheerfully than the two large wax candles; or, if aught could rival them, it was the flaming bickering faggots in the chimney, that sent at once their gleam and their warmth through the snug apartment; which, notwithstanding the general antiquity of its appearance, was not wanting in the least convenience that modern habits rendered either necessary or desirable.

"This is an old-fashioned sleeping apartment, General," said the young lord; "but I hope you will find nothing that makes you envy your old tobacco-cask."

"I am not particular respecting my lodgings," replied the General; "yet, were I to make any choice, I would prefer this chamber by many degrees to the gayer and more modern rooms of your family mansion. Believe me, that when I unite its modern air of comfort with its venerable antiquity, and recollect that it is your lordship's property, I shall feel in better quarters here than if I were in the best hotel London could afford."

"I trust—I have no doubt—that you will find yourself as comfortable as I wish you, my dear General," said the young nobleman; and once more bidding his guest good-night, he shook him by the hand and withdrew.

The General again looked round him, and internally congratulating himself on his return to peaceful life, the comforts of which were endeared by the recollection of the hardships and dangers he had lately sustained, undressed himself, and prepared himself for a luxurious night's rest.

Here, contrary to the custom of this species of tale, we leave the General in possession of his apartment until the next morning.

The company assembled for breakfast at an early hour, but without the appearance of General Browne, who seemed the guest that Lord Woodville was desirous of honouring above all whom his hospitality had assembled around him. He more than once expressed surprise at the General's absence, and at length sent a servant to make inquiry after him. The man brought back information that General Browne had been walking abroad since an early hour of the morning, in defiance of the weather, which was misty and ungenial.

"The custom of a soldier," said the young nobleman to his friends; "many of them acquire habitual vigilance, and cannot sleep after the early hour at which their duty usually commands them to be alert."

Yet the explanation which Lord Woodville thus offered to the company seemed hardly satisfactory to his own mind, and it was in a fit of silence and abstraction that he awaited the return of the General. It took place near an hour after the breakfast-bell had rung. He looked fatigued and feverish. His hair, the powdering and arrangement of which was at this time one of the most important occupations of a man's whole day, and marked his fashion as much as in the present time the tying of a cravat or the want of one, was dishevelled, uncurled, void of powder, and dank with dew. His clothes were huddled on with a careless negligence, remarkable in a military man, whose real or supposed duties are usually held to include some attention to the toilet; and his looks were haggard and ghastly in a peculiar degree.

"So you have stolen a march upon us this morning, my dear General," said Lord Woodville; "or you have not found your bed so much to your mind as I had hoped and you seemed to expect. How did you rest last night?"

"Oh, excellently well! remarkably well! never better in my life," said General Browne rapidly, and yet with an air of embarrassment which was obvious to his friend. He then hastily swallowed a cup of tea, and, neglecting or refusing whatever else was offered, seemed to fall into a fit of abstraction.

"You will take the gun to-day, General?" said his friend and host, but had to repeat the question twice ere he received the abrupt answer, "No, my lord; I am sorry I cannot have the honour of spending another day with your lordship; my post-horses are ordered, and will be here directly."

All who were present showed surprise, and Lord Woodville immediately replied, "Post-horses, my good friend! what can you possibly want with them, when you promised to stay with me quietly for at least a week?"

"I believe," said the General, obviously much embarrassed, "that I might, in the pleasure of my first meeting with your lordship, have said something about stopping here a few days; but I have since found it altogether impossible."

"That is very extraordinary," answered the young nobleman. "You seemed quite disengaged yesterday, and you cannot have had a summons to-day; for our post has not come up from the town, and therefore you cannot have received any letters."

General Browne, without giving any further explanation, muttered something of indispensable business, and insisted on the absolute necessity of his departure in a manner which silenced all opposition on the part of his host, who saw that his resolution was taken, and forbore further importunity.

"At least, however," he said, "permit me, my dear Browne, since go you will or must, to show you the view from the terrace, which the mist, that is now rising, will soon display."

He threw open a sash window, and stepped down upon the terrace as he spoke. The General followed him mechanically, but seemed little to attend to what his host was saying, as, looking across an extended and rich prospect, he pointed out the different objects worthy of observation. Thus they moved on till Lord Woodville had attained his purpose of drawing his guest entirely apart from the rest of the company, when, turning round upon him with an air of great solemnity, he addressed him thus: "Richard Browne, my old and very dear friend, we are now alone. Let me conjure you to answer me upon the word of a friend and the honour of a soldier. How did you in reality rest during last night?"

"Most wretchedly indeed, my lord," answered the General in the same tone of solemnity; "so miserably, that I would not run the risk of such a second night, not only for all the lands belonging to this castle, but for all the country which I see from this elevated point of view."

"This is most extraordinary," said the young lord, as if speaking to himself; "then there must be something in the reports concerning that apartment." Again turning to the General, he said, "For God's sake, my dear friend, be candid with me, and let me know the disagreeable particulars which have befallen you under a roof where, with consent of the owner, you should have met nothing save comfort."

The General seemed distressed by this appeal, and paused a moment before he replied. "My dear lord," he at length said, "what happened to me last night is of a nature so peculiar and so unpleasant that I could hardly bring myself to detail it even to your lordship, were it not that, independent of my wish to gratify any request of yours, I think that sincerity on my part may lead to some explanation about a circumstance equally painful and mysterious. To others the communication I am about to make might place me in the light of a weak-minded, superstitious fool, who suffered his own imagination to delude and bewilder him ; but you have known me in childhood. and youth, and will not suspect me of having adopted in manhood the feelings and frailties from which my early years were free." Here he paused, and his friend replied, " Do not doubt my perfect confidence in the truth of your communication, however strange it may be," replied Lord Woodville ; " I know your firmness of disposition too well to suspect you could be made the object of imposition, and am aware that your honour and your friendship will equally deter you from exaggerating whatever you may have witnessed."

" Well, then," said the General, " I will proceed with my story as well as I can, relying upon your candour, and yet distinctly feeling that I would rather face a battery than recall to my mind the odious recollections of last night."

He paused a second time, and then, perceiving that Lord Woodville remained silent and in an attitude of attention, he commenced, though not without obvious reluctance, the history of his night's adventures in the Tapestried Chamber.

" I undressed and went to bed so soon as your lordship left me yesterday evening; but the wood in the chimney, which nearly fronted my bed, blazed brightly and cheerfully, and, aided by a hundred exciting recollections of my childhood and youth, which had been recalled by the unexpected pleasure of meeting your lordship, prevented me from falling immediately asleep. I ought, however, to say that these reflections were all of a pleasant and agreeable kind, grounded on a sense of having for a time exchanged the labour, fatigues, and dangers of my profession for the enjoyments of a peaceful life, and

the reunion of those friendly and affectionate ties which I
had torn asunder at the rude summons of war.

"While such pleasing reflections were stealing over
my mind, and gradually lulling me to slumber, I was
suddenly aroused by a sound like that of the rustling of
a silken gown and the tapping of a pair of high-heeled
shoes, as if a woman were walking in the apartment. Ere
I could draw the curtain to see what the matter was, the
figure of a little woman passed between the bed and the
fire. The back of this form was turned to me, and I
could observe from the shoulders and neck it was that of
an old woman, whose dress was an old-fashioned gown
which, I think, ladies call a sacque; that is, a sort
of robe completely loose in the body, but gathered
into broad plaits upon the neck and shoulders, which
fall down to the ground and terminate in a species of
train.

"I thought the intrusion singular enough, but never
harboured for a moment the idea that what I saw was
anything more than the mortal form of some old woman
about the establishment, who had a fancy to dress like
her grandmother, and who, having perhaps (as your lordship mentioned that you were rather straitened for room)
been dislodged from her chamber for my accommodation,
had forgotten the circumstance, and returned by twelve
to her old haunt. Under this persuasion I moved myself
in bed and coughed a little, to make the intruder sensible
of my being in possession of the premises. She turned
slowly round, but, gracious Heaven! my lord, what a
countenance did she display to me! There was no longer
any question what she was, or any thought of her
being a living being. Upon a face which wore the fixed

features of a corpse were imprinted the traces of the vilest and most hideous passions which had animated her while she lived. The body of some atrocious criminal seemed to have been given up from the grave and the soul restored from the penal fire, in order to form for a space a union with the ancient accomplice of its guilt. I started up in bed, and sat upright, supporting myself on my palms, as I gazed on this horrible spectre. The hag made, as it seemed, a single and swift stride to the bed where I lay, and squatted herself down upon it, in precisely the same attitude which I had assumed in the extremity of horror, advancing her diabolical countenance within half a yard of mine, with a grin which seemed to intimate the malice and the derision of an incarnate fiend."

Here General Browne stopped, and wiped from his brow the cold perspiration with which the recollection of his horrible vision had covered it.

"My lord," he said, "I am no coward. I have been in all the mortal dangers incidental to my profession, and I may truly boast that no man ever knew Richard Browne dishonour the sword he wears; but in these horrible circumstances, under the eyes and, as it seemed, almost in the grasp of an incarnation of an evil spirit, all firmness forsook me, all manhood melted from me like wax in the furnace, and I felt my hair individually bristle. The current of my life-blood ceased to flow, and I sank back in a swoon, as very a victim to panic terror as ever was a village girl or a child of ten years old. How long I lay in this condition I cannot pretend to guess.

"But I was roused by the castle clock striking one, so loud that it seemed as if it were in the very room.

It was some time before I dared open my eyes, lest they should again encounter the horrible spectacle. When, however, I summoned courage to look up, she was no longer visible. My first idea was to pull my bell, wake the servants, and remove to a garret or a hay-loft, to be insured against a second visitation. Nay, I will confess the truth, that my resolution was altered, not by the shame of exposing myself, but by the fear that, as the bell-cord hung by the chimney, I might, in making my way to it, be again crossed by the fiendish hag, who, I figured to myself, might be still lurking about some corner of the apartment.

"I will not pretend to describe what hot and cold fever-fits tormented me for the rest of the night, through broken sleep, weary vigils, and that dubious state which forms the neutral ground between them. A hundred terrible objects appeared to haunt me; but there was the great difference betwixt the vision which I have described and those which followed, that I knew the last to be deceptions of my own fancy and over-excited nerves.

" Day at last appeared, and I rose from my bed ill in health and humiliated in mind. I was ashamed of myself as a man and a soldier, and still more so at feeling my own extreme desire to escape from the haunted apartment, which, however, conquered all other considerations; so that, huddling on my clothes with the most careless haste, I made my escape from your lordship's mansion, to seek in the open air some relief to my nervous system, shaken as it was by this horrible rencontre with a visitant —for such I must believe her—from the other world. Your lordship has now heard the cause of my discomposure, and of my sudden desire to leave your hospitable castle. In other places I trust we may often meet; but God protect me from ever spending a second night under that roof!"

Strange as the General's tale was, he spoke with such a deep air of conviction that it cut short all the usual commentaries which are made on such stories. Lord Woodville never once asked him if he was sure he did not dream of the apparition, or suggested any of the possibilities by which it is fashionable to explain supernatural appearances, as wild vagaries of the fancy or deceptions of the optic nerves. On the contrary, he seemed deeply impressed with the truth and reality of what he had heard, and after a considerable pause regretted, with much appearance of sincerity, that his early friend should in his house have suffered so severely.

"I am the more sorry for your pain, my dear Browne," he continued, "that it is the unhappy, though most unexpected, result of an experiment of my own! You must know that, for my father and grandfather's time at least, the apartment which was assigned to you last night had been shut on account of reports that it was disturbed by supernatural sights and noises. When I came, a few weeks since, into possession of the estate, I thought the accommodation which the castle afforded for my friends was not extensive enough to permit the inhabitants of the invisible world to retain possession of a comfortable sleeping apartment. I therefore caused the Tapestried Chamber, as we call it, to be opened; and, without destroying its air of antiquity, I had such new articles of furniture placed in it as became the modern times. Yet, as the opinion that the room was haunted very strongly prevailed among the domestics, and was also known in the neighbourhood and to many of my friends, I feared some prejudice might be entertained by the first occupant of the Tapestried Chamber, which might tend to revive the evil report which it had laboured under, and so disappoint my purpose of rendering it a useful part of the house. I must confess, my dear Browne, that your arrival yesterday, agreeable to me for a thousand reasons besides, seemed the most favourable opportunity of removing the unpleasant rumours which attached to the room, since your courage was indubitable, and your mind free of any preoccupation on the subject. I could not, therefore, have chosen a more fitting subject for my experiment."

"Upon my life," said General Browne somewhat hastily, "I am infinitely obliged to your lordship—very particularly indebted indeed. I am likely to remember for some time the consequences of the experiment, as your lordship is pleased to call it."

"Nay, now you are unjust, my dear friend," said Lord Woodville. "You have only to reflect for a single moment, in order to be convinced that I could not augur the possibility of the pain to which you have been so unhappily exposed. I was yesterday morning a complete sceptic on the subject of supernatural appearances. Nay, I am sure that, had I told you what was said about that room, those very reports would have induced you, by your own choice, to select it for your accommodation. It was my misfortune, perhaps my error, but really cannot be termed my fault, that you have been afflicted so strangely."

"Strangely indeed!" said the General, resuming his

good temper; "and I acknowledge that I have no right
to be offended with your lordship for treating me like
what I used to think myself—a man of some firmness
and courage. But I see my post-horses are arrived,
and I must not detain your lordship from your amusement."

"Nay, my old friend," said Lord Woodville, "since
you cannot stay with us another day, which, indeed, I
can no longer urge, give me at least half-an-hour more.
You used to love pictures, and I have a gallery of portraits, some of them by Vandyke, representing ancestry
to whom this property and castle formerly belonged. I
think that several of them will strike you as possessing
merit."

General Browne accepted the invitation, though somewhat unwillingly. It was evident he was not to breathe
freely or at ease till he left Woodville Castle far behind
him. He could not refuse his friend's invitation, however; and the less so that he was a little ashamed of the
peevishness which he had displayed towards his well-
meaning entertainer.

The General, therefore, followed Lord Woodville
through several rooms into a long gallery hung with
pictures, which the latter pointed out to his guest, telling
the names and giving some account of the personages
whose portraits presented themselves in progression.
General Browne was but little interested in the details
which these accounts conveyed to him. They were,
indeed, of the kind which are usually found in an old
family gallery. Here was a Cavalier who had ruined
the estate in the royal cause; there a fine lady who had
reinstated it by contracting a match with a wealthy

K

Roundhead. There hung a gallant who had been in danger for corresponding with the exiled court at Saint Germains; here one who had taken arms for William at the Revolution; and there a third that had thrown his weight alternately into the scale of Whig and Tory.

While Lord Woodville was cramming these words into his guest's ear "against the stomach of his sense," they gained the middle of the gallery, when he beheld General Browne suddenly start, and assume an attitude of the utmost surprise, not unmixed with fear, as his eyes were caught and suddenly riveted by a portrait of an old lady in a sacque, the fashionable dress of the end of the seventeenth century.

"There she is!" he exclaimed; "there she is, in form and features, though inferior in demoniac expression to the accursed hag who visited me last night!"

"If that be the case," said the young nobleman, "there can remain no longer any doubt of the horrible reality of your apparition. That is the picture of a wretched ancestress of mine, of whose crimes a black and fearful catalogue is recorded in a family history in my charter-chest. The recital of them would be too horrible; it is enough to say that in yon fatal apartment incest and unnatural murder were committed. I will restore it to the solitude to which the better judgment of those who preceded me had consigned it; and never shall any one, so long as I can prevent it, be exposed to a repetition of the supernatural horrors which could shake such courage as yours."

Thus the friends, who had met with such glee, parted in a very different mood, Lord Woodville to command the Tapestried Chamber to be unmantled and the door built up, and General Browne to seek in some less beautiful country, and with some less dignified friend, forgetfulness of the painful night which he had passed in Woodville Castle.

VII

RIP VAN WINKLE

[A POSTHUMOUS WRITING OF DIEDRICH
KNICKERBOCKER]

By Washington Irving

" By Woden, God of Saxons,
From whence comes Wensday, that is Wodensday,
Truth is a thing that ever I will keep
Unto thylke day in which I can creep into
My sepulchre——"   —Cartwright.

WHOEVER has made a voyage up the Hudson must
remember the Kaatskill Mountains.   They are a dis-
membered branch of the great Appalachian family, and
are seen away to the west of the river, swelling up to a
noble height, and lording it over the surrounding country.
Every change of season, every change of weather, indeed,
every hour of the day, produces some change in the
magical hues and shapes of these mountains, and they
are regarded by all the good wives, far and near, as perfect barometers.   When the weather is fair and settled,
they are clothed in blue and purple, and print their bold
outlines on the clear evening sky ; but sometimes, when
the rest of the landscape is cloudless, they will gather a

hood of grey vapours about their summits, which, in the last rays of the setting sun, will glow and light up like a crown of glory.

At the foot of these fairy mountains, the voyager may have descried the light smoke curling up from a village, whose shingle-roofs gleam among the trees, just where the blue tints of the upland melt away into the fresh green of the nearer landscape. It is a little village, of great antiquity, having been founded by some of the Dutch colonists, in the early times of the province, just about the beginning of the government of the good Peter Stuyvesant (may he rest in peace !), and there were some of the houses of the original settlers standing within a few years, built of small yellow bricks brought from Holland, having latticed windows and gable fronts, sur-mounted with weathercocks.

In that same village, and in one of these very houses (which, to tell the precise truth, was sadly time-worn and weather-beaten), there lived many years since, while the country was yet a province of Great Britain, a simple, good-natured fellow, of the name of Rip Van Winkle. He was a descendant of the Van Winkles who figured so gallantly in the chivalrous days of Peter Stuyvesant, and accompanied him to the siege of Fort Christina. He inherited, however, but little of the martial character of his ancestors. I have observed that he was a simple, good-natured man ; he was, moreover, a kind neighbour, and an obedient, henpecked husband. Indeed, to the latter circumstance might be owing that meekness of spirit which gained him such universal popularity; for those men are most apt to be obsequious and conciliating abroad, who are under the discipline of shrews at home.

Their tempers, doubtless, are rendered pliant and malleable in the fiery furnace of domestic tribulation, and a curtain lecture is worth all the sermons in the world for teaching the virtues of patience and long-suffering. A termagant wife may, therefore, in some respects, be considered a tolerable blessing ; and if so, Rip Van Winkle was thrice blessed.

Certain it is that he was a great favourite among all the good wives of the village, who, as usual with the amiable sex, took his part in all family squabbles, and never failed, whenever they talked those matters over in their evening gossipings, to lay all the blame on Dame Van Winkle. The children of the village, too, would shout with joy whenever he approached. He assisted at their sports, made their playthings, taught them to fly kites and shoot marbles, and told them long stories of ghosts, witches, and Indians. Whenever he went dodging about the village, he was surrounded by a troop of them, hanging on his skirts, clambering on his back, and playing a thousand tricks on him with impunity ; and not a dog would bark at him throughout the neighbourhood.

The great error in Rip's composition was an insuperable aversion to all kinds of profitable labour. It could not be from the want of assiduity or perseverance, for he would sit on a wet rock, with a rod as long and heavy as a Tartar's lance, and fish all day without a murmur, even though he should not be encouraged by a single nibble. He would carry a fowling-piece on his shoulder for hours together, trudging through woods and swamps, and up hill and down dale, to shoot a few squirrels or wild pigeons. He would never refuse to assist a neighbour even in the roughest toil, and was a foremost man at all

country frolics, for husking Indian corn, or building stone
fences ; the women of the village, too, used to employ
him to run their errands, and to do such little odd jobs
as their less obliging husbands would not do for them.
In a word, Rip was ready to attend to anybody's business
but his own ; but as to doing family duty, and keeping
his farm in order, he found it impossible.

In fact, he declared it was of no use to work on his
farm ; it was the most pestilent little piece of ground in
the whole country ; everything about it went wrong, and
would go wrong, in spite of him.   His fences were continually falling to pieces ; his cow would either go astray,
or get among the cabbages ; weeds were sure to grow
quicker in his fields than anywhere else ; the rain always
made a point of setting in just as he had some outdoor
work to do ; so that, though his patrimonial estate had
dwindled away under his management, acre by acre, until
there was little more left than a mere patch of Indian corn
and potatoes, yet it was the worst-conditioned farm in the
neighbourhood.

His children, too, were as ragged and wild as if they
belonged to nobody.   His son Rip, an urchin begotten
in his own likeness, promised to inherit the habits, with
the old clothes of his father.   He was generally seen
trooping like a colt at his mother's heels, equipped in
a pair of his father's cast-off galligaskins, which he had
much ado to hold up with one hand, as a fine lady does
her train in bad weather.

Rip Van Winkle, however, was one of those happy
mortals, of foolish, well-oiled dispositions, who take the
world easy, eat white bread or brown, whichever can be
got with least thought or trouble, and would rather

starve on a penny than work for a pound. If left to himself, he would have whistled life away in perfect contentment; but his wife kept continually dinning in his ears about his idleness, his carelessness, and the ruin he was bringing on his family. Morning, noon, and night, her tongue was incessantly going, and everything he said or did was sure to produce a torrent of household eloquence. Rip had but one way of replying to all lectures of the kind, and that, by frequent use, had grown into a habit. He shrugged his shoulders, shook his head, cast up his eyes, but said nothing. This, however, always provoked a fresh volley from his wife; so that he was fain to draw off his forces, and take to the outside of the house—the only side which, in truth, belongs to a henpecked husband.

Rip's sole domestic adherent was his dog Wolf, who was as much henpecked as his master; for Dame Van Winkle regarded them as companions in idleness, and even looked upon Wolf with an evil eye, as the cause of his master's going so often astray. True it is, in all points of spirit befitting an honourable dog he was as courageous an animal as ever scoured the woods—but what courage can withstand the ever-during and all-besetting terrors of a woman's tongue? The moment Wolf entered the house his crest fell, his tail drooped to the ground, or curled between his legs; he sneaked about with a gallows air, casting many a sidelong glance at Dame Van Winkle, and at the least flourish of a broomstick or ladle, he would fly to the door with yelping precipitation.

Times grew worse and worse with Rip Van Winkle as years of matrimony rolled on; a tart temper never

mellows with age, and a sharp tongue is the only edged
tool that grows keener with constant use. For a long
while he used to console himself, when driven from home,
by frequenting a kind of perpetual club of the sages,
philosophers, and other idle personages of the village,
which held its sessions on a bench before a small inn,
designated by a rubicund portrait of his Majesty George
the Third. Here they used to sit in the shade through
a long lazy summer's day, talking listlessly over village
gossip, or telling endless sleepy stories about nothing.
But it would have been worth any statesman's money to
have heard the profound discussions that sometimes took
place, when by chance an old newspaper fell into their
hands from some passing traveller. How solemnly they
would listen to the contents, as drawled out by Derrick
Van Bummel, the schoolmaster, a dapper learned little
man, who was not to be daunted by the most gigantic
word in the dictionary; and how sagely they would deli-
berate upon public events some months after they had
taken place.

The opinions of this junto were completely controlled
by Nicholas Vedder, a patriarch of the village, and landlord of the inn, at the door of which he took his seat
from morning till night, just moving sufficiently to avoid
the sun and keep in the shade of a large tree, so that
the neighbours could tell the hour by his movements as
accurately as by a sundial. It is true he was rarely heard
to speak, but smoked his pipe incessantly. His adherents,
however (for every great man has his adherents), perfectly
understood him, and knew how to gather his opinions.
When anything that was read or related displeased him,
he was observed to smoke his pipe vehemently, and to

send forth short, frequent, and angry puffs, but when pleased he would inhale the smoke slowly and tranquilly, and emit it in light and placid clouds; and sometimes, taking the pipe from his mouth, and letting the fragrant vapour curl about his nose, would gravely nod his head in token of perfect approbation.

From even this stronghold the unlucky Rip was at length routed by his termagant wife, who would suddenly break in upon the tranquillity of the assemblage and call the members all to naught; nor was that august personage, Nicholas Vedder himself, sacred from the daring tongue of this terrible virago, who charged him outright with encouraging her husband in habits of idleness.

Poor Rip was at last reduced almost to despair, and his only alternative, to escape from the labour of the farm and clamour of his wife, was to take gun in hand and stroll away into the woods. Here he would sometimes seat himself at the foot of a tree, and share the contents of his wallet with Wolf, with whom he sympathised as a fellow-sufferer in persecution. "Poor Wolf," he would say, "thy mistress leads thee a dog's life of it; but never mind, my lad, whilst I live thou shalt never want a friend to stand by thee!" Wolf would wag his tail, look wistfully in his master's face, and if dogs can feel pity, I verily believe he reciprocated the sentiment with all his heart.

In a long ramble of the kind on a fine autumnal day, Rip had unconsciously scrambled to one of the highest parts of the Kaatskill Mountains. He was after his favourite sport of squirrel-shooting, and the still solitudes had echoed and re-echoed with the reports of his gun. Panting and fatigued, he threw himself, late in the afternoon, on a green knoll, covered with mountain herbage, that crowned the brow of a precipice. From an opening between the trees he could overlook all the lower country for many a mile of rich woodland. He saw at a distance the lordly Hudson, far, far below him, moving on its silent but majestic course, with the reflection of a purple cloud, or the sail of a lagging bark, here and there sleeping on its glassy bosom, and at last losing itself in the blue highlands.

On the other side he looked down into a deep mountain glen, wild, lonely, and shagged, the bottom filled with fragments from the impending cliffs, and scarcely lighted by the reflected rays of the setting sun. For some time Rip lay musing on this scene; evening was gradually advancing; the mountains began to throw their long blue shadows over the valleys; he saw that it would be dark long before he could reach the village, and he heaved a heavy sigh when he thought of encountering the terrors of Dame Van Winkle.

As he was about to descend, he heard a voice from a distance, hallooing, " Rip Van Winkle! Rip Van Winkle!" He looked round, but could see nothing but a crow winging its solitary flight across the mountain. He thought his fancy must have deceived him, and turned again to descend, when he heard the same cry ring through the still evening air, " Rip Van Winkle! Rip Van Winkle!"—at the same time Wolf bristled up his back, and, giving a loud growl, skulked to his master's side, looking fearfully down into the glen. Rip now felt a vague apprehension stealing over him; he looked anxiously in the same direction, and perceived a strange figure slowly toiling up the rocks, and bending under the weight of something he carried on his back. He was surprised to see any human being in this lonely and unfrequented place; but supposing it to be some one of the neighbourhood in need of his assistance, he hastened down to yield it.

On nearer approach he was still more surprised at the singularity of the stranger's appearance. He was a short, square-built old fellow, with thick bushy hair and a grizzled beard. His dress was of the antique Dutch fashion —a cloth jerkin, strapped round the waist, several pairs of breeches, the outer one of ample volume, decorated with rows of buttons down the sides, and bunches at the knees. He bore on his shoulder a stout keg, that seemed full of liquor, and made signs for Rip to approach and assist him with the load. Though rather shy and distrustful of this new acquaintance, Rip complied with his usual alacrity; and, mutually relieving each other, they clambered up a narrow gully, apparently the dry bed of a mountain torrent. As they ascended, Rip every now and then heard long rolling peals, like distant thunder, that seemed to issue out of a deep ravine, or rather cleft, between lofty rocks, toward which their rugged path conducted. He paused for an instant, but supposing it to be the muttering of one of those transient thunder-showers which often take place in mountain heights, he proceeded. Passing through the ravine they came to a hollow, like a small amphitheatre, surrounded by perpendicular precipices, over the brinks of which impending trees shot their branches, so that you only caught glimpses of the azure sky and the bright evening cloud. During the whole time Rip and his companion had laboured on in silence, for though the former marvelled greatly what could be the object of carrying a keg of liquor up this wild mountain, yet there was something strange and incomprehensible about the unknown that inspired awe and checked familiarity.

On entering the amphitheatre, new objects of wonder presented themselves. On a level spot in the centre was a company of odd-looking personages playing at ninepins. They were dressed in a quaint outlandish fashion; some wore short doublets, others jerkins, with long knives in their belts, and most of them had enormous breeches, of similar style with that of the guide's. Their visages, too, were peculiar : one had a large head, broad face, and small piggish eyes ; the face of another seemed to consist entirely of nose, and was surmounted by a white sugar-loaf hat, set off with a little red cock's tail. They all had beards, of various shapes and colours. There was one who seemed to be the commander. He was a stout old gentleman, with a weather-beaten countenance ; he wore a laced doublet, broad belt and hanger, high-crowned hat and feather, red stockings, and high-heeled shoes, with roses in them. The whole group reminded Rip of the figures in an old Flemish painting, in the parlour of Dominie Van Shaick, the village parson, and which had been brought over from Holland at the time of the settlement.

What seemed particularly odd to Rip was that, though these folks were evidently amusing themselves, yet they maintained the gravest faces, the most mysterious silence, and were, withal, the most melancholy party of pleasure he had ever witnessed. Nothing interrupted the stillness of the scene but the noise of the balls, which, whenever they were rolled, echoed along the mountains like rumbling peals of thunder.

As Rip and his companion approached them, they suddenly desisted from their play, and stared at him with such fixed, statue-like gaze, and such strange, uncouth, lustre-like countenances, that his heart turned within him, and his knees smote together. His companion now emptied the contents of the keg into large flagons, and made signs to him to wait upon the company. He obeyed with fear and trembling; they quaffed the liquor in profound silence, and then returned to their game.

By degrees Rip's awe and apprehension subsided. He even ventured, when no eye was fixed upon him, to taste the beverage, which, he found, had much of the flavour of excellent Hollands. He was naturally a thirsty soul, and was soon tempted to repeat the draught. One taste provoked another; and he reiterated his visits to the flagon so often, that at length his senses were overpowered, his eyes swam in his head, his head gradually declined, and he fell into a deep sleep.

On waking, he found himself on the green knoll whence he had first seen the old man of the glen. He rubbed his eyes—it was a bright sunny morning. The birds were hopping and twittering among the bushes, and the eagle was wheeling aloft and breasting the pure mountain breeze. "Surely," thought Rip, "I have not slept here all night." He recalled the occurrences before he fell asleep. The strange man with the keg of liquor —the mountain ravine—the wild retreat among the rocks —the woe-begone party at ninepins—the flagon—"oh! that flagon! that wicked flagon!" thought Rip; "what excuse shall I make to Dame Van Winkle?"

He looked round for his gun, but in place of the clean, well-oiled fowling-piece, he found an old firelock lying by him, the barrel incrusted with rust, the lock falling off, and the stock worm-eaten. He now suspected that the grave roysterers of the mountain had put a trick upon him, and, having dosed him with liquor, had robbed him of his gun. Wolf, too, had disappeared, but he might have strayed away after a squirrel or partridge. He whistled after him, and shouted his name, but all in vain; the echoes repeated his whistle and shout, but no dog was to be seen.

He determined to revisit the scene of the last evening's gambol, and, if he met with any of the party, to demand his dog and gun. As he rose to walk, he found himself stiff in the joints, and wanting in his usual activity. "These mountain beds do not agree with me," thought Rip; "and if this frolic should lay me up with a fit of rheumatism, I shall have a blessed time with Dame Van Winkle." With some difficulty he got down into the glen; he found the gully up which he and his companion had ascended the preceding evening; but, to his astonishment, a mountain stream was now foaming down it—leaping from rock to rock, and filling the glen with babbling murmurs. He, however, made shift to scramble up its sides, working his toilsome way through thickets of birch, sassafras, and wild-hazel, and sometimes tripped up or entangled by the wild grape-vines that twisted their coils or tendrils from tree to tree, and spread a kind of network in his path.

At length he reached where the ravine had opened through the cliffs to the amphitheatre, but no traces of such opening remained. The rocks presented a high impenetrable wall, over which the torrent came tumbling in a sheet of feathery foam, and fell into a broad deep basin, black from the shadows of the surrounding forest. Here, then, poor Rip was brought to a stand. He again called and whistled after his dog; he was only answered by the cawing of a flock of idle crows, sporting high in air about a dry tree that overhung a sunny precipice; and who, secure in their elevation, seemed to look down and scoff at the poor man's perplexities. What was to be done?—the morning was passing away, and Rip felt famished for want of his breakfast. He grieved to give up his dog and his gun; he dreaded to meet his wife; but it would not do to starve among the mountains. He shook his head, shouldered the rusty firelock, and, with a heart full of trouble and anxiety, turned his steps homeward.

As he approached the village he met a number of people, but none whom he knew, which somewhat surprised him, for he had thought himself acquainted with every one in the country round. Their dress, too, was of a different fashion from that to which he was accustomed. They all stared at him with equal marks of surprise, and, whenever they cast their eyes upon him, invariably stroked their chins. The constant recurrence of this gesture induced Rip, involuntarily, to do the same —when, to his astonishment, he found his beard had grown a foot long!

He had now entered the skirts of the village. A troop of strange children ran at his heels, hooting after him, and pointing at his grey beard. The dogs, too, not one of whom he recognised for an old acquaintance, barked at him as he passed; the very village was altered —it was larger and more populous. There were rows of houses which he had never seen before, and those which had been his familiar haunts had disappeared. Strange names were over the doors—strange faces at the windows—everything was strange. His mind now misgave him; he began to doubt whether both he and the world around him were not bewitched. Surely this was his native village, which he had left but the day before. There stood the Kaatskill Mountains—there ran the silver Hudson at a distance—there was every hill and dale precisely as it had always been. Rip was sorely perplexed. "That flagon last night," thought he, "has addled my poor head sadly!"

It was with some difficulty that he found his way to his own house, which he approached with silent awe, expecting every moment to hear the shrill voice of Dame Van Winkle. He found the house gone to decay—the roof fallen in, the windows shattered, and the doors off the hinges. A half-starved dog that looked like Wolf was skulking about it. Rip called him by his name, but the cur snarled, showed his teeth, and passed on. This was an unkind cut indeed. "My very dog," sighed poor Rip, "has forgotten me!"

He entered the house, which, to tell the truth, Dame Winkle had always kept in neat order. It was empty, forlorn, and apparently abandoned. The desolateness overcame all his connubial fears; he called loudly for his wife and children; the lonely chambers rang for a moment with his voice, and then all again was silence.

He now hurried forth, and hastened to his old resort, the village inn—but it too was gone. A large rickety wooden building stood in its place, with great gaping windows, some of them broken and mended with old hats and petticoats, and over the door was painted, "The

L

Union Hotel, by Jonathan Doolittle." Instead of the great tree that used to shelter the quiet little Dutch inn of yore, there was now reared a tall naked pole, with something on the top that looked like a red nightcap, and from it was fluttering a flag, on which was a singular assemblage of stars and stripes—all this was strange and incomprehensible. He recognised on the sign, however, the ruby face of King George, under which he had smoked so many a peaceful pipe; but even this was singularly metamorphosed. The red coat was changed for one of blue and buff, a sword was held in the hand instead of a sceptre, the head was decorated with a cocked hat, and underneath was painted, in large characters, GENERAL WASHINGTON.

There was, as usual, a crowd of folks about the door, but none that Rip recollected. The very character of the people seemed changed. There was a busy, bustling, disputatious tone about it, instead of the accustomed phlegm and drowsy tranquillity. He looked in vain for the sage Nicholas Vedder, with his broad face, double chin, and fair long pipe, uttering clouds of tobacco smoke instead of idle speeches; or Van Bummel, the school-master, doling forth the contents of an ancient news-paper. In place of these, a lean, bilious-looking fellow, with his pockets full of handbills, was haranguing vehemently about rights of citizens—elections—members of Congress—liberty—Bunker's Hill—heroes of seventy-six—and other words, which were a perfect Babylonish jargon to the bewildered Van Winkle.

The appearance of Rip, with his long grizzled beard, his rusty fowling-piece, his uncouth dress, and an army of women and children at his heels, soon attracted the

attention of the tavern politicians. They crowded round
him, eyeing him from head to foot with great curiosity.
The orator bustled up to him, and, drawing him partly
aside, inquired " On which side he voted ? " Rip stared
in vacant stupidity. Another short but busy little fellow
pulled him by the arm, and, rising on tiptoe, inquired in
his ear, " Whether he was a Federal or a Democrat ? "
Rip was equally at a loss to comprehend the question;
when a knowing, self-important old gentleman, in a sharp
cocked hat, made his way through the crowd, putting
them to the right and left with his elbows as he passed,
and planting himself before Van Winkle, with one arm
akimbo, the other resting on his cane, his keen eyes and
sharp hat penetrating, as it were, into his very soul,
demanded in an austere tone, " What brought him to
the election with a gun on his shoulder and a mob at
his heels; and whether he meant to breed a riot in the
village ? "—" Alas! gentlemen," cried Rip, somewhat
dismayed, " I am a poor quiet man, a native of the
place, and a loyal subject of the king, God bless
him ! "

Here a general shout burst from the bystanders—
" A Tory! a Tory! a spy! a refugee! hustle him!
away with him ! " It was with great difficulty that the
self-important man in the cocked hat restored order;
and, having assumed a tenfold austerity of brow, demanded again of the unknown culprit what he came
there for, and whom he was seeking ? The poor man
humbly assured him that he meant no harm, but merely
came there in search of some of his neighbours, who used
to keep about the tavern.

" Well, who are they ? Name them."

Rip bethought himself a moment and inquired, "Where's Nicholas Vedder?"

There was a silence for a little while, when an old man replied in a thin piping voice, "Nicholas Vedder! why, he is dead and gone these eighteen years! There was a wooden tombstone in the churchyard that used to tell all about him, but that's rotten and gone too."

"Where's Brom Dutcher?"

"Oh, he went off to the army in the beginning of the war; some say he was killed at the storming of Stony Point, others say he was drowned in a squall at the foot of Antony's Nose. I don't know; he never came back again."

"Where's Van Bummel, the schoolmaster?"

"He went off to the wars too, was a great militia general, and is now in Congress."

Rip's heart died away at hearing of these sad changes in his home and friends, and finding himself thus alone in the world. Every answer puzzled him too, by treating of such enormous lapses of time, and of matters which he could not understand: war—Congress—Stony Point; he had no courage to ask after any more friends, but cried out in despair, "Does nobody here know Rip Van Winkle?"

"Oh, Rip Van Winkle!" exclaimed two or three. "Oh, to be sure! that's Rip Van Winkle yonder, leaning against the tree."

Rip looked, and beheld a precise counterpart of himself as he went up the mountain: apparently as lazy, and certainly as ragged. The poor fellow was now completely confounded. He doubted his own identity, and whether he was himself or another man. In the midst of his bewilderment, the man in the cocked hat demanded who he was, and what was his name?

"God knows," exclaimed he, at his wit's end; "I'm not myself—I'm somebody else—that's me yonder—no —that's somebody else got into my shoes—I was myself last night, but I fell asleep on the mountain, and they've changed my gun, and everything's changed, and I am changed, and I can't tell what's my name, or who I am!"

The bystanders began now to look at each other, nod, wink significantly, and tap their fingers against their foreheads. There was a whisper also about securing the gun, and keeping the old fellow from doing mischief, at the very suggestion of which the self-important man in the cocked hat retired with some precipitation. At this critical moment a fresh comely woman pressed through the throng to get a peep at the grey-bearded man. She had a chubby child in her arms, which, frightened at his looks, began to cry. "Hush, Rip," cried she, "hush, you little fool, the old man won't hurt you." The name of the child, the tone of her voice, all awakened a train of recollections in his mind.

"What is your name, my good woman?" asked he.

"Judith Gardenier."

"And your father's name?"

"Ah, poor man, Rip Van Winkle was his name, but it's twenty years since he went away from home with his gun, and never has been heard of since; his dog came home without him, but whether he shot himself, or was carried away by the Indians, nobody can tell. I was then but a little girl."

Rip had but one question more, but he put it with a faltering voice—

"Where's your mother?"

"Oh, she too had died but a short time since; she broke a blood-vessel in a fit of passion at a New England pedlar."

There was a drop of comfort, at least, in this intelligence. The honest man could contain himself no longer. He caught his daughter and her child in his arms. "I am your father!" cried he. "Young Rip Van Winkle once, old Rip Van Winkle now! Does nobody know poor Rip Van Winkle?"

All stood amazed, until an old woman, tottering out from among the crowd, put her hand to her brow, and peering under it into his face for a moment, exclaimed, "Sure enough! it is Rip Van Winkle; it is himself! Welcome home again, old neighbour. Why, where have you been these twenty long years?"

Rip's story was soon told, for the whole twenty years had been to him but as one night. The neighbours stared when they heard it; some were seen to wink at each other, and put their tongues in their cheeks; and the self-important man in the cocked hat, who, when the alarm was over, had returned to the field, screwed down the corners of his mouth, and shook his head—upon which there was a general shaking of the head throughout the assemblage.

It was determined, however, to take the opinion of old Peter Vanderdonk, who was seen slowly advancing up the road. He was a descendant of the historian of that name, who wrote one of the earliest accounts of the province. Peter was the most ancient inhabitant of the village, and well versed in all the wonderful events and traditions of the neighbourhood. He recollected Rip at once, and corroborated his story in the most satisfactory manner. He assured the company that it was a fact, handed down from his ancestor the historian, that the Kaatskill Mountains had always been haunted by strange beings. That it was affirmed that the great Hendrick Hudson, the first discoverer of the river and country, kept a kind of vigil there every twenty years with his crew of the *Half-moon*; being permitted in this way to revisit the scenes of his enterprise, and keep a guardian eye upon the river and the great city called by his name. That his father had once seen them in their old Dutch dresses playing at ninepins in a hollow of the mountain; and that he himself had heard, one summer afternoon, the sound of their balls like distant peals of thunder.

To make a long story short, the company broke up, and returned to the more important concerns of the election. Rip's daughter took him home to live with her; she had a snug, well-furnished house, and a stout, cheery farmer for her husband, whom Rip recollected for one of the urchins that used to climb upon his back. As to Rip's son and heir, who was the ditto of himself, seen leaning against the tree, he was employed to work on the farm; but evinced an hereditary disposition to attend to anything else but his business.

Rip now resumed his old walks and habits; he soon found many of his former cronies, though all rather the worse for the wear and tear of time, and preferred making friends among the rising generation, with whom he soon grew into great favour.

Having nothing to do at home, and being arrived at that happy age when a man can be idle with impunity, he took his place once more on the bench at the inn door, and was reverenced as one of the patriarchs of the village, and a chronicle of the old times "before the war." It was some time before he could get into the regular track of gossip, or could be made to comprehend the strange events that had taken place during his torpor. How that there had been a revolutionary war—that the country had thrown off the yoke of old England—and that, instead of being a subject of his Majesty George the Third, he was now a free citizen of the United States. Rip, in fact, was no politician; the changes of states and empires made but little impression on him; but there was one species of despotism under which he had long groaned, and that was—petticoat government. Happily that was at an end; he had got his neck out of the yoke of matrimony, and could go in and out whenever he pleased without dreading the tyranny of Dame Van Winkle. Whenever her name was mentioned, however, he shook his head, shrugged his shoulders, and cast up his eyes, which might pass either for an expression of resignation to his fate or joy at his deliverance.

He used to tell his story to every stranger that arrived at Mr. Doolittle's hotel. He was at first observed to vary on some points every time he told it, which was, doubtless, owing to his having so recently awaked. It at last settled down to precisely the tale I have related, and not a man, woman, or child in the neighbourhood but knew it by heart. Some always pretended to doubt the reality of it, and insisted that Rip had been out of his head, and that this was one point on which he always remained flighty. The old Dutch inhabitants, however, almost universally gave it full credit. Even to this day they never hear a thunderstorm of a summer afternoon

about the Kaatskill, but they say Hendrick Hudson and
his crew are at their game of ninepins; and it is a
common wish of all henpecked husbands in the neighbourhood, when life hangs heavy on their hands, that
they might have a quieting draught out of Rip Van
Winkle's flagon.

VIII

MY KINSMAN, MAJOR MOLINEUX

By Nathaniel Hawthorne

AFTER the kings of Great Britain had assumed the right
of appointing the colonial governors, the measures of the
latter seldom met with the ready and general approbation which had been paid to those of their predecessors
under the original charters.   The people looked with
most jealous scrutiny to the exercise of power which did
not emanate from themselves, and they usually rewarded
their rulers with slender gratitude for the compliances by
which, in softening their instructions from beyond the
sea, they had incurred the reprehension of those who gave
them.   The annals of Massachusetts Bay will inform us
that of six governors in the space of about forty years
from the surrender of the old charter, under James II.,
two were imprisoned by a popular insurrection ; a third,
as Hutchinson inclines to believe, was driven from the
province by the whizzing of a musket-ball ; a fourth, in
the opinion of the same historian, was hastened to his
grave by continual bickerings with the House of Re-
presentatives ; and the remaining two, as well as their
successors, till the Revolution, were favoured with few and
brief intervals of peaceful sway.   The inferior members

of the court party, in times of high political excitement,
led scarcely a more desirable life. These remarks may
serve as a preface to the following adventures, which
chanced upon a summer night, not far from a hundred
years ago. The reader, in order to avoid a long and dry
detail of colonial affairs, is requested to dispense with an
account of the train of circumstances that had caused
much temporary inflammation of the popular mind.

It was near nine o'clock of a moonlight evening, when
a boat crossed the ferry with a single passenger, who had
obtained his conveyance at that unusual hour by the promise of an extra fare. While he stood on the landing
place, searching in either pocket for the means of ful-
filling his agreement, the ferryman lifted a lantern, by the
aid of which, and the newly-risen moon, he took a very
accurate survey of the stranger's figure. He was a youth
of barely eighteen years, evidently country-bred, and now,
as it should seem, upon his first visit to town. He was
clad in a coarse grey coat, well-worn, but in excellent
repair; his under-garments were durably constructed of
leather, and fitted tight to a pair of serviceable and well-
shaped limbs; his stockings of blue yarn were the incon-
trovertible work of a mother or a sister; and on his head
was a three-cornered hat, which in its better days had
perhaps sheltered the graver brow of the lad's father.
Under his left arm was a heavy cudgel, formed of an oak
sapling, and retaining a part of the hardened root; and
his equipment was completed by a wallet, not so abun-
dantly stocked as to incommode the vigorous shoulders on
which it hung. Brown, curly hair, well-shaped features,
and bright, cheerful eyes were Nature's gifts, and worth
all that art could have done for his adornment.

The youth, one of whose names was Robin, finally
drew from his pocket the half of a little province bill of
five shillings, which, in the depreciation of that sort of
currency, did but satisfy the ferryman's demand, with the
surplus of a sexangular piece of parchment, valued at
threepence. He then walked forward into the town, with
as light a step as if his day's journey had not already
exceeded thirty miles, and with as eager an eye as if he
were entering London city, instead of the little metro-
polis of a New England colony. Before Robin had proceeded far, however, it occurred to him that he knew not
whither to direct his steps ; so he paused, and looked up
and down the narrow street, scrutinising the small and
mean wooden buildings that were scattered on either
side.

"This low hovel cannot be my kinsman's dwelling,"
thought he, "nor yonder old house, where the moonlight enters at the broken casement ; and truly I see none
hereabouts that might be worthy of him. It would have
been wise to inquire my way of the ferryman, and doubtless he would have gone with me, and earned a shilling
from the major for his pains. But the next man I meet
will do as well."

He resumed his walk, and was glad to perceive that
the street now became wider, and the houses more
respectable in their appearance. He soon discerned a
figure moving on moderately in advance, and hastened
his steps to overtake it. As Robin drew nigh, he saw
that the passenger was a man in years, with a full periwig of grey hair, a wide-skirted coat of dark cloth, and
silk stockings rolled above his knees. He carried a long
and polished cane, which he struck down perpendicularly

before him at every step; and at regular intervals he uttered two successive hems, of a peculiarly solemn and sepulchral intonation. Having made these observations, Robin laid hold of the skirt of the old man's coat, just when the light from the open door and windows of a barber's shop fell upon both their figures.

"Good evening to you, honoured sir," said he, making a low bow, and still retaining his hold of the skirt. "I pray you tell me whereabouts is the dwelling of my kinsman, Major Molineux."

The youth's question was uttered very loudly; and one of the barbers, whose razor was descending on a well-soaped chin, and another who was dressing a Ramillies wig, left their occupations and came to the door. The citizen, in the meantime, turned a long-favoured countenance upon Robin, and answered him in a tone of excessive anger and annoyance. His two sepulchral hems, however, broke into the very centre of his rebuke with most singular effect, like a thought of the cold grave obtruding among wrathful passions.

"Let go my garment, fellow! I tell you I know not the man you speak of. What! I have authority, I have—hem, hem—authority; and if this be the respect you show for your betters, your feet shall be brought acquainted with the stocks by daylight to-morrow morning!"

Robin released the old man's skirt, and hastened away, pursued by an ill-mannered roar of laughter from the barber's shop. He was at first considerably surprised by the result of his question, but, being a shrewd youth, soon thought himself able to account for the mystery.

"This is some country representative," was his conclusion, "who has never seen the inside of my kinsman's door, and lacks the breeding to answer a stranger civilly. The man is old, or verily I might be tempted to turn back and smite him on the nose. Ah, Robin, Robin! even the barber's boys laugh at you for choosing such a guide! You will be wiser in time, friend Robin."

He now became entangled in a succession of crooked and narrow streets, which crossed each other, and meandered at no great distance from the water-side. The smell of tar was obvious to his nostrils, the masts of vessels pierced the moonlight above the tops of the buildings, and the numerous signs, which Robin paused to read, informed him that he was near the centre of business. But the streets were empty, the shops were closed, and lights were visible only in the second storeys of a few dwelling-houses. At length, on the corner of a narrow lane, through which he was passing, he beheld the broad countenance of a British hero swinging before the door of an inn, whence proceeded the voices of many guests. The casement of one of the lower windows was thrown back, and a very thin curtain permitted Robin to distinguish a party at supper, round a well-furnished table. The fragrance of the good cheer steamed forth into the outer air, and the youth could not fail to recollect that the last remnant of his travelling stock of provision had yielded to his morning appetite, and that noon had found and left him dinnerless.

"Oh, that a parchment threepenny might give me a right to sit down at yonder table!" said Robin with a sigh. "But the major will make me welcome to the best of his victuals; so I will even step boldly in, and inquire my way to his dwelling."

He entered the tavern, and was guided by the murmur
of voices and the fumes of tobacco to the public room.
It was a long and low apartment, with oaken walls,
grown dark in the continual smoke, and a floor which
was thickly sanded, but of no immaculate purity. A
number of persons—the larger part of whom appeared
to be mariners, or in some way connected with the sea
—occupied the wooden benches or leather-bottomed
chairs, conversing on various matters, and occasionally
lending their attention to some topic of general interest.
Three or four little groups were draining as many bowls
of punch, which the West India trade had long since
made a familiar drink in the colony. Others, who had
the appearance of men who lived by regular and laborious
handicraft, preferred the insulated bliss of an unshared
potation, and became more taciturn under its influence.
Nearly all, in short, evinced a predilection for the Good
Creature in some of its various shapes, for this is a vice
to which, as Fast-day sermons of a hundred years ago
will testify, we have a long hereditary claim. The only
guests to whom Robin's sympathies inclined him were
two or three sheepish countrymen, who were using the
inn something after the fashion of a Turkish caravansary;
they had gotten themselves into the darkest corner of the
room, and, heedless of the nicotian atmosphere, were
supping on the bread of their own ovens, and the bacon
cured in their own chimney-smoke. But though Robin
felt a sort of brotherhood with these strangers, his eyes
were attracted from them to a person who stood near the
door, holding whispered conversation with a group of ill-
dressed associates. His features were separately striking
almost to grotesqueness, and the whole face left a deep

impression on the memory. The forehead bulged out into a double prominence, with a vale between; the nose came boldly forth in an irregular curve, and its bridge was of more than a finger's breadth; the eyebrows were deep and shaggy, and the eyes glowed beneath them like fire in a cave.

While Robin deliberated of whom to inquire respecting his kinsman's dwelling, he was accosted by the inn-keeper, a little man in a stained white apron, who had come to pay his professional welcome to the stranger. Being in the second generation from a French Protestant, he seemed to have inherited the courtesy of his parent nation; but no variety of circumstances was ever known to change his voice from the one shrill note in which he now addressed Robin.

"From the country, I presume, sir?" said he, with a profound bow. "Beg leave to congratulate you on your arrival, and trust you intend a long stay with us. Fine town here, sir, beautiful buildings, and much that may interest a stranger. May I hope for the honour of your commands in respect to supper?"

"The man sees a family likeness! the rogue has guessed that I am related to the major!" thought Robin, who had hitherto experienced little superfluous civility.

All eyes were now turned on the country lad, standing at the door, in his worn three-cornered hat, grey coat, leather breeches, and blue yarn stockings, leaning on an oaken cudgel, and bearing a wallet on his back.

Robin replied to the courteous innkeeper, with such an assumption of confidence as befitted the major's relative. "My honest friend," he said, "I shall make it a point to patronise your house on some occasion, when"—

here he could not help lowering his voice—"when I may have more than a parchment threepence in my pocket. My present business," continued he, speaking with lofty confidence, "is merely to inquire my way to the dwelling of my kinsman, Major Molineux."

There was a sudden and general movement in the room, which Robin interpreted as expressing the eagerness of each individual to become his guide. But the innkeeper turned his eyes to a written paper on the wall, which he read, or seemed to read, with occasional recurrences to the young man's figure.

"What have we here?" said he, breaking his speech into little dry fragments. "'Left the house of the subscriber, bounden servant, Hezekiah Mudge;—had on, when he went away, grey coat, leather breeches, master's third-best hat. One pound currency reward to whosoever shall lodge him in any jail of the province.' Better trudge, boy, better trudge!"

Robin had begun to draw his hand towards the lighter end of the oak cudgel, but a strange hostility in every countenance induced him to relinquish his purpose of breaking the courteous innkeeper's head. As he turned to leave the room, he encountered a sneering glance from the bold-featured personage whom he had before noticed; and no sooner was he beyond the door, than he heard a general laugh, in which the innkeeper's voice might be distinguished, like the dropping of small stones into a kettle.

"Now, is it not strange," thought Robin, with his usual shrewdness, "is it not strange that the confession of an empty pocket should outweigh the name of my kinsman, Major Molineux? Oh, if I had one of those

M

grinning rascals in the woods, where I and my oak sapling grew up together, I would teach him that my arm
is heavy, though my purse be light ! "

On turning the corner of the narrow lane, Robin found
himself in a spacious street, with an unbroken line of
lofty houses on each side, and a steepled building at the
upper end, whence the ringing of a bell announced the
hour of nine. The light of the moon, and the lamps
from the numerous shop-windows, discovered people pro-
menading on the pavement, and amongst them Robin
hoped to recognise his hitherto inscrutable relative. The
result of his former inquiries made him unwilling to
hazard another in a scene of such publicity, and he
determined to walk slowly and silently up the street,
thrusting his face close to that of every elderly gentleman, in search of the major's lineaments. In his progress
Robin encountered many gay and gallant figures. Em-
broidered garments of showy colours, enormous periwigs,
gold-laced hats, and silver-hilted swords, glided past him,
and dazzled his optics. Travelled youths, imitators of
the European fine gentleman of the period, trod jauntily
along, half-dancing to the fashionable tunes which they
hummed, and making poor Robin ashamed of his quiet
and natural gait. At length, after many pauses to examine the gorgeous display of goods in the shop-windows,
and after suffering some rebukes for the impertinence of
his scrutiny into people's faces, the major's kinsman found
himself near the steepled building, still unsuccessful in
his search. As yet, however, he had seen only one side of
the thronged street ; so Robin crossed, and continued the
same sort of inquisition down the opposite pavement,
with stronger hopes than the philosopher seeking an

honest man, but with no better fortune. He had arrived about midway towards the lower end, from which his course began, when he overheard the approach of some one, who struck down a cane on the flag-stones at every step, uttering, at regular intervals, two sepulchral hems.

"Mercy on us!" quoth Robin, recognising the sound.

Turning a corner, which chanced to be close at his right hand, he hastened to pursue his researches in some other part of the town. His patience now was wearing low, and he seemed to feel more fatigue from his rambles since he crossed the ferry, than from his journey of several days on the other side. Hunger also pleaded loudly within him, and Robin began to balance the propriety of demanding, violently, and with lifted cudgel, the necessary guidance from the first solitary passenger whom he should meet. While a resolution to this effect was gaining strength, he entered a street of mean appearance, on either side of which a row of ill-built houses was straggling towards the harbour. The moonlight fell upon no passenger along the whole extent, but in the third domicile which Robin passed there was a half-opened door, and his keen glance detected a woman's garment within.

"My luck may be better here," said he to himself.

Accordingly, he approached the door, and beheld it shut closer as he did so; yet an open space remained, sufficing for the fair occupant to observe the stranger, without a corresponding display on her part. All that Robin could discern was a strip of scarlet petticoat, and the occasional sparkle of an eye, as if the moonbeams were trembling on some bright thing.

"Pretty mistress," for I may call her so with a good conscience, thought the shrewd youth, since I know nothing to the contrary,—"my sweet pretty mistress, will you be kind enough to tell me whereabouts I must seek the dwelling of my kinsman, Major Molineux?"

Robin's voice was plaintive and winning, and the female, seeing nothing to be shunned in the handsome country youth, thrust open the door and came forth into the moonlight. She was a dainty little figure, with a white neck, round arms, and a slender waist, at the extremity of which her scarlet petticoat jutted out over a hoop, as if she were standing in a balloon. Moreover, her face was oval and pretty, her hair dark beneath the little cap, and her bright eyes possessed a sly freedom which triumphed over those of Robin.

"Major Molineux dwells here," said this fair woman.

Now, her voice was the sweetest Robin had heard that night, the airy counterpart of a stream of melted silver; yet he could not help doubting whether that sweet voice spoke Gospel truth. He looked up and down the mean street, and then surveyed the house before which they stood. It was a small, dark edifice of two storeys, the second of which projected over the lower floor, and the front apartment had the aspect of a shop for petty commodities.

"Now truly I am in luck," replied Robin cunningly, "and so indeed is my kinsman, the major, in having so pretty a housekeeper. But I prithee trouble him to step to the door; I will deliver him a message from his friends in the country, and then go back to my lodgings at the inn."

"Nay, the major has been abed this hour or more," said the lady of the scarlet petticoat; "and it would be to little purpose to disturb him to-night, seeing his evening draught was of the strongest. But he is a kind-hearted man, and it would be as much as my life's worth to let a kinsman of his turn away from the door. You are the good old gentleman's very picture, and I could swear that was his rainy-weather hat. Also he has garments very much resembling those leather small-clothes. But come in, I pray, for I bid you hearty welcome in his name."

So saying, the fair and hospitable dame took our hero by the hand; and the touch was light, and the force was gentleness, and though Robin read in her eyes what he did not hear in her words, yet the slender-waisted woman in the scarlet petticoat proved stronger than the athletic country youth. She had drawn his half-willing footsteps nearly to the threshold, when the opening of a door in the neighbourhood startled the major's housekeeper, and, leaving the major's kinsman, she vanished speedily into her own domicile. A heavy yawn preceded the appearance of a man, who, like the Moonshine of Pyramus and Thisbe, carried a lantern, needlessly aiding his sister luminary in the heavens. As he walked sleepily up the street, he turned his broad, dull face on Robin, and displayed a long staff, spiked at the end.

"Home, vagabond, home!" said the watchman, in accents that seemed to fall asleep as soon as they were uttered. "Home, or we'll set you in the stocks by peep of day!"

"This is the second hint of the kind," thought Robin.

"I wish they would end my difficulties by setting me there to-night."

Nevertheless, the youth felt an instinctive antipathy towards the guardian of midnight order, which at first prevented him from asking his usual question. But just when the man was about to vanish behind the corner, Robin resolved not to lose the opportunity, and shouted lustily after him—

"I say, friend! will you guide me to the house of my kinsman, Major Molineux?"

The watchman made no reply, but turned the corner and was gone; yet Robin seemed to hear the sound of drowsy laughter stealing along the solitary street. At that moment, also, a pleasant titter saluted him from the open window above his head; he looked up, and caught the sparkle of a saucy eye; a round arm beckoned to him, and next he heard light footsteps descending the staircase within. But Robin, being of the household of a New England clergyman, was a good youth, as well as a shrewd one; so he resisted temptation, and fled away.

He now roamed desperately and at random through the town, almost ready to believe that a spell was on him, like that by which a wizard of his country had once kept three pursuers wandering, a whole winter night, within twenty paces of the cottage which they sought. The streets lay before him, strange and desolate, and the lights were extinguished in almost every house. Twice, however, little parties of men, among whom Robin distinguished individuals in outlandish attire, came hurrying along; but though on both occasions they paused to address him, such intercourse did not at all enlighten his perplexity. They did but utter

a few words in some language of which Robin knew
nothing, and perceiving his inability to answer, bestowed
a curse upon him in plain English and hastened away.
Finally, the lad determined to knock at the door of every
mansion that might appear worthy to be occupied by his
kinsman, trusting that perseverance would overcome the
fatality that had hitherto thwarted him.   Firm in this
resolve, he was passing beneath the walls of a church,
which formed the corner of two streets, when, as he
turned into the shade of its steeple, he encountered a
bulky stranger, muffled in a cloak.   The man was proceeding with the speed of earnest business, but Robin
planted himself full before him, holding the oak cudgel
with both hands across his body, as a bar to further
passage.

"Halt, honest man, and answer me a question,"
said he, very resolutely.   "Tell me, this instant,
whereabouts is the dwelling of my kinsman, Major
Molineux?"

"Keep your tongue between your teeth, fool, and
let me pass!" said a deep, gruff voice, which Robin
partly remembered.   "Let me pass, I say, or I'll strike
you to the earth!"

"No, no, neighbour!" cried Robin, flourishing his
cudgel, and then thrusting its larger end close to the
man's muffled face.   "No, no, I'm not the fool you
take me for, nor do you pass till I have an answer to
my question.   Whereabouts is the dwelling of my kinsman, Major Molineux?"

The stranger, instead of attempting to force his
passage, stepped back into the moonlight, unmuffled his
face, and stared full into that of Robin.

"Watch here an hour, and Major Molineux will pass by," said he.

Robin gazed with dismay and astonishment on the unprecedented physiognomy of the speaker. The forehead with its double prominence, the broad hooked nose, the shaggy eyebrows, and fiery eyes, were those which he had noticed at the inn, but the man's complexion had undergone a singular, or, more properly, a twofold change. One side of the face blazed an intense red, while the other was black as midnight, the division line being in the broad bridge of the nose; and a mouth which seemed to extend from ear to ear was black or red, in contrast to the colour of the cheek. The effect was as if two individual devils, a fiend of fire and a fiend of darkness, had united themselves to form this infernal visage. The stranger grinned in Robin's face, muffled his parti-coloured features, and was out of sight in a moment.

"Strange things we travellers see!" ejaculated Robin.

He seated himself, however, upon the steps of the church door, resolving to wait the appointed time for his kinsman. A few moments were consumed in philosophical speculations upon the species of man who had just left him; but having settled this point, shrewdly, rationally, and satisfactorily, he was compelled to look elsewhere for his amusement. And first he threw his eyes along the street. It was of more respectable appearance than most of those into which he had wandered, and the moon, creating, like the imaginative power, a beautiful strangeness in familiar objects, gave something of romance to a scene that might not have possessed it in the light of day. The irregular and often quaint architecture of

the houses, some of whose roofs were broken into numerous little peaks, while others ascended, steep and narrow,
into a single point, and others again were square; the
pure snow-white of some of their complexions, the aged
darkness of others, and the thousand sparklings, reflected
from bright substances in the walls of many; these matters engaged Robin's attention for a while, and then
began to grow wearisome.   Next he endeavoured to
define the forms of distant objects, starting away, with
almost ghostly indistinctness, just as his eye appeared to
grasp them; and finally, he took a minute survey of an
edifice which stood on the opposite side of the street,
directly in front of the church door where he was sta-
tioned.   It was a large, square mansion, distinguished
from its neighbours by a balcony, which rested on tall
pillars, and by an elaborate Gothic window communi-
cating therewith.

"Perhaps this is the very house I have been seeking,"
thought Robin.

Then he strove to speed away the time by listening
to a murmur which swept continually along the street,
yet was scarcely audible, except to an unaccustomed ear
like his; it was a low, dull, dreamy sound, compounded
of many noises, each of which was at too great a distance
to be separately heard.   Robin marvelled at this snore
of a sleeping town, and marvelled more whenever its
continuity was broken by now and then a distant shout,
apparently loud where it originated.   But altogether it
was a sleep-inspiring sound, and to shake off its drowsy
influence Robin arose and climbed a window-frame that
he might view the interior of the church.   There the
moonbeams came trembling in, and fell down upon the

deserted pews, and extended along the quiet aisles. A fainter yet more awful radiance was hovering around the pulpit, and one solitary ray had dared to rest upon the opened page of the great Bible. Had nature, in that deep hour, become a worshipper in the house which man had builded? Or was that heavenly light the visible sanctity of the place—visible because no earthly and impure feet were within the walls? The scene made Robin's heart shiver with a sensation of loneliness stronger than he had ever felt in the remotest depths of his native woods; so he turned away, and sat down again before the door. There were graves around the church, and now an uneasy thought obtruded into Robin's breast. What if the object of his search, which had been so often and so strangely thwarted, were all the time mouldering in his shroud? What if his kinsman should glide through yonder gate, and nod and smile to him in dimly passing by?

"Oh, that any breathing thing were here with me!" said Robin.

Recalling his thoughts from this uncomfortable track, he sent them over forest, hill, and stream, and attempted to imagine how that evening of ambiguity and weariness had been spent by his father's household. He pictured them assembled at the door, beneath the tree, the great old tree, which had been spared for its huge twisted trunk and venerable shade, when a thousand leafy brethren fell. There, at the going down of the summer sun, it was his father's custom to perform domestic worship, that the neighbours might come and join with him like brothers of the family, and that the wayfaring man might pause to drink at that fountain, and keep his heart

pure by freshening the memory of home. Robin distinguished the seat of every individual of the little
audience; he saw the good man in the midst, holding
the Scriptures in the golden light that fell from the
western clouds; he beheld him close the book, and all
rise up to pray. He heard the old thanksgivings for
daily mercies, the old supplications for their continuance,
to which he had so often listened in weariness, but which
were now among his dear remembrances. He perceived
the slight inequality of his father's voice when he came
to speak of the absent one; he noted how his mother
turned her face to the broad and knotted trunk; how his
elder brother scorned, because the beard was rough upon
his upper lip, to permit his features to be moved; how
the younger sister drew down a low-hanging branch
before her eyes; and how the little one of all, whose
sports had hitherto broken the decorum of the scene,
understood the prayer for her playmate, and burst into
clamorous grief. Then he saw them go in at the door;
and when Robin would have entered also, the latch
tinkled into its place, and he was excluded from his
home.

"Am I here or there?" cried Robin, starting; for
all at once, when his thoughts had become visible and
audible in a dream, the long, wide solitary street shone
out before him.

He aroused himself, and endeavoured to fix his attention steadily upon the large edifice which he had surveyed
before. But still his mind kept vibrating between fancy
and reality; by turns, the pillars of the balcony length-
ened into the tall, bare stems of pines, dwindled down to
human figures, settled again into their true shape and

size, and then commenced a new succession of changes.
For a single moment, when he deemed himself awake, he
could have sworn that a visage—one which he seemed to
remember, yet could not absolutely name as his kinsman's
—was looking towards him from the Gothic window.
A deeper sleep wrestled with and nearly overcame him,
but fled at the sound of footsteps along the opposite
pavement. Robin rubbed his eyes, discerned a man
passing at the foot of the balcony, and addressed him in
a loud, peevish, and lamentable cry.

"Hallo, friend! must I wait here all night for my
kinsman, Major Molineux?"

The sleeping echoes awoke, and answered the voice;
and the passenger, barely able to discern a figure sitting
in the oblique shade of the steeple, traversed the street
to obtain a nearer view. He was himself a gentleman
in his prime, of open, intelligent, cheerful, and altogether
prepossessing countenance. Perceiving a country youth,
apparently homeless and without friends, he accosted him
in a tone of real kindness, which had become strange to
Robin's ears.

"Well, my good lad, why are you sitting here?" inquired he. "Can I be of service to you in any way?"

"I am afraid not, sir," replied Robin despondingly;
"yet I shall take it kindly, if you'll answer me a single
question. I've been searching half the night for one
Major Molineux; now, sir, is there really such a person
in these parts, or am I dreaming?"

"Major Molineux! The name is not altogether
strange to me," said the gentleman, smiling. "Have
you any objection to telling me the nature of your
business with him?"

Then Robin briefly related that his father was a clergyman, settled on a small salary, at a long distance back in the country, and that he and Major Molineux were brothers' children. The major, having inherited riches and acquired civil and military rank, had visited his cousin, in great pomp, a year or two before; had manifested much interest in Robin and an elder brother, and, being childless himself, had thrown out hints respecting the future establishment of one of them in life. The elder brother was destined to succeed to the farm which his father cultivated in the interval of sacred duties; it was therefore determined that Robin should profit by his kinsman's generous intentions, especially as he seemed to be rather the favourite, and was thought to possess other necessary endowments.

"For I have the name of being a shrewd youth," observed Robin, in this part of his story.

"I doubt not you deserve it," replied his new friend good-naturedly; "but pray proceed."

"Well, sir, being nearly eighteen years old, and well-grown, as you see," continued Robin, drawing himself up to his full height, "I thought it high time to begin the world. So my mother and sister put me in handsome trim, and my father gave me half the remnant of his last year's salary, and five days ago I started for this place to pay the major a visit. But, would you believe it, sir! I crossed the ferry a little after dark, and have yet found nobody that would show me the way to his dwelling;—only, an hour or two since, I was told to wait here, and Major Molineux would pass by."

"Can you describe the man who told you this?" inquired the gentleman.

"Oh, he was a very ill-favoured fellow, sir," replied Robin, "with two great bumps on his forehead, a hook nose, fiery eyes,—and, what struck me as the strangest, his face was of two different colours. Do you happen to know such a man, sir?"

"Not intimately," answered the stranger, "but I chanced to meet him a little time previous to your stopping me. I believe you may trust his word, and that the major will very shortly pass through this street. In the meantime, as I have a singular curiosity to witness your meeting, I will sit down here upon the steps and bear you company."

He seated himself accordingly, and soon engaged his companion in animated discourse. It was but of brief continuance, however, for a noise of shouting, which had long been remotely audible, drew so much nearer that Robin inquired its cause.

"What may be the meaning of this uproar?" asked he. "Truly, if your town be always as noisy, I shall find little sleep while I am an inhabitant."

"Why, indeed, friend Robin, there do appear to be three or four riotous fellows abroad to-night," replied the gentleman. "You must not expect all the stillness of your native woods here in our street. But the watch will shortly be at the heels of these lads, and——"

"Ay, and set them in the stocks by peep of day," interrupted Robin, recollecting his own encounter with the drowsy lantern-bearer. "But, dear sir, if I may trust my ears, an army of watchmen could never make head against such a multitude of rioters. There were at least a thousand voices went up to make that one shout."

"May not a man have several voices, Robin, as well as two complexions?" said his friend.

"Perhaps a man may; but heaven forbid that a woman should!" responded the shrewd youth, thinking of the seductive tones of the major's housekeeper.

The sounds of a trumpet in some neighbouring street now became so evident and continual that Robin's curiosity was strongly excited. In addition to the shouts, he heard frequent bursts from many instruments of discord, and a wild and confused laughter filled up the intervals. Robin rose from the steps, and looked wistfully towards a point whither several people seemed to be hastening.

"Surely some prodigious merry-making is going on," exclaimed he. "I have laughed very little since I left home, sir, and should be sorry to lose an opportunity. Shall we step round the corner by that darkish house and take our share of the fun?"

"Sit down again, sit down, good Robin," replied the gentleman, laying his hand on the skirt of the grey coat. "You forget that we must wait here for your kinsman; and there is reason to believe that he will pass by in the course of a very few moments."

The near approach of the uproar had now disturbed the neighbourhood; windows flew open on all sides; and many heads, in the attire of the pillow, and confused by sleep suddenly broken, were protruded to the gaze of whoever had leisure to observe them. Eager voices hailed each other from house to house, all demanding the explanation which not a soul could give. Half-dressed men hurried towards the unknown commotion, stumbling as they went over the stone steps, that thrust themselves into the narrow foot-walk. The shouts, the laughter, and the tuneless bray, the antipodes of music, came onwards with increasing din, till scattered individuals, and then denser bodies, began to appear round a corner at the distance of a hundred yards.

"Will you recognise your kinsman if he passes in this crowd?" inquired the gentleman.

"Indeed, I cannot warrant it, sir; but I'll take my stand here, and keep a bright look-out," answered Robin, descending to the outer edge of the pavement.

A mighty stream of people now emptied into the street, and came rolling slowly towards the church. A single horseman wheeled the corner in the midst of them, and close behind him came a band of fearful wind instruments, sending forth a fresher discord, now that no intervening buildings kept it from the ear. Then a redder light disturbed the moonbeams, and a dense multitude of torches shone along the street, concealing, by their glare, whatever object they illuminated. The single horseman, clad in a military dress, and bearing a drawn sword, rode onward as the leader, and, by his fierce and variegated countenance, appeared like war personified: the red of one cheek was an emblem of fire and sword; the blackness of the other betokened the mourning that attends them. In his train were wild figures in the Indian dress, and many fantastic shapes without a model, giving the whole march a visionary air, as if a dream had broken forth from some feverish brain, and were sweeping visibly through the midnight streets. A mass of people, inactive, except as applauding spectators, hemmed the procession in; and several women ran along the side-walk, piercing the confusion of heavier sounds with their shrill voices of mirth or terror.

"The double-faced fellow has his eye upon me," muttered Robin, with an indefinite but an uncomfortable idea that he was himself to bear a part in the pageantry.

The leader turned himself in the saddle, and fixed his glance full upon the country youth, as the steed went slowly by. When Robin had freed his eyes from those fiery ones, the musicians were passing before him, and the torches were close at hand; but the unsteady brightness of the latter formed a veil which he could not penetrate. The rattling of wheels over the stones sometimes found its way to his ear, and confused traces of a human form appeared at intervals, and then melted into the vivid light. A moment more, and the leader thundered a command to halt; the trumpets vomited a horrid breath, and then held their peace; the shouts and laughter of the people died away, and there remained only a universal hum, allied to silence. Right before Robin's eyes was an uncovered cart. There the torches blazed the brightest, there the moon shone out like day, and there, in tar-and-feathery dignity, sat his kinsman, Major Molineux!

He was an elderly man, of large and majestic person, and strong, square features, betokening a steady soul; but steady as it was, his enemies had found means to shake it. His face was pale as death, and far more ghastly; the broad forehead was contracted in his agony, so that his eyebrows formed one grizzled line; his eyes were red and wild, and the foam hung white upon his quivering lip. His whole frame was agitated by a quick and continued tremor, which his pride strove to quell,

N

even in those circumstances of overwhelming humiliation. But perhaps the bitterest pang of all was when his eyes met those of Robin; for he evidently knew him on the instant, as the youth stood witnessing the foul disgrace of a head grown grey with honour. They stared at each other in silence, and Robin's knees shook, and his hair bristled, with a mixture of pity and terror. Soon, however, a bewildering excitement began to seize upon his mind; the preceding adventures of the night, the unexpected appearance of the crowd, the torches, the confused din, and the hush that followed, the spectre of his kinsman reviled by that great multitude,—all this, and, more than all, a perception of tremendous ridicule in the whole scene, affected him with a sort of mental inebriety. At that moment a voice of sluggish merriment saluted Robin's ears; he turned instinctively, and just behind the corner of the church stood the lantern-bearer, rubbing his eyes, and drowsily enjoying the lad's amazement. Then he heard a peal of laughter like the ringing of silvery bells; a woman twitched his arm, a saucy eye met his, and he saw the lady of the scarlet petticoat. A sharp, dry cachinnation appealed to his memory, and, standing on tiptoe in the crowd, with his white apron over his head, he beheld the courteous little innkeeper. And lastly, there sailed over the heads of the multitude a great, broad laugh, broken in the midst by two sepulchral hems; thus, " Haw, haw, haw,—hem, hem,—haw, haw, haw, haw ! "

The sound proceeded from the balcony of the opposite edifice, and thither Robin turned his eyes. In front of the Gothic window stood the old citizen, wrapped in a wide gown, his grey periwig exchanged for a nightcap, which was thrust back from his forehead, and his silk stockings hanging about his legs. He supported himself on his polished cane in a fit of convulsive merriment, which manifested itself on his solemn old features like a funny inscription on a tombstone. Then Robin seemed to hear the voices of the barbers, of the guests of the inn, and of all that had made sport of him that night. The contagion was spreading among the multitude, when, all at once, it seized upon Robin, and he sent forth a shout of laughter that echoed through the streets; every man shook his sides, every man emptied his lungs, but Robin's shout was the loudest there. The cloud-spirits peeped from their silvery islands, as the congregated mirth went roaring up the sky! The Man in the Moon heard the far bellow; "Oho," quoth he, "the old earth is frolicsome to-night!"

When there was a momentary calm in that tempestuous sea of sound, the leader gave the sign, the procession resumed its march. On they went, like fiends that throng in mockery around some dead potentate, mighty no more, but majestic still in his agony. On they went, in counterfeited pomp, in senseless uproar, in frenzied merriment, trampling all on an old man's heart. On swept the tumult, and left a silent street behind.

. . . .

"Well, Robin, are you dreaming?" inquired the gentleman, laying his hand on the youth's shoulder.

Robin started, and withdrew his arm from the stone post to which he had instinctively clung, as the living stream rolled by him. His cheek was somewhat pale, and his eye not quite as lively as in the earlier part of the evening.

"Will you be kind enough to show me the way to the ferry?" said he, after a moment's pause.

"You have, then, adopted a new subject of inquiry?" observed his companion, with a smile.

"Why, yes, sir," replied Robin, rather dryly. "Thanks to you, and to my other friends, I have at last met my kinsman, and he will scarce desire to see my face again. I begin to grow weary of a town life, sir. Will you show me the way to the ferry?"

"No, my good friend, Robin—not to-night at least," said the gentleman. "Some few days hence, if you wish it, I will speed you on your journey. Or, if you prefer to remain with us, perhaps, as you are a shrewd youth, you may rise in the world without the help of your kinsman, Major Molineux."

IX

THE FALL OF THE HOUSE OF USHER

By Edgar Allan Poe

" Son cœur est un luth suspendu ;
Sitôt qu'on le touche il résonne."
—De Beranger.

DURING the whole of a dull, dark, and soundless day in the autumn of the year, when the clouds hung oppressively low in the heavens, I had been passing alone, on horseback, through a singularly dreary tract of country, and at length found myself, as the shades of the evening drew on, within view of the melancholy House of Usher. I know not how it was, but, with the first glimpse of the building, a sense of insufferable gloom pervaded my spirit. I say insufferable, for the feeling was unrelieved by any of that half-pleasurable, because poetic, sentiment with which the mind usually receives even the sternest natural images of the desolate or terrible. I looked upon the scene before me—upon the mere house, and the simple landscape features of the domain—upon the bleak walls—upon the vacant eye-like windows—upon a few rank sedges—and upon a few white trunks of decayed trees—with an utter depression of soul which I can compare to no earthly sensation more properly than to the after-dream of the reveller upon opium—the bitter lapse into everyday life—the hideous dropping off of the veil. There was an iciness, a sinking, a sickening of the heart—an unredeemed dreariness of thought which no goading of the imagination could torture into aught of the sublime. What was it—I paused to think—what was it that so unnerved me in the contemplation of the House of Usher? It was a mystery all insoluble; nor could I grapple with the shadowy fancies that crowded upon me as I pondered. I was forced to fall back upon the unsatisfactory conclusion, that while, beyond doubt, there *are* combinations of very simple natural objects which have the power of thus affecting us, still the analysis of this power lies among considerations beyond our depth. It was possible, I reflected, that a mere different arrangement of the particulars of the scene, of the details of the picture, would be sufficient to modify, or perhaps to annihilate its capacity for sorrowful impression; and, acting upon this idea, I reined my horse to the precipitous brink of a black and lurid tarn that lay in unruffled lustre by the dwelling, and gazed down—but with a shudder even more thrilling than before—upon the remodelled and inverted images of the grey sedge, and the ghastly tree-stems, and the vacant and eye-like windows.

Nevertheless, in this mansion of gloom I now proposed to myself a sojourn of some weeks. Its proprietor, Roderick Usher, had been one of my boon companions in boyhood; but many years had elapsed since our last meeting. A letter, however, had lately reached me in a distant part of the country—a letter from him—which,

in its wildly importunate nature, had admitted of no
other than a personal reply.   The MS. gave evidence of
nervous agitation.   The writer spoke of acute bodily
illness—of a mental disorder which oppressed him—and
of an earnest desire to see me, as his best and indeed his
only personal friend, with a view of attempting, by the
cheerfulness of my society, some alleviation of his malady.
It was the manner in which all this, and much more, was
said—it was the apparent *heart* that went with his request
—which allowed me no room for hesitation, and I accordingly obeyed forthwith what I still considered a very
singular summons.

Although, as boys, we had been even intimate associates, yet I really knew little of my friend.   His reserve
had been always excessive and habitual.   I was aware,
however, that his very ancient family had been noted,
time out of mind, for a peculiar sensibility of temperament, displaying itself, through long ages, in many works
of exalted art, and manifested, of late, in repeated deeds
of munificent, yet unobtrusive charity, as well as in a
passionate devotion to the intricacies, perhaps even more
than to the orthodox and easily recognisable beauties of
musical science.   I had learned, too, the very remarkable
fact, that the stem of the Usher race, all time-honoured
as it was, had put forth, at no period, any enduring
branch ; in other words, that the entire family lay in the
direct line of descent, and had always, with very trifling
and very temporary variation, so lain.   It was this deficiency, I considered, while running over in thought the
perfect keeping of the character of the premises with the
accredited character of the people, and while speculating
upon the possible influence which the one, in the long

lapse of centuries, might have exercised upon the other—
it was this deficiency, perhaps, of collateral issue, and
the consequent undeviating transmission, from sire to
son, of the patrimony with the name, which had, at
length, so identified the two as to merge the original
title of the estate in the quaint and equivocal appellation
of the "House of Usher"—an appellation which seemed
to include, in the minds of the peasantry who used it,
both the family and the family mansion.

I have said that the sole effect of my somewhat
childish experiment—that of looking down within the
tarn—had been to deepen the first singular impression.
There can be no doubt that the consciousness of the
rapid increase of my superstition—for why should I not
so term it?—served mainly to accelerate the increase
itself. Such, I have long known, is the paradoxical law
of all sentiments having terror as a basis. And it might
have been for this reason only, that, when I again uplifted
my eyes to the house itself, from its image in the pool,
there grew in my mind a strange fancy—a fancy so ridiculous, indeed, that I but mention it to show the vivid
force of the sensations which oppressed me. I had so
worked upon my imagination as really to believe that
about the whole mansion and domain there hung an
atmosphere peculiar to themselves and their immediate
vicinity—an atmosphere which had not affinity with the
air of heaven, but which had reeked up from the decayed
trees, and the grey wall, and the silent tarn—a pestilent
and mystic vapour, dull, sluggish, faintly discernible, and
leaden-hued.

Shaking off from my spirit what *must* have been a
dream, I scanned more narrowly the real aspect of the

building. Its principal feature seemed to be that of an
excessive antiquity. The discoloration of ages had been
great. Minute fungi overspread the whole exterior,
hanging in a fine tangled web-work from the eaves. Yet
all this was apart from any extraordinary dilapidation.
No portion of the masonry had fallen; and there appeared to be a wild inconsistency between its still perfect
adaptation of parts, and the crumbling condition of the
individual stones. In this there was much that reminded
me of the specious totality of old woodwork which has
rotted for long years in some neglected vault, with no
disturbance from the breath of the external air. Beyond
this indication of extensive decay, however, the fabric
gave little token of instability. Perhaps the eye of a
scrutinising observer might have discovered a barely per-
ceptible fissure, which, extending from the roof of the
building in front, made its way down the wall in a zigzag direction, until it became lost in the sullen waters of
the tarn.

Noticing these things, I rode over a short causeway
to the house. A servant in waiting took my horse, and
I entered the Gothic archway of the hall. A valet, of
stealthy step, thence conducted me, in silence, through
many dark and intricate passages in my progress to the
studio of his master. Much that I encountered on the
way contributed, I know not how, to heighten the vague
sentiments of which I have already spoken. While the
objects around me—while the carvings of the ceilings,
the sombre tapestries of the walls, the ebon blackness
of the floors, and the phantasmagoric armorial trophies
which rattled as I strode, were but matters to which, or
to such as which, I had been accustomed from my infancy

—while I hesitated not to acknowledge how familiar was all this—I still wondered to find how unfamiliar were the fancies which ordinary images were stirring up. On one of the staircases I met the physician of the family. His countenance, I thought, wore a mingled expression of low cunning and perplexity. He accosted me with trepidation and passed on. The valet now threw open a door and ushered me into the presence of his master.

The room in which I found myself was very large and lofty. The windows were long, narrow, and pointed, and at so vast a distance from the black oaken floor as to be altogether inaccessible from within. Feeble gleams of encrimsoned light made their way through the trellised panes, and served to render sufficiently distinct the more prominent objects around; the eye, however, struggled in vain to reach the remoter angles of the chamber, or the recesses of the vaulted and fretted ceiling. Dark draperies hung upon the walls. The general furniture was profuse, comfortless, antique, and tattered. Many books and musical instruments lay scattered about, but failed to give any vitality to the scene. I felt that I breathed an atmosphere of sorrow. An air of stern, deep, and irredeemable gloom hung over and pervaded all.

Upon my entrance, Usher arose from a sofa on which he had been lying at full length, and greeted me with a vivacious warmth which had much in it, I at first thought, of an overdone cordiality—of the constrained effort of the *ennuyé* man of the world. A glance, however, at his countenance convinced me of his perfect sincerity. We sat down; and for some moments, while he spoke not, I gazed upon him with a feeling half of pity, half of awe. Surely, man had never before so terribly altered, in so brief a period, as had Roderick Usher! It was with difficulty that I could bring myself to admit the identity of the wan being before me with the companion of my early boyhood. Yet the character of his face had been at all times remarkable. A cadaverousness of complexion; an eye large, liquid, and luminous beyond comparison; lips somewhat thin and very pallid, but of a surpassingly beautiful curve; a nose of a delicate Hebrew model, but with a breadth of nostril unusual in similar formations; a finely moulded chin, speaking, in its want of prominence, of a want of moral energy; hair of a more than web-like softness and tenuity;—these features, with an inordinate expansion above the regions of the temple, made up altogether a countenance not easily to be forgotten. And now in the mere exaggeration of the prevailing character of these features, and of the expression they were wont to convey, lay so much of change that I doubted to whom I spoke. The now ghastly pallor of the skin, and the now miraculous lustre of the eye, above all things startled and even awed me. The silken hair, too, had been suffered to grow all unheeded, and as, in its wild gossamer texture, it floated rather than fell about the face, I could not, even with effort, connect its Arabesque expression with any idea of simple humanity.

In the manner of my friend I was at once struck with an incoherence—an inconsistency; and I soon found this to arise from a series of feeble and futile struggles to overcome an habitual trepidancy—an excess of nervous agitation. For something of this nature I had indeed been prepared, no less by his letter than by reminiscences of certain boyish traits, and by conclusions deduced from his peculiar physical conformation and temperament. His action was alternately vivacious and sullen. His voice varied rapidly from a tremulous indecision (when the animal spirits seemed utterly in abeyance) to that species of energetic concision—that abrupt, weighty, unhurried, and hollow-sounding enunciation — that leaden, self-balanced, and perfectly modulated guttural utterance, which may be observed in the lost drunkard, or the irreclaimable eater of opium during the periods of his most intense excitement.

It was thus that he spoke of the object of my visit, of his earnest desire to see me, and of the solace he expected me to afford him. He entered at some length into what he conceived to be the nature of his malady. "It was," he said, "a constitutional and a family evil, and one for which he despaired to find a remedy—a mere nervous affection," he immediately added, "which would undoubtedly soon pass off." It displayed itself in a host of unnatural sensations. Some of these, as he detailed them, interested and bewildered me; although, perhaps, the terms and the general manner of their narration had their weight. He suffered much from a morbid acuteness of the senses; the most insipid food was alone endurable; he could wear only garments of certain texture; the odours of all flowers were oppressive; his eyes were tortured by even a faint light; and there were but peculiar sounds, and these from stringed instruments, which did not inspire him with horror.

To an anomalous species of terror I found him a bounden slave. "I shall perish," said he, "I *must* perish in this deplorable folly. Thus, thus, and not otherwise, shall I be lost.   I dread the events of the future, not in themselves but in their results.   I shudder at the thought of any, even the most trivial, incident, which may operate upon this intolerable agitation of soul.   I have, indeed, no abhorrence of danger, except in its absolute effect—in terror.   In this unnerved, in this pitiable, condition I feel that the period will sooner or later arrive when I must abandon life and reason together, in some struggle with the grim phantasm—FEAR."

I learned, moreover, at intervals, and through broken and equivocal hints, another singular feature of his mental condition.   He was enchained by certain superstitious impressions in regard to the dwelling which he tenanted, and whence, for many years, he had never ventured forth —in regard to an influence whose supposititious force was conveyed in terms too shadowy here to be re-stated—an influence which some peculiarities in the mere form and substance of his family mansion had, by dint of long sufferance, he said, obtained over his spirit—an effect which the *physique* of the grey walls and turrets, and of the dim tarn into which they all looked down, had, at length, brought about upon the *morale* of his existence.

He admitted, however, although with hesitation, that much of the peculiar gloom which thus afflicted him could be traced to a more natural and far more palpable origin—to the severe and long-continued illness—indeed to the evidently approaching dissolution — of a tenderly beloved sister, his sole companion for long years, his last and only relative on earth.   "Her decease," he said, with a bitterness which I can never forget, "would leave him (him, the hopeless and the frail) the last of the ancient race of the Ushers."   While he spoke, the Lady Madeline (for so was she called) passed through a remote portion of the apartment, and, without having noticed my presence, disappeared. I regarded her with an utter astonishment, not unmingled with dread; and yet I found it impossible to account for such feelings. A sensation of stupor oppressed me as my eyes followed her retreating steps. When a door, at length, closed upon her, my glance sought instinctively and eagerly the countenance of the brother, but he had buried his face in his hands, and I could only perceive that a far more than ordinary wanness had overspread the emaciated fingers through which trickled many passionate tears.

The disease of the Lady Madeline had long baffled the skill of her physicians. A settled apathy, a gradual wasting away of the person, and frequent although transient affections of a partially cataleptical character were the unusual diagnosis. Hitherto she had steadily borne up against the pressure of her malady, and had not betaken herself finally to bed; but on the closing in of the evening of my arrival at the house, she succumbed (as her brother told me at night with inexpressible agitation) to the prostrating power of the destroyer; and I learned that the glimpse I had obtained of her person would thus probably be the last I should obtain—that the lady, at least while living, would be seen by me no more.

For several days ensuing, her name was unmentioned by either Usher or myself; and during this period I was busied in earnest endeavours to alleviate the melancholy of my friend. We painted and read together, or I listened, as if in a dream, to the wild improvisations of his speaking guitar. And thus, as a closer and still closer intimacy admitted me more unreservedly into the recesses of his spirit, the more bitterly did I perceive the futility of all attempt at cheering a mind from which darkness, as if an inherent positive quality, poured forth upon all objects of the moral and physical universe in one unceasing radiation of gloom.

I shall ever bear about me a memory of the many solemn hours I thus spent alone with the master of the House of Usher.   Yet I should fail in any attempt to convey an idea of the exact character of the studies, or of the occupations, in which he involved me, or led me the way.   An excited and highly distempered ideality threw a sulphureous lustre over all.   His long improvised dirges will ring for ever in my ears.   Among other things, I hold painfully in mind a certain singular perversion and amplification of the wild air of the last waltz of Von Weber.   From the paintings over which his elaborate fancy brooded, and which grew, touch by touch, into vaguenesses at which I shuddered the more thrillingly, because I shuddered knowing not why—from these paintings (vivid as their images now are before me) I would in vain endeavour to educe more than a small portion which should lie within the compass of merely written words.   By the utter simplicity, by the nakedness of his designs, he arrested and overawed attention.   If ever mortal painted an idea, that mortal was Roderick Usher. For me, at least, in the circumstances then surrounding me, there arose out of the pure abstractions which the hypochondriac contrived to throw upon his canvas, an intensity of intolerable awe, no shadow of which felt I ever yet in the contemplation of the certainly glowing yet too concrete reveries of Fuseli.

One of the phantasmagoric conceptions of my friend,

partaking not so rigidly of the spirit of abstraction, may be shadowed forth, although feebly, in words. A small picture presented the interior of an immensely long and rectangular vault or tunnel, with low walls, smooth, white, and without interruption or device. Certain accessory points of the design served well to convey the idea that this excavation lay at an exceeding depth below the surface of the earth. No outlet was observed in any portion of its vast extent, and no torch or other artificial source of light was discernible; yet a flood of intense rays rolled throughout, and bathed the whole in a ghastly and inappropriate splendour.

I have just spoken of that morbid condition of the auditory nerve which rendered all music intolerable to the sufferer, with the exception of certain effects of stringed instruments. It was, perhaps, the narrow limits to which he thus confined himself upon the guitar which gave birth, in great measure, to the fantastic character of his performances. But the fervid *facility* of his *impromptus* could not be so accounted for. They must have been, and were, in the notes, as well as in the words of his wild fantasias (for he not unfrequently accompanied himself with rhymed verbal improvisations), the result of that intense mental collectedness and concentration to which I have previously alluded as observable only in particular moments of the highest artificial excitement. The words of one of these rhapsodies I have easily remembered. I was, perhaps, the more forcibly impressed with it as he gave it, because in the under or mystic current of its meaning, I fancied that I perceived, and for the first time, a full consciousness on the part of Usher of the tottering of his lofty reason

upon her throne. The verses, which were entitled
"The Haunted Palace," ran very nearly, if not accurately, thus—

I.

" In the greenest of our valleys,
   By good angels tenanted,
Once a fair and stately palace—
   Radiant palace—reared its head.
In the monarch Thought's dominion—
   It stood there !
Never seraph spread a pinion
   Over fabric half so fair.

II.

Banners yellow, glorious, golden,
   On its roof did float and flow
(This—all this—was in the olden
   Time long ago) ;
And every gentle air that dallied,
   In that sweet day,
Along the ramparts plumed and pallid,
   A wingèd odour went away.

III.

Wanderers in that happy valley
   Through two luminous windows saw
Spirits moving musically
   To a lute's well-tunèd law ;
Round about a throne, where sitting
   (Porphyrogene !)
In state his glory well befitting,
   The ruler of the realm was seen.

IV.

And all with pearl and ruby glowing
   Was the fair palace door,
Through which came flowing, flowing, flowing,
   And sparkling evermore,

O

A troop of Echoes whose sweet duty
   Was but to sing,
In voices of surpassing beauty,
   The wit and wisdom of their king.

v.

But evil things, in robes of sorrow,
   Assailed the monarch's high estate;
(Ah, let us mourn, for never morrow
   Shall dawn upon him, desolate!)
And, round about his home, the glory
   That blushed and bloomed
Is but a dim-remembered story
   Of the old time entombed.

vi.

And travellers now within that valley,
   Through the red-litten windows see
Vast forms that move fantastically
   To a discordant melody;
While, like a rapid ghastly river,
   Through the pale door,
A hideous throng rush out for ever,
   And laugh—but smile no more."

I well remember that suggestions arising from this ballad led us into a train of thought wherein there became manifest an opinion of Usher's, which I mention not so much on account of its novelty (for other men [1] have thought thus), as on account of the pertinacity with which he maintained it. This opinion, in its general form, was that of the sentience of all vegetable things. But, in his disordered fancy, the idea had assumed a more daring character, and trespassed, under certain con-

[1] Watson, Dr. Percival, Spallanzani, and especially the Bishop of Llandaff.—See "Chemical Essays," vol. v.

ditions, upon the kingdom of inorganisation.   I lack
words to express the full extent, or the earnest *abandon*
of his persuasion.   The belief, however, was connected
(as I have previously hinted) with the grey stones of the
home of his forefathers.   The conditions of the sentence
had been here, he imagined, fulfilled in the method of
collocation of these stones—in the order of their arrangement, as well as in that of the many fungi which overspread them, and of the decayed trees which stood around
—above all, in the long undisturbed endurance of this
arrangement, and in its reduplication in the still waters
of the tarn.   Its evidence—the evidence of the sentience
—was to be seen, he said (and I here started as he spoke),
in the gradual yet certain condensation of an atmosphere
of their own about the waters and the walls.   The
result was discoverable, he added, in that silent yet
importunate and terrible influence which for centuries
had moulded the destinies of his family, and which made
him what I now saw him—what he was.   Such opinions
need no comment, and I will make none.

Our books—the books which for years had formed
no small portion of the mental existence of the invalid—
were, as might be supposed, in strict keeping with this
character of phantasm.   We pored together over such
works as the " Ververt et Chartreuse " of Gresset ; the
" Belphegor " of Machiavelli ; the " Heaven and Hell "
of Swedenborg ; the " Subterranean Voyage of Nicholas
Klimm " by Holberg ; the " Chiromancy " of Robert
Fludd, of Jean D'Indaginé, and of De la Chambre ; the
" Journey into the Blue Distance " of Tieck ; and the
" City of the Sun " of Campanella.   One favourite
volume was a small octavo edition of the " Directorium

Inquisitorium," by the Dominican Eymeric de Gironne; and there were passages in Pomponius Mela about the old African Satyrs and Œgipans, over which Usher would sit dreaming for hours. His chief delight, however, was found in the perusal of an exceedingly rare and curious book in quarto Gothic—the manual of a forgotten church —the *Vigiliæ Mortuorum secundum Chorum Ecclesiæ Maguntinæ.*

I could not help thinking of the wild ritual of this work, and of its probable influence upon the hypochondriac, when, one evening, having informed me abruptly that the Lady Madeline was no more, he stated his intention of preserving her corpse for a fortnight (previously to its final interment) in one of the numerous vaults within the main walls of the building. The worldly reason, however, assigned for this singular proceeding was one which I did not feel at liberty to dispute. The brother had been led to his resolution (so he told me) by consideration of the unusual character of the malady of the deceased, of certain obtrusive and eager inquiries on the part of her medical men, and of the remote and exposed situation of the burial-ground of the family. I will not deny that when I called to mind the sinister countenance of the person whom I met upon the staircase, on the day of my arrival at the house, I had no desire to oppose what I regarded as at best but a harmless, and by no means an unnatural, precaution.

At the request of Usher, I personally aided him in the arrangements for the temporary entombment. The body having been encoffined, we two alone bore it to its rest. The vault in which we placed it (and which had been so long unopened that our torches, half-smothered

in its oppressive atmosphere, gave us little opportunity
for investigation) was small, damp, and entirely without
means of admission for light; lying, at great depth,
immediately beneath that portion of the building in
which was my own sleeping apartment.   It had been
used, apparently, in remote feudal times, for the worst
purposes of a donjon-keep, and, in later days, as a place
of deposit for powder, or some other highly combustible
substance, as a portion of its floor, and the whole interior
of a long archway through which we reached it, were
carefully sheathed with copper.   The door, of massive
iron, had been also similarly protected.   Its immense
weight caused an unusually sharp, grating sound, as it
moved upon its hinges.

Having deposited our mournful burden upon tressels
within this region of horror, we partially turned aside
the yet unscrewed lid of the coffin, and looked upon the
face of the tenant.   A striking similitude between the
brother and sister now first arrested my attention; and
Usher, divining, perhaps, my thoughts, murmured out
some few words from which I learned that the deceased
and himself had been twins, and that sympathies of a
scarcely intelligible nature had always existed between
them.   Our glances, however, rested not long upon the
dead—for we could not regard her unawed.   The disease
which had thus entombed the lady in the maturity of
youth, had left, as usual in all maladies of a strictly
cataleptical character, the mockery of a faint blush upon
the bosom and the face, and that suspiciously lingering
smile upon the lip which is so terrible in death.   We
replaced and screwed down the lid, and, having secured
the door of iron, made our way, with toil, into the

scarcely less gloomy apartments of the upper portion of the house.

And now, some days of bitter grief having elapsed, an observable change came over the features of the mental disorder of my friend. His ordinary manner had vanished. His ordinary occupations were neglected or forgotten. He roamed from chamber to chamber with hurried, unequal, and objectless step. The pallor of his countenance had assumed, if possible, a more ghastly hue— but the luminousness of his eye had utterly gone out. The once occasional huskiness of his tone was heard no more; and a tremulous quaver, as if of extreme terror, habitually characterised his utterance. There were times, indeed, when I thought his unceasingly agitated mind was labouring with some oppressive secret, to divulge which he struggled for the necessary courage. At times, again, I was obliged to resolve all into the mere inexplicable vagaries of madness, for I beheld him gazing upon vacancy for long hours, in an attitude of the profoundest attention, as if listening to some imaginary sound. It was no wonder that his condition terrified—that it affected me. I felt creeping upon me, by slow yet certain degrees, the wild influences of his own fantastic yet impressive superstitions.

It was, especially, upon retiring to bed late in the night of the seventh or eighth day after the placing of the Lady Madeline within the donjon, that I experienced the full power of such feelings. Sleep came not near my couch—while the hours waned and waned away. I struggled to reason off the nervousness which had dominion over me. I endeavoured to believe that much, if not all of what I felt, was due to the bewildering influ-

ence of the gloomy furniture of the room—of the dark
and tattered draperies, which, tortured into motion by
the breath of a rising tempest, swayed fitfully to and
fro upon the walls, and rustled uneasily about the deco-
rations of the bed. But my efforts were fruitless. An
irrepressible tremor gradually pervaded my frame; and,
at length, there sat upon my very heart an incubus of
utterly causeless alarm. Shaking this off with a gasp and
a struggle, I uplifted myself upon the pillows, and,
peering earnestly within the intense darkness of the
chamber, hearkened—I know not why, except that an
instinctive spirit prompted me—to certain low and indefinite sounds which came, through the pauses of the
storm, at long intervals, I knew not whence. Overpowered by an intense sentiment of horror, unaccountable
yet unendurable, I threw on my clothes with haste (for I
felt that I should sleep no more during the night), and
endeavoured to arouse myself from the pitiable condition
into which I had fallen, by pacing rapidly to and fro
through the apartment.

I had taken but few turns in this manner, when a
light step on an adjoining staircase arrested my attention. I presently recognised it as that of Usher. In an
instant afterwards he rapped, with a gentle touch, at my
door, and entered, bearing a lamp. His countenance was,
as usual, cadaverously wan—but, moreover, there was a
species of mad hilarity in his eyes—an evidently restrained
hysteria in his whole demeanour. His air appalled me—
but anything was preferable to the solitude which I had
so long endured, and I even welcomed his presence as a
relief.

"And you have not seen it?" he said abruptly, after

having stared about him for some moments in silence—
"you have not then seen it?—but stay! you shall."
Thus speaking, and having carefully shaded his lamp,
he hurried to one of the casements, and threw it freely
open to the storm.

The impetuous fury of the entering gust nearly lifted
us from our feet. It was, indeed, a tempestuous yet
sternly beautiful night, and one wildly singular in its
terror and its beauty. A whirlwind had apparently
collected its force in our vicinity; for there were frequent and violent alterations in the direction of the
wind; and the exceeding density of the clouds (which
hung so low as to press upon the turrets of the house)
did not prevent our perceiving the lifelike velocity with
which they flew careering from all points against each
other, without passing away into the distance. I say
that even their exceeding density did not prevent our
perceiving this—yet we had no glimpse of the moon or
stars, nor was there any flashing forth of the lightning.
But the under surfaces of the huge masses of agitated
vapour, as well as all terrestrial objects immediately
around us, were glowing in the unnatural light of a
faintly luminous and distinctly visible gaseous exhalation
which hung about and enshrouded the mansion.

"You must not—you shall not behold this!" said
I, shuddering, to Usher, as I led him, with a gentle
violence, from the window to a seat. "These appearances, which bewilder you, are merely electrical pheno-
mena, not uncommon — or it may be that they have
their ghastly origin in the rank miasma of the tarn.
Let us close this casement; the air is chilling and dangerous to your frame. Here is one of your favourite

romances.   I will read and you shall listen ; and so we
will pass away this terrible night together."

The antique volume which I had taken up was the
"Mad Trist" of Sir Launcelot Canning; but I had called it
a favourite of Usher's more in sad jest than in earnest ; for,
in truth, there is little in its uncouth and unimaginative
prolixity which could have had interest for the lofty and
spiritual ideality of my friend.   It was, however, the only
book immediately at hand, and I indulged a vague hope
that the excitement which now agitated the hypochondriac
might find relief (for the history of mental disorder is
full of similar anomalies) even in the extremeness of the
folly which I should read.   Could I have judged, indeed,
by the wild overstrained air of vivacity with which he
hearkened, or apparently hearkened, to the words of the
tale, I might well have congratulated myself upon the
success of my design.

I had arrived at that well-known portion of the story
where Ethelred, the hero of the Trist, having sought in
vain for peaceable admission into the dwelling of the
hermit, proceeds to make good an entrance by force.
Here, it will be remembered, the words of the narrative
run thus :—

"And Ethelred, who was by nature of a doughty
heart, and who was now mighty withal, on account of
the powerfulness of the wine which he had drunken,
waited no longer to hold parley with the hermit, who,
in sooth, was of an obstinate and maliceful turn, but,
feeling the rain upon his shoulders, and fearing the rising
of the tempest, uplifted his mace outright, and, with
blows, made quickly room in the plankings of the door
for his gauntleted hand ; and now pulling therewith stur-

dily, he so cracked, and ripped, and tore all asunder, that the noise of the dry and hollow-sounding wood alarmed and reverberated throughout the forest."

At the termination of this sentence I started and, for a moment, paused; for it appeared to me (although I at once concluded that my excited fancy had deceived me) —it appeared to me that, from some very remote portion of the mansion, there came, indistinctly to my ears, what might have been, in its exact similarity of character, the echo (but a stifled and dull one certainly) of the very cracking and ripping sound which Sir Launcelot had so particularly described. It was, beyond doubt, the coincidence alone which had arrested my attention; for, amid the rattling of the sashes of the casements, and the ordinary commingled noises of the still increasing storm, the sound, in itself, had nothing, surely, which should have interested or disturbed me. I continued the story:—

"But the good champion Ethelred, now entering within the door, was sore enraged and amazed to perceive no signal of the maliceful hermit; but, in the stead thereof, a dragon of a scaly and prodigious demeanour, and of fiery tongue, which sate in guard before a palace of gold, with a floor of silver: and upon the wall there hung a shield of shining brass with this legend enwritten—

Who entereth herein, a conqueror hath bin;
Who slayeth the dragon, the shield he shall win.

And Ethelred uplifted his mace, and struck upon the head of the dragon, which fell before him, and gave up his pesty breath, with a shriek so horrid and harsh, and withal so piercing, that Ethelred had fain to close his ears with his hands against the dreadful noise of it, the like whereof was never heard before."

Here again I paused abruptly, and now with a feeling of wild amazement, for there could be no doubt whatever that, in this instance, I did actually hear (although from what direction it proceeded I found it impossible to say) a low and apparently distant but harsh, protracted, and most unusual screaming or grating sound, the exact counterpart of what my fancy had already conjured up for the dragon's unnatural shriek as described by the romancer.

Oppressed, as I certainly was, upon the occurrence of this second and most extraordinary coincidence, by a thousand conflicting sensations, in which wonder and extreme terror were predominant, I still retained sufficient presence of mind to avoid exciting, by any observation, the sensitive nervousness of my companion. I was by no means certain that he had noticed the sounds in question; although, assuredly, a strange alteration had, during the last few minutes, taken place in his demeanour. From a position fronting my own, he had gradually brought round his chair, so as to sit with his face to the door of the chamber; and thus I could but partially perceive his features, although I saw that his lips trembled as if he were murmuring inaudibly. His head had dropped upon his breast, yet I knew that he was not asleep, from the wide and rigid opening of the eye as I caught a glance of it in profile. The motion of his body, too, was at variance with this idea, for he rocked from side to side with a gentle yet constant and uniform sway. Having rapidly taken notice of all this, I resumed the narrative of Sir Launcelot, which thus proceeded:

"And now, the champion, having escaped from the terrible fury of the dragon, bethinking himself of the brazen shield, and of the breaking up of the enchantment which was upon it, removed the carcass from out of the way before him, and approached valorously over the silver pavement of the castle to where the shield was upon the wall; which in sooth tarried not for his full coming, but fell down at his feet upon the silver floor, with a mighty great and terrible ringing sound."

No sooner had these syllables passed my lips than—as if a shield of brass had indeed, at the moment, fallen heavily upon a floor of silver—I became aware of a distinct, hollow, metallic, and clangorous, yet apparently muffled reverberation. Completely unnerved, I leaped to my feet; but the measured rocking movement of Usher was undisturbed. I rushed to the chair in which he sat. His eyes were bent fixedly before him, and throughout his whole countenance there reigned a stony rigidity. But, as I placed my hand upon his shoulder, there came a strong shudder over his whole person; a sickly smile quivered about his lips; and I saw that he spoke in a low, hurried, and gibbering murmur, as if unconscious of my presence. Bending closely over him, I at length drank in the hideous import of his words.

"Not hear it?—yes, I hear it, and *have* heard it. Long—long—long—many minutes, many hours, many days, have I heard it—yet I dared not—oh, pity me, miserable wretch that I am!—I dared not—I *dared* not speak! *We have put her living in the tomb!* Said I not that my senses were acute? I *now* tell you that I heard her first feeble movements in the hollow coffin. I heard them—many, many days ago—yet I dared not—

I dared not speak! And now—to-night—Ethelred—
ha! ha!—the breaking of the hermit's door, and the
death-cry of the dragon, and the clangour of the shield—
say, rather, the rending of her coffin, and the grating of
the iron hinges of her prison, and her struggles within
the coppered archway of the vault! Oh! whither shall
I fly? Will she not be here anon? Is she not hurrying
to upbraid me for my haste? Have I not heard her
footstep on the stair? Do I not distinguish that heavy and
horrible beating of her heart? Madman!"—here he
sprang furiously to his feet, and shrieked out his syllables,
as if in the effort he were giving up his soul—"*Madman!
I tell you that she now stands without the door!*"

As if in the superhuman energy of his utterance there
had been found the potency of a spell, the huge antique
panels to which the speaker pointed threw slowly back,
upon the instant, their ponderous and ebony jaws. It
was the work of the rushing gust—but then without
those doors there *did* stand the lofty and enshrouded
figure of the Lady Madeline of Usher. There was blood
upon her white robes, and the evidence of some bitter
struggle upon every portion of her emaciated frame. For
a moment she remained trembling and reeling to and fro
upon the threshold—then, with a low moaning cry, fell
heavily inward upon the person of her brother, and in
her violent and now final death-agonies, bore him to
the floor a corpse, and a victim to the terrors he had
anticipated.

From that chamber, and from that mansion, I fled
aghast. The storm was still abroad in all its wrath as
I found myself crossing the old causeway. Suddenly
there shot along the path a wild light, and I turned to

see whence a gleam so unusual could have issued ; for the vast house and its shadows were alone behind me. The radiance was that of the full, setting, and blood-red moon, which now shone vividly through that once barely discernible fissure, of which I have before spoken as extending from the roof of the building, in a zigzag direction, to the base. While I gazed, this fissure rapidly widened —there came a fierce breath of the whirlwind—the entire orb of the satellite burst at once upon my sight—my brain reeled as I saw the mighty walls rushing asunder—there was a long tumultuous shouting sound like the voice of a thousand waters—and the deep and dank tarn at my feet closed sullenly and silently over the fragments of the House of Usher.

X

THE "OLD BACHELOR'S" NIGHTCAP

By Hans Christian Andersen

THERE is a street in Copenhagen which is known by the curious name of Hysken Street. But why is it called so? and what can Hysken mean? It is really a German word, though one would not think so. "Häuschen" the street ought to be called, and that means "small houses." For in this street, for many years, the houses were just like the wooden booths you may still see in the market-places; a little bigger they were, indeed, and they had windows, but then these windows were only made of horn or bladder-skin, for at that time glass windows were too dear for them to be seen in every house. Those days are so long gone by, that my grandfather's grandfather, whenever he spoke of them, always called them "the old, old days;" it was hundreds of years ago.

The rich merchants of Bremen and Lübeck used to trade with Copenhagen; not going thither themselves, but sending their clerks, who lived in the wooden booths in the "Street of Small Houses," and sold their ale and spices; many kinds of good German ale, and all sorts of spices, saffron, anise, ginger, and above all, pepper. It

was this that they chiefly sold, so that the German clerk
in Denmark was called a " pepper dealer." Before they
left home they had to promise that they would not marry
while they were away; many of them, too, were very old,
and they had to look after themselves, find for themselves, and light their own fires, if they had any; so it
was that some of them grew such queer old fellows, with
their own peculiar thoughts and ways; and it is because
of them that men who grow old without having married
are called " Pebersvend," or " Pepper-dealers." All this
can be seen and understood in this story.

People make fun of the pepper-dealers, bidding them
go put their nightcaps on, pull them down over their
eyes, and go to bed—

> " Oh fie ! you pepper-seller !
> Put up your green umbrella !
> Go to bed with your nightcap on,
> Put out your light, and you'll have none ! "

Yes, that is what they sing about them ! They laugh
at the pepper-dealer and his nightcap, just because they
know nothing about either one or the other. Alas! it
is a nightcap no one need wish for! And why so?
Well, listen, and you shall hear.

In the "Street of Small Houses," in the old times,
there was no pavement; people stumbled out of one hole
into another, as though it were a dirty cart-track, and it
was very narrow. The booths stood close beside each
other, and with so little distance between the two rows,
that in the summer time they stretched a sail from one
side of the street to the other, and then the air was more
full than ever of the spicy smells of pepper and saffron
and ginger.

Behind the counters there stood no brisk young clerks; no, they were mostly old fellows, who did not go dressed, as you would think, in a wig or nightcap, with knee-breeches and waistcoat, or a coat buttoned up to the chin, just as we have seen our great-grandfathers painted; no, the pepper-dealers had no money to get themselves painted, but all the same they would have made a picture well worth the having, as they stood behind their counters, or as they went to church on holy-days. They wore high-crowned hats, with wide brims, and often the youngest clerks stuck a feather in as well; the woollen shirt was hidden under a falling linen collar, the coat was closely buttoned up, and the cloak hung loosely over it; the trousers were tucked into the square-toed shoes, for they wore no stockings. In their belts they carried a table-knife and spoon, and a big knife as well for protection, as was very needful in those times.

Just in this way old Anthony, the oldest clerk in the whole street, went clad on feast days, only he wore no high-crowned hat, but a kind of bonnet, under which he drew on a nightcap—a regular nightcap, which he was so used to wearing, that he actually had two of the same kind.

He made just the figure to paint, he was so thin, so wrinkled about the mouth and eyes; he had long knotted fingers and bushy grey eyebrows, while over his left eye there hung a great tuft of hair. It was not handsome, but it made him the more remarkable. People knew of him that he had come from Bremen, where his employer lived, but that he had not been born there. His home had been in Thuringia, in the town of Eisenach, under the Wartburg. Old Anthony did not speak much of all this, but he thought the more.

P

The old clerks in the street did not often meet together; each one lived in his little house, that was closed early in the evening, when all looked very dismal. Only a dull faint light shone through the little horn window in the roof, while within sat the old fellow often on his bed, with his old German song-book, and sang his evening hymn, or else trotted about down below, putting all to rights among his wares. It was certainly not very pleasant; to be a stranger in a strange land is a bitter lot; no one takes much account of you, unless you happen to get in their way.

Sometimes on a very dark night, when there was rain or mist, it was very dreary and deserted. There were no lights to be seen, except one very little one, right at the top of the street, before a picture of the Blessed Virgin, that was painted on the wall. You could hear the sound of the waves ceaselessly splashing and beating against the wooden piles, out at Slotsholm, past the turn at the far end of the street. Such evenings would be long and lonely if there was nothing to do. Packing and unpacking, making paper bags and polishing scales—these things were not to be done every day; something else must be found, and this old Anthony did; he himself mended his clothes and patched his shoes. When at last he went to bed, still with his nightcap on, he had only to pull it a little farther down; but in a minute he was sure to push it up again, to see if the light was properly put out; then he would feel for it, pinch the wick, and then turn round to the other side, pulling his nightcap down. Then something else would be sure to occur to him; whether every coal was quite burned out and quenched in the little fire-pan downstairs, and whether some tiny spark might not remain, and, by setting light to something, work him great mischief. At that thought he would get out of bed and creep to the ladder, for it could not be called a stair, and when he reached the fire-pan there would not be a spark to be seen, so that he must just go back again. But as soon as he had got half way he would begin to wonder if the doors were all fast and the shutters bolted; so his poor thin legs must carry him back to see, and, as he crept back to bed, he froze, and his teeth chattered, for the last nip the cold gives one is always the sharpest.

Then he would pull the bedclothes higher up, and his nightcap farther down over his eyes, and turn away his thoughts from the day's work and business. But small comfort he would get, for then came old memories and hung their curtains up, and sometimes they brought pins as well, which pricked sadly. "Oh, oh!" cry the poor souls who lie awake, when the pins are driven sharply in, and tears fall from their eyes. All these things came to poor old Anthony, and he wept hot tears like the clearest pearls; they fell down over the coverlet and on to the floor, with a sound as if pain were breaking the strings of the heart. When the tear vanished, then a flame sprang in its place, and lit up a picture of life that had never faded from his heart. If he wiped his eyes with his nightcap the tear and the picture would be crushed, but the source of them remained, for it lay in his heart. The pictures did not come in the same order as in the life whose reflection they were; the most painful ones came oftenest, but the happy ones were the saddest to him, for they cast the deepest shadow.

"How beautiful are the beech-woods of Denmark!"

they say; but more beautiful seemed to Anthony the beech-woods around the Wartburg; mightier and more venerable seemed to him the old oaks round the great castle, where the climbing plants hung in festoons on the granite rocks of the cliffs. Sweeter to him its apple-blossoms than any in the Danish land; he could still distinctly smell their pure fragrance. Then a tear rose and fell, and the light shone; he saw plainly two little children, a boy and a girl, playing. The boy had rosy cheeks, yellow curling hair, and honest blue eyes—it was the rich merchant's son, little Anthony himself. The little girl had brown eyes and black hair; bright and clever she looked; it was the Burgomaster's daughter, Molly. The two children were playing with an apple; they shook it and listened to the pips rattling inside. Then they cut it in two, and each of them had half; they ate it up and the pips as well, all but one, which they must put into the earth, said the little girl.

"Then you will see that something will come up, something you would never expect; a whole apple-tree will come up, only not at once."

And they planted the pip in a flower-pot; both of them were very busy over it; the boy made a hole in the earth with his finger, the little girl put in the pip, and they both pushed the earth back over it.

"Now you must not take it out in the morning to see if it has a root," she said; "one must never do that! I did it with my flowers, only twice, just to see if they were growing, for then I knew no better, and the flowers died."

Anthony kept the flower-pot, and every morning, all through the winter, he looked at it; but there was nothing to be seen but the brown earth. Soon, however, came the spring, and the sun shone as warm as could be, and then there peeped out of the flower-pot two small green leaves.

"That is me and Molly!" said Anthony. "That is wonderful! that is beautiful!"

Soon there came out a third leaf. Who could that be for? But there came another and yet another! Every day it grew stronger and stronger, and the plant became a little tree. And all this was pictured in a single tear that was brushed away and disappeared; but it might come again from its source—from old Anthony's heart.

Near Eisenach there is a great ridge of stony mountains; one of them stands out from the rest with a rounded top, bare of trees or bushes or grass. This one is called the Venusberg, and within it lives Lady Venus, a goddess of heathen times; Lady Holle she is called now, and that every child in Eisenach knows. She it was who enticed the noble knight, Tannhäuser, the Minnesinger, into her mountain, away from the minstrels of the Wartburg.

Little Molly and Anthony sometimes found themselves on the mountain, and once she said to him, "Dare you climb up and say, 'Lady Holle! Lady Holle! look out, here is Tannhäuser!'" But Anthony did not dare; Molly did; but she only said the words "Lady Holle, Lady Holle!" out loud and clearly, the rest she said so softly under her breath, that Anthony was quite sure she had said nothing at all.

Yet so bold as she looked, and so saucy, just as she did sometimes when she and some other little girls met him in the gardens; then they all would try and kiss him, just because he didn't like it, and would try to knock them away: then she alone would dare to do it.

"I may kiss him!" she would say proudly, and throw her arms round his neck. That was just her vanity, and Anthony would put up with it, and never think of it twice. How pretty she was, and how daring! Lady Holle in the mountain was beautiful too, but her beauty was that of a tempting witch. The highest beauty was that of the holy Elizabeth, the pious Thuringian princess, the guardian saint of the land, whose good deeds, remembered in tale and legend, have made famous many a place; her picture hung in the chapel with silver lamps all around; but Molly was not in the least like her.

The apple-tree that the two children had planted grew year by year, till at length it was so tall it must be transplanted into the garden, out in the fresh air, where the dew fell and the sun shone warm. There it gained strength to stand against the winter, and after the winter's hard trial was over, it covered itself with blossoms for very joy. In the autumn it had two apples, one for Molly and one for Anthony; it could hardly do less.

As the tree grew, so did Molly, and she was as fresh as an apple-blossom. But not for much longer could Anthony look on this flower. Everything alters, everything changes! Molly's father left the old home, and Molly followed him far away — nowadays indeed it would only be a journey of a few hours, but at that time it took more than a night and a day to travel so far eastward from Eisenach, that lay on the furthest border of Thuringia, to the town that is still called Weimar.

Then Molly wept and Anthony wept; but all the

tears ran into one big one, that had joy's red lovely light.
Molly had told him that she thought more of him than
of all the splendours of Weimar.

One year went by, then two, then three; and in all
that time there came two letters. The first was brought
by a carrier, the second by a traveller. It was a hard
journey, a long road winding past towns and villages.

How often had not Anthony and Molly listened
together to the story of Tristan and Isolde, and just so
often he had likened himself to Tristan, although the
name meant "born in sorrow," which he himself certainly
was not; nor would he ever have to say, as Tristan did,
"She has forgotten me!" But yet Isolde had not really
forgotten the friend of her heart, and when they were
both dead, and buried side by side in the churchyard, two
linden trees grew out of their graves high over the church
roof, and mixed their flowering branches there. That was
so pretty, thought Anthony, but so sad! but it could never
be sad with him and Molly, and he whistled a verse of
the Minnesinger, Walther von der Vogelweide :—

> " Under the linden tree,
> There by the heath."

And this, too, he thought so beautiful—

> " Out in the woods, in the quiet dale,
>   Tandaradai !
> Sang to himself a nightingale ! "

This verse was always in his head, and he sang and
whistled it one moonshiny night as he, on horseback in
the deep-sunk road, set off for Weimar to visit Molly ;

unexpected he wished to come, and so he arrived unexpected.

He had a welcome! wine filled high in the great tankards, lively company of the very best, a beautiful chamber, and a soft bed; and yet it was not what he had so often thought and dreamed of. He did not understand himself, and he did not understand the others. But we can understand it! One can live in a house and family, and yet not become one of them. People can talk together as one talks in a stage-coach, know each other as one does in a stage-coach, weary each other, and each man wish either himself or his good neighbour away. Something of all this Anthony felt.

"I am an honourable girl," said Molly to him, "and I will tell you all. Everything has changed since we were children; all is different both within and without, and custom and one's own will have no power over the heart! Anthony! I would not have an enemy in you; now, when I am going far away, believe me, I have always kind thoughts of you; but as to loving you as I now know one can love another, that I have never done! and you will have to get used to it! Farewell, Anthony!"

And Anthony, too, said farewell; tears came to his eyes, but he understood that he was no longer Molly's friend. Hot iron and cold iron both take the skin from our lips with the same sensation when we kiss them, and Anthony burnt as fiercely now in hatred as he had in love.

In less than four and twenty hours Anthony was at home again in Eisenach, but the horse that he rode was quite ruined. "What does it matter?" he said; "I am ruined, and I will ruin everything that can remind me of her—Lady Holle, Lady Venus, thou heathen woman!

I will tear down and break the apple-tree, and pull it up by the roots; never more shall it blossom or bear fruit!"

But he never struck down the tree, for he himself was stricken down by a fever, and lay on his bed. What could help him up again? A medicine came that was powerful enough, the bitterest possible, as he found whose sick body and shrinking soul were alike wrung by it. Anthony's father was no longer the rich merchant; dark days, days of trial, stood at the door; misfortune rushed in and overwhelmed in its floods the once prosperous house. His father was now a poor man, and trouble and sorrow crushed him. So that Anthony had something else to think of beside nursing his grief and rage against Molly. He must be both father and mother in the house; must give orders and assistance, act with decision, and at last go out into the wide world and work for his bread.

He came to Bremen, endured want and dark days—days which sometimes harden the heart, and sometimes make it soft, only too soft. How far different was the world and the people in it from what he had thought them in the days of his childhood! What to him now were the Minnesinger's verses? Just a tinkling of words, mere wasted breath; yes, that was what he thought! Sometimes, however, their music stole into his soul, and he became gentle of heart again.

"God's will is best," he would say then. "How well it was that Molly's heart did not cleave to me. Whatever should we have done now that the luck has turned. She sent me away before she knew or dreamed of the misfortunes that have come upon me. That was the will of Heaven for me; everything is for the best; everything is ordered wisely; she could not help it, and yet I have been so bitter against her."

And the years went by. Anthony's father was dead, and strangers lived in his father's house. But Anthony was to see it again, for his rich employer sent him travelling on business, and so he came to his native town—Eisenach. The old Wartburg stood up there on the mountain just the same, with the great stones, the "monk and the nun"; the huge oak-trees spread the same beauty over all as in his childhood. The Venusberg stood up bare and grey from among the valleys. How willingly he would have called: "Lady Holle, Lady Holle! open your mountain; I will stay with you in my own land!"

But that was a wicked thought, and he made the sign of the cross on his bosom. Then a little bird sang in the bushes, and the old song came into his head—

> " Out in the woods, in the quiet dale,
>   Tandaradai!
> Sang to himself a nightingale!"

He remembered so much, now when he saw his old home, that he had to look through tears. His father's house stood as before, but the garden was changed. A new road cut off one corner of it, and the apple-tree, that he had never torn down, stood there still, but now outside the garden, and on the other side of the road. Still the sun shone there, and the dew fell there, and it bore fruit, so the branches were weighed down to the ground.

"Ay, it thrives!" said he; "well for it!"

One of the great branches had been broken, rough hands had plucked at it, for it stood on the public road.

"Men may break off its blossoms without saying thank you; they may steal the fruit and break the boughs. If one might speak so of a tree—it was never foretold at the cradle that it should stand like this. Its story opened so fairly, and now what is its lot? Forsaken and forgotten, a garden tree in a ditch by a public road! There it stands with no protection, plundered and torn! Not yet has it faded, but year by year its blossoms will be fewer, its fruit less and less, until at last—ay, then its story will be done!"

So thought Anthony as he stood under the tree, and so he thought many a night in his lonely little room in the wooden booth in the strange town of Copenhagen, whither his rich employer, the Bremen merchant, had sent him, on condition that he should not marry.

"Marry! ha, ha!" and he laughed bitterly to himself.

The winter came early, and it froze hard; out of doors there was a snow-storm, so that every one who could stayed indoors. So it happened that Anthony's neighbour over the way never noticed that his booth had not been opened for two whole days, and that he himself had not been seen, for who would go out in such weather when he could stay at home?

Those were grey, dark days, and in houses where the windows were not made of glass twilight and pitch dark reigned by turns. Old Anthony had not left his bed for two days, he had no strength for it. For a long time past the hard weather had benumbed his limbs. Forsaken lay the old bachelor; he could not help himself, barely could he reach to the water-jug he had placed by his bedside, and now the last drop was gone. No fever or sickness had brought him down, nothing but old age. It was all the time dark night in the little corner where he lay. A little spider, that he could not see, worked busily, and spun his web just overhead, so that there should be at least a little fresh new shroud for his face when the old man should close his eyes.

Slowly and drearily time went by; he had no tears to shed, and he felt no pain; Molly never came into his thoughts; he had a feeling as though the world and its bustle was nothing to him, as though he lay beyond it, and no one remembered him. Now and then it seemed to him that he felt hunger and thirst;—yes! he was sure that he did!—but no one came to comfort him, no one would come. Then he thought of all those who had ever suffered hardship, and he remembered how the holy Elizabeth, when she lived on the earth, she, the heroine of his home and his childhood, the noble Duchess of Thuringia, the lofty lady, went herself into the poorest cabin, and brought hope and comfort to the sick. Her good deeds shone in his thoughts; he remembered how she had come and spoken words of consolation to those who suffered, how she bound up the wounds of the miserable and brought food to the hungry, although often rebuked for it by her stern husband. Then he remembered a tale about her; how, when she came with her basket packed full of wine and bread, her husband, who watched her comings and goings, strode up in anger, and asked her what it was that she was carrying, whereupon in terror she answered that it was but roses she had plucked in the garden. At that he tore off the cloth, and

a miracle had been worked for the good queen; and the
wine and bread and everything in the basket lay there
changed into roses.

So lived this princess in the thoughts of old Anthony;
so she stood in living colour before his weary eyes, beside
his bed in the poor wooden booth in the Danish land.
He bared his head, looked up into her kind eyes, and all
around was a glory of light, and roses spread themselves
through the room and smelt so sweet. Then, too, came
the peculiar delicious perfume of the apple-blossom, and
he saw the blooming branches of an apple-tree waving
over him—it was the tree that he and Molly had planted
from the little kernel.

The tree scattered its perfumed petals over his hot
forehead and cooled it; they fell on his parched lips,
and it was like refreshing bread and wine; they fell
on his breast, and then he felt peaceful and ready to
slumber.

"I will go to sleep," he murmured; "sleep will do
me good, and in the morning I shall get up again quite
strong. How lovely! how beautiful! The apple-tree,
planted in love, I see again in heavenly beauty!"

And so he slept.

The next day, the third day that his booth had been
shut, the snow ceased falling, and the neighbour opposite
went over to visit old Anthony, as he had not yet shown
himself. There he lay stretched dead on his pallet, with
his old nightcap clasped tightly in his two hands. But
he did not have this one on in his coffin—he had a new
one, clean and white.

Where were now the tears that he had shed? Where
were the pearls? They remained in the nightcap—for

the real ones are not lost in the wash—yes, they remained
with the nightcap, thrown aside and forgotten—the old
thoughts, the old dreams, they were all there in the Old
Bachelor's Nightcap. Never wish yourself such a one!
It would make your forehead hot, cause your pulse to
beat stronger, and bring you dreams that would seem to
you real. And so found the first person who put it on,
and that was half a century after, and it was the Burgomaster himself, as he sat quite safe indoors with his wife
and eleven children; directly it was upon his head he
dreamed of unhappy love, of bankruptcy, and starvation.

"Hallo! how hot the nightcap is!" he said, and
pulled it off, and then there fell a pearl, and then
another, that tinkled on the floor, and broke in a flash
of light. "That is the rheumatism!" said the Burgomaster; "it makes my eyes swim!" But it was the
tears wept half a century ago, wept by old Anthony
from Eisenach.

To every one who afterwards put this cap on his
head there came straightway visions and dreams. His
own history grew into Anthony's, and became a whole
new tale; so that there are many which others can tell,
now that we have told the first one, whose last word
is—Never wish for yourself a "Bachelor's Nightcap."

www.ingramcontent.com/pod-product-compliance
Lightning Source LLC
Chambersburg PA
CBHW030817020726
47499CB00006B/1954